John Masefield

JOHN MASEFIELD was born in 1878 in Ledbury, England. Orphaned at an early age, he was raised by his uncle, who sent him into training aboard a sailing ship when he was thirteen to "toughen him up." Four years later he abandoned his ship in New York City and for the next two years lived as a vagabond, taking whatever jobs he could find. During this time he studied the work of Chaucer and other English poets. Ill health forced him to return to England in 1897, determined to be a writer.

John Masefield wrote articles and literary reviews for several newspapers. His first book of poems, *Salt Water Ballads*, was published in 1902. He went on to publish a great number of poetry collections, novels, plays, and essays, and was renowned especially for his rousing tales of adventure told in long narrative verse. By the time *The Midnight Folk* and its sequel, *The Box of Delights*, were published, he had become famous as a master storyteller.

In 1930 King George V appointed John Masefield poet laureate. As the official poet of England, he composed verse for royal and public events, while continuing to publish books, until his death in 1967.

YEARLING CLASSICS

Works of lasting literary merit by English
and American classic and contemporary writers.

HANS BRINKER, OR THE SILVER SKATES, Mary Mapes Dodge
EIGHT COUSINS, OR THE AUNT HILL,
Louisa May Alcott
FIVE LITTLE PEPPERS AND HOW THEY GREW, Margaret Sidney
THE MIDNIGHT FOLK, John Masefield
FIVE CHILDREN AND IT, E. Nesbit
THE PRINCE AND THE PAUPER, Mark Twain
THE PRINCESS AND THE GOBLIN, George MacDonald
ROSE IN BLOOM, Louisa May Alcott
TOM'S MIDNIGHT GARDEN, Philippa Pearce
LITTLE LORD FAUNTLEROY, Frances Hodgson Burnett
THE BOOK OF DRAGONS, E. Nesbit
REBECCA OF SUNNYBROOK FARM, Kate Douglas Wiggin

YEARLING BOOKS are designed especially to entertain and
enlighten young people. Charles F. Reasoner, Professor
Emeritus of Children's Literature and Reading, New York
University, is consultant to this series.

For a complete listing of all Yearling titles, write to
Dell Publishing Co., Inc., Promotion Department,
P.O. Box 3000, Pine Brook, N.J. 07058.

The
Midnight Folk

John Masefield

With an Afterword by Madeleine L'Engle

Published by
Dell Publishing Co., Inc.
1 Dag Hammarskjold Plaza
New York, New York 10017

For J. & L.

Yearling ® TM 913705, Dell Publishing Co., Inc.

ISBN: 0-440-45631-2

RL: 6.7

Printed in the United States of America
First Yearling Classic printing
November 1985

10 9 8 7 6 5 4 3 2 1

W

The
Midnight Folk

*I*t had been an unhappy day for little Kay Harker. To begin with, at breakfast time the governess had received a letter from his guardian, Sir Theopompus, the chemical powder merchant, to say that he would be there for lunch, but would like lunch at 2 P.M., as the trains did not suit. This made the governess cross, or as she called it, "put out." On giving the order to Jane, the cook, for a very good lunch at two o'clock, instead of one, Jane was put out, for it was her afternoon off and she did not like to be put upon. Ellen, the maid, was also put out, because if you have lunch so late, it is teatime before you have finished washing up. Jane and Ellen between them put the governess much further out, and then it was lesson time: divinity, French, history, and Latin.

Divinity was easy, as it was about Noah's Ark. French was fairly easy, as it was about the cats of the daughter of the gardener. History was not at all easy, as it was all about beastly Odo. He longed for Odo to come into the room, saying, "I'm Odo," so that he could jolly well shut him up with, "Well, O don't." He got knapped on the knuckles rather tartly over history. Then came Latin. That morning it was all adjectives, especially a loathsome adjective called *acer, acris, acre,* "sharp" or "piercing." It was that that put *him* out.

It came right at the end of lessons, that was the worst of it. As he was longing to be out of doors, he was always looking out of the window, watching the pigeons. He had to repeat *acer* line by line, in a sort of catechism.

> *The governess:* What is "sharp"?
> *Kay:* Acer
> *The governess:* Feminine?
> *Kay:* Acris.
> *The governess:* Neuter?
> *Kay:* Acre.
> *The governess:* Now the nominative, all genders.
> *Kay:* Acer, *acris, acre.*
> *The governess:* Meaning?
> *Kay:* "Sharp."
> *The governess:* Or? What else can it mean?
> *Kay:* "Piercing."
> *The governess:* Accusative?
> *Kay:* Acrem . . . *acris, acre.*

Here the governess scowled rather and would not say if he were right. Instead, she said, "Genitive?" But how was he to leap at the genitive when he could not tell if his taking-off point, the accusative, were sound? Besides, had it a genitive? Could you say "Of sharp"? What would be the genitive? Could it be *acrae, acri, acri*? That didn't sound right. What did sound right? Not quite *acrorum, acrarum, acrorum.*

"Well," the governess said, "what is the genitive?"

"Acrostic, acrostic, acrostic?"

"What?"

"Acrumpet, acrumpet, acrumpet."

"You're a very idle, impertinent little boy," the governess said. "You will write it all out five times, and I shall tell your guardian, Sir Theopompus, when he comes. Now go and have your milk, but not your biscuit—you haven't deserved one. And mind you come to lunch with washed hands."

The governess's Christian names were Sylvia and Daisy. Kay had read a poem about Sylvia and had decided that it was not swains who commended this one, but Mrs. Tattle and Mrs. Gossip. He loved daisies because the closer one looked at them the more beautiful they seemed, yet this daisy was like a rhododendron. She was big, handsome, and with something of a flaunting manner, which turned into a flounce when she was put out.

She left the schoolroom with something of a flounce after passing this sentence about the no biscuit with his milk. He had had his biscuit stopped before, more than once. He had invented a dodge for making up for the loss of biscuit. He used to go to the kitchen cupboard, where the raisins were kept, and get a handful of raisins instead. Ellen was his devoted friend, and Jane thought that raisins were very good for him.

But this morning, alas, things had gone badly in the house, and Ellen and Jane were cross. When he put his hand into the blue paper bag for the raisins, Jane stopped him.

"Now, Master Kay," she said, "you put down those raisins, or I shall tell your governess about you. You go taking those raisins and then it's put down to me. You've got plenty of good plain food without going stuffing yourself. That's how little boys get a stoppage. And I don't want you bothering about in my kitchen when I'm as busy as I am. I've put your milk in the dining room long ago."

There was nothing for it but to go.

In the dining room another trouble showed. There, on the sideboard, with his head in the tumbler of milk, which was tilted so that he was lapping the last remnants of it, was Blackmalkin, one of the three cats. Kay shooed him away, but three quarters of the milk had gone, and Kay would not drink what was left, because the cat had breathed in it, and Kay had heard that a cat's breath always gave you consumption.

He went into the garden without milk or biscuit. Before he

could settle down to any game, he was called indoors to wash his hands and then to put on a Sunday collar ready for Sir Theopompus. He loathed Sir Theopompus, a stout, red-faced man with eyes staring out of his head, as though he were at the point of choking. The worst of Sir Theopompus's coming was that there was always a lovely dinner, but "no contentment therewith," only the scowl of Sylvia Daisy if he did anything wrong.

Presently Sir Theopompus arrived in his fluttery way, with his gold-rimmed spectacles, his umbrella with the gold band, and his gold watch and chain. The governess presented her reports, but mercifully never said anything about the Latin adjective. Sir Theopompus didn't say much to Kay, happily, but from time to time would ask some question, such as "Are you enjoying your history? Got as far as the first reform bill yet? And what is your opinion of Lord Palmerston as a statesman, hey?" Then, after some more talk and another helping of goose, he would switch on to geography. "Know all about latitude and longitude, hey? What latitude are you in now, do you suppose?"

Towards the end of dinner, when he was shiny with his lunch, Sir Theopompus asked, "And what are you going to be, my young man? Got any plans yet?"

"I was rather hoping that I could be a jockey," Kay said timidly.

A look of displeasure came upon Miss Sylvia Daisy's face.

"Not thinking of being a sailor, like your great-grandpapa?" Sir Theopompus said. "Do you know about your great-grandpapa?"

"Yes, I know something," Kay said.

"Oh! and what do you know?" said the governess very sweetly.

"He was a sea captain," Kay said, "and went a lot to the West Indies and Santa Barbara."

"Yes," Sir Theopompus broke in, "and he took away the Santa Barbara treasure worth about a million pounds, as some think, and his crew mutinied, put him ashore, and ran away with it. Pretty pickings for a crew of seamen. Of course, some say," Sir Theopompus added as he rose from his chair, "some say that your great-grandpapa brought that treasure home with him and hid it somewhere. Have you come upon any treasure in your grubbings?"

"No," Kay said.

"Well, I'll tell you what I'll do," Sir Theopompus said. "If you'll find that treasure and tell me where it is, I'll go an honest halves with you."

"But it wouldn't be an honest halves," Kay said, "because you'd have done none of the work and all the treasure belongs to the Santa Barbara priests."

"Oh, so that's the line you're going on," Sir Theopompus said. "Now, you cut, for I've got to talk business here."

Kay went out into the garden and amused himself until teatime, wondering what the two could find to talk about, though he supposed that it was mostly about himself. Tea was very early, although lunch had been so late, because Sir Theopompus had to catch the 4:30.

Tea, with Sir Theopompus there, was a dismal function in the drawing room, with the tea set known as the Lowestoft and the stiff rosewood chairs which Kay was to be sure not to scratch.

"Well, have you found the treasure, hey?" Sir Theopompus asked.

Kay said that he had not.

"It seems to me," Sir Theopompus said, "that you're making this young man something of a moony. When I was a young fellow, by George, the thought of treasure would have set me going, I know. Don't you want to find it, hey?"

"Everybody says that it was never here, sir," Kay said.

"Oh, no," Sir Theopompus answered. "But a good many say that it was here and is here somewhere. Those West India merchants were a pretty odd lot of fellows, if you ask me. A lot of piracy and slaving going on there. I daresay your great-grandpapa was no better than his time, and a million pounds is a big temptation in the path of a man who's been just a merchant skipper."

"Sir, he was a very good man," Kay said. "His portrait is in the schoolroom."

"Well, he was a very good man, was he?" Sir Theopompus said. "He didn't bring back the treasure that he was trusted with. We know what to call men of that stamp in the City, by George!"

The day had been full of contrariety. Now something in the day and in Sir Theopompus combined to Kay's ruin.

"Well, I don't care," he said. "You oughtn't to condemn a man who isn't here to answer."

"By George," Sir Theopompus said, "we shall have to put you into Parliament."

He went rather turkey-cocky about the gills, snorted, and said that he had to catch his train. When the wheels of the fly had scrunched along the gravel out of the gate, the governess turned upon him.

"What a very impertinent little boy you are, Kay," she said. "Not only to me this morning, but to your kind guardian, who has come here specially and solely to see how you are getting on. It would have done you good if he had boxed your ears soundly and sent you packing."

"I don't care," Kay said. "He oughtn't to have said that about Great-grandpapa Harker, because it isn't true."

"You are a wicked little boy, Kay," the governess said. "You will go straight to bed this minute, without your bread and milk."

The little boy went upstairs to his room, in the old part of the house. There were oak beams in the ceiling, the floor was all oak plank. The bed was big and old, valanced to the floor, and topped by a canopy. Kay was very much afraid of it at going-to-bed time because so many tigers could get underneath it, to wait till he was asleep, but tonight he did not mind, because it was still only sunset. He had two windows in his room. One looked out on a garden, where Nibbins, the black cat, was watching some birds; the other looked out over a field, where there was a sheep trough. He did not like the look of the trough in the long grass, because it looked so like a puma with its ears cocked. Beyond the field he could see the stable, where Benjamin the highwayman had once lived.

Now, in his room there were two doors leading to different passages, which was terrible after dark, because of footsteps. On the wall were two colored prints, "The Meet" and "Full Cry," one on each side of the fireplace. Over the washhand stand, as it was called, were two old pistols wired to nails. They were called Great-grandpapa Harker's pistols, and Kay was to be sure never to touch them, because they might go off. Then, on the other side of the room, there was the dressing table, valanced to the floor, which made a very good secret room, where nobody ever looked for you. In the corner, near this, on a shelf on the wall, stood an old model of a ship, which Kay was never to touch, because boys are so destructive. This was the model of Great-grandpapa Harker's ship, the *Plunderer*, which had disappeared with the missing treasure so long before.

A very terrible thing about the fireplace was the stone hearth "as big as three men could lift," Jane said. Ellen said that a stone like that was a sure sign that somebody had been murdered and buried there, and that if Kay wasn't a good boy, he would come out and warn him. Cook said once she had seen him come out and he was all in black, which was a sure sign. "And he wanted to speak," she said, "only it wasn't his time."

This night the rooks were very noisy at their going to roost. The peacocks were screaming, and the brook at the end of the garden could be heard. "It is going to rain," Kay thought. He lingered over his undressing because he hoped that Ellen or Jane would smuggle him some bread and milk when the governess went to supper. But it was Ellen's evening alone, when she always did her ironing, and Jane was out.

By and by the sun went down behind the wooded camp, known as King Arthur's Round Table, where King Arthur was supposed to ride at full moon. When the sun had gone, all the world glowed for a while; but it was not wise to wait till the glow had gone, because so soon the dusk began, when the owls would come, and the footsteps would begin, and the tigers would stir under the bed and put out their paws, and the scratchings would scrape under the floor. He knew that he had not been good and that "he" might "come out and warn him." He got into the bed with a leap, because then you dodged the paws. He got well under the clothes for a minute, to make sure that he was not pursued. Luckily none of the tigers had heard him. The worst of it was that tigers look out for wicked little boys. When Kay came from under the bedclothes he could not be sure that there was not a tiger lying in the canopy above him. It was sagged down, just as though a tiger were there. If it were to give way, the tiger would fall right on top of him. Or very likely it was not a tiger but a python, for that is what pythons do.

Now it became darker, so that he could see a few stars. Footsteps passed in the house, sometimes close to his door, so that gleams of candlelight crossed the ceiling. Very strange creakings sounded in the house. There were scutterings to and fro, and scraping scratchings. By and by he heard the governess, who had finished her supper, come to the room beneath him, the library, as she usually did in the evenings. He was cross with her for stopping his bread and milk, but glad that she was there. She opened the piano and began to play. Usually she played things without any tune, which she said he couldn't understand yet because they were classical. This night she played something that had a sort of tune, and then began to sing to it in a very beautiful voice, so that he was rapt away at once into joy. There were not any more tigers, nor pythons— only a mouse gnawing in the wainscot. Or was it someone playing on a guitar and humming some song about a treasure?

After a time he did not think that it was a guitar, but a voice calling to him: "Kay, Kay, wake up." Waking up, he rubbed his eyes. It was broad daylight, but no one was there. Someone was scraping and calling inside the wainscot, just below where the pistols hung. There was something odd about the daylight—it was brighter than usual. All things looked more real than usual. "Can't you open the door, Kay?" the voice asked. There never had been a door there, but now that Kay looked, there was a little door, all studded with knops of iron. Just as he got down to it, it opened towards him. There was Nibbins, the black cat.

"Come along, Kay," Nibbins said. "We can just do it while they're at the banquet. But don't make more noise than you must."

Kay peeped through the door. It opened from a little narrow passage in the thickness of the wall.

"Where does it lead to?" he asked.

"Come and see," Nibbins said.

Kay slipped on his slippers and followed Nibbins into the little passage. Nibbins closed the door behind him and bolted it.

"I'll lead the way," he said. "Mind the stairs: they're a bit worn, for the smugglers used to use these passages. But there's lots of light. Take my paw as we go up."

They went up some stairs in the thickness of the wall. Then a panel slid up in front of them and they came out onto the top landing. Nibbins closed the panel behind them. It was dark night there on the landing, except for a little moonlight. The house was very still, but looking down over the banisters into the hall, Kay thought that he saw a shadow, wearing a ruff and a long sword, standing in the moonlight. The cuckoo clock in the nursery struck twelve.

"All the house is sound asleep," Nibbins said. "Jane and Ellen are in there in those two rooms. They little know what goes on among us midnight folk. Give us a hand with this ringbolt, will you?"

In the oak planks of the floor there was a trapdoor, which Kay had never seen before. Together they pulled it up. Beneath was a ladder leading down into a passage brightly lit like the other.

"Close the trap after you," Nibbins said as he went down.

They went along a passage into a little room all hung with swords and banners.

"This is the guardroom," Nibbins said. "Some of the swords

are still here. The guards went away a long time ago. Least said, soonest mended—it's not for me to blame anybody. There are their names cut on the wall."

Kay read some of the names:

Robin Pointnose	Dogg	Petter Horse	
Eduardo da Vinci	P. Dogg	Tom	Ernest
Salado da Vinci	Jack	John	Jemima
Bruno Bree	Peterkin	Lenda	Maria
Snowball	James	Peter Gillian	Susan
G. L. Brown Bear	Squirrel	Wm. Brown	Peter

Alas, Kay knew those names only too well: they were the names of his beloved companions of old, before there had been any governess or Sir Theopompus. They had been his toys, of bears, dogs, rabbits, cats, horses, and boys. They had all been packed away long ago, when the governess came, because, as he had heard her tell Ellen, "they will only remind him of the past." They were locked up somewhere, he thought, yet he often feared that they had been given away to other children, who would not know them or be kind to them.

"Why do you call them the guards, Nibs?" he asked.

"Why, because they were the guards," Nibbins said. "I told them they ought not to go, but Edward said that he had got a clue and had to follow it up."

"What had he got a clue to?" Kay asked.

"The Harker treasure," he said. "I begged him to leave half the guards, but he said, 'No, I'll only be away a week or two.' So away they went, with the horse and cart, the big tent that takes to pieces, and all the hammocks and guns. Edward had his sword, the cocked hat, the coat with the piping, and his striped trousers, so you can see that he thought it important. But as to his being away only a week, he has been away a year or more, and not a word has come from any of them."

"I'm afraid they are all dead," Kay said. "I wish they weren't."

"Things have gone to rack and ruin without them," Nibbins said. "What with witchcraft and that. Of course I'm only a cat, but I've got eyes, and a cat can look at a king. Still, least said, soonest mended. Now, come along, this way, down these steps. Now, do you see these eyeholes? They are cut in the portraits on the walls of one of the rooms. You can look down, if you like."

Kay looked down through the eyeholes of Grandmama Harker's portrait into the drawing room, which was shuttered dark, except for some moonlight coming from the upper panes. This moonlight fell upon the table, where the red and white ivory chessmen were playing chess by themselves. They had come out of the box and ranged themselves. The kings called out the moves, but generally they asked the queens first. The pieces and pawns which had been taken stood beside the board, giving cheers for their own sides and uttering little cries of warning.

"Well played, Red."

"Now, White Knight, why don't you take him?"

"Oh, Your Majesty, look out for the bishop."

"Oh, well played, Your Grace. Well played indeed."

"That'll be mate in three moves if you do that, Red."

"Will it really? Yes, my dear, I suppose it will. I'd better not do it then. What would you suggest?" etc.

While Kay was watching, Nibbins put a paw on his arm.

"Don't speak," he said. "Mrs. Pouncer is going to sing. Come along quietly. You'll enjoy this."

He led Kay along a narrow corridor to another passage, where there were more eyelet holes. Kay looked through the eyes of Great-grandmama Siskin's portrait into the dining room, but what did he see?

There were seven old witches in tall black hats and long scarlet cloaks sitting round the table at a very good supper: the cold goose and chine which had been hot at middle-day dinner, and the plum cake which had been new for tea. They were very piggy in their eating (picking the bones with their fingers, etc.) and they had almost finished the marsala. The old witch who sat at the head of the table tapped with her crooked-headed stick and removed her tall, pointed hat. She had a hooky nose and chin, and very bright eyes.

"Dear Pouncer is going to sing to us," another witch said.

"Hear, hear," the other witches said. "Dear Pouncer, sing."

"But you must join in the chorus, sisters. Shall it be the old song, dear Nightshade?"

"Yes, yes. The old song."

Mrs. Pouncer cleared her throat and began:

> "When the midnight strikes in the belfry dark
> And the white goose quakes at the fox's bark,
> We saddle the horse that is hayless, oatless,
> Hoofless and pranceless, kickless and coatless,
> We canter off for a midnight prowl . . .

"Chorus, dear sisters . . .

> "Whoo-hoo-hoo, says the hook-eared owl."

All the witches put back their heads to sing the chorus:

> "Whoo-hoo-hoo, says the hook-eared owl."

It seemed to Kay that they were looking straight at him. Nibbins's eyes gleamed with joy.

"I can't resist this song," he said. "I never could. It was this song, really, that got me into this way of life."

"But I don't know what it means. What is the horse that is hayless?"

"Aha," Nibbins said. "Well, we've time while they're at this song: it has nine times nine verses. But you ought to stay for some more whoo-hoos. Doesn't it give you the feel of the moon in the treetops?: 'Whoo-hoo-hoo, says the hook-eared owl.' Come along quietly."

*N*ibbins led the way up some more stairs, till he came to an open door, through which Kay saw the stars. "Why, this is the roof," he said. He saw how strange the roof was, close to, like this, with the twisted brick chimneys standing guard, with their cowls still spinning. He seemed very far from the ground.

"This is what they mean," Nibbins said. "Just open that middle chimney, will you?"

"But it is a chimney—it won't open."

"No, it isn't. There's a bobbin on it—pull that. It's their stable."

Kay scrambled up to the middle chimney of the three nearest to him. Sure enough, there was a bobbin on it. He pulled it, the latch came up, the chimney opened like a door. There inside was a cupboard in which stood one besom, one stable broom, one straw broom, one broom broom, and three kitchen brooms, each with a red headstall marked with magic.

"Take the besom and the broom broom," Nibbins said, "and pitch the others over the gutter."

Kay pitched the five over the gutter. They whinnied as they fell onto the garden path, but nobody seemed to notice.

"Now let us mount and ride," Nibbins said. "But first we'll shut the door."

He was going to shut the door into the house, when the noise of the song suddenly became much louder. Somebody at the banquet said "Hush" suddenly. The singing stopped. The witches were holding their door open, listening.

"They've heard us," Nibbins said. "Mount, Kay, and ride. Mount, catch him by the bridle, say, '*Sessa*,' and point him where you want to go. Watch me."

Nibbins mounted the besom, Kay the broom broom. Just as he was mounted, he heard the sharp voice of Mrs. Pouncer calling from the foot of the stairs.

> "Night glider, tell,
> Are ill things well?"

Kay saw the besom toss up its head. It began to say:

> "Save, mistress, save,
> From white thief and black knave. . . ."

but before he could finish, both Nibbins and Kay said "*Sessa*" and pointed their horses towards the wood. Kay heard the witches clattering up the stairs on their high-heeled shoes. Looking back, he saw them all clustered on the roof shaking their fists and sticks, but already they were far away, for the two broom horses were rushing through the air so fast that soon the house was out of sight. As they went over the elm boughs, they came so close to the top twigs that some young rooks woke in the rookery and cried "Kaa" at them.

It was merry to be so high in the air. Kay could see the village, with hardly a light in it, and the flashing of the brook where it went over the fall. Near the ponds many little lights were twinkling. Kay wondered what they could be. A couple of white owls drifted up alongside Kay like moths. He could see their burning yellow eyes.

"We'll race you to the upper wood," they said.

"All right," Kay said. "Come up, horse."

The brooms were much faster than the owls: soon they were well ahead.

"You keep clear of Wicked Hill," the owls cried. They said something more, but the brooms were too far in front for the riders to hear.

"We'll land here, if you don't mind," Nibbins said. "I'd like to speak with a friend, if he's anywhere about. Point his head down to the quarry there."

When they had landed in the quarry, they tied the brooms to two spindle trees. "It must be spindle trees," Nibbins said. The quarry was bright in the moonlight and much overgrown with hazels and gorse.

"What is Wicked Hill," Kay asked, "that we are to keep clear of?"

"They told us to keep clear of it, did they?" Nibbins said. "That shows that there is something on. . . . However, this is where my friend lives, if he's not on his rounds." He led the way towards the quarry end, where there was much tumbled stone worn into a track by feet. A warm strong scent was blowing about the place, more like a taste than a smell. The ground was white with little bones. Something that looked like washing hung upon the gorse bushes. It was not washing, though—it was rabbit skins hung up to dry. Someone with a most unpleasant voice was doing something with the rabbit skins, and singing as he worked. He was either folding the dry ones or hanging more fresh.

His song was not a nice one.

"I crept out of covert and what did I see?
    Ow-ow-ow-diddle-ow!
But seven fat bunnies, each waiting for me.
With a poacher's noosey, catch the fat goosey, Ho says
    Rollicum Bitem.

" 'O pretty bunnies, let's come for a stroll.'
      'Oh, no, no, no; you're a fox.'
'A fox, pretty dears?—can't you see I'm a mole?'
With a weasely, stoaty, snap at his throaty, Ho says
      Rollicum Bitem.

" 'Let's dance, one by one, arm in arm, as dear friends.'
      'Oh, certainly, sir, if you please.'
So seven fat bunnies had seven sweet ends . . .
Hay for a hennerel, snug in my dennerel, Ho says
      Rollicum Bitem."

The song stopped suddenly. Kay heard no sound of footsteps, but suddenly two very bright green eyes were shining at him above some glittering teeth.

"It's all right, Bitem old boy," Nibbins said. "It's only Nibs. This is my friend, Kay. Mr. Kay, Mr. Lightfoot, Mr. Rollicum Bitem Lightfoot."

"Oh, it's you, Nibs! Pleased to meet you, Mr. Kay. Come in, won't you? Sorry I didn't recognize you at once. This way." He led the way to what looked like the mouth of a cave in the quarry face. "It will be dark for you," he said to Kay. "You'll find some glowworms on the shelf there, if you want a light."

Kay took a glowworm from the shelf. By the light of this he was able to see where he was going. The two others went down the passage in front of him. It was a rough, dark, narrow passage, with many twists in it. Everywhere there was this strong, rich scent, so like a taste. There were many rabbit skins about, as well as feathers.

"Mr. Bitem deals in game," Nibbins said. "I have to consult him about some rabbiting."

Mr. Bitem led them into his study, which was also his bedroom and larder. "Bachelor's quarters," he said. "A bit rough and ready, but then I'm only here in the winter, really. Would you care to pick a wing or anything? No? I've some nice fowl, cold. And there's a bit of duck under the floor there. No? Well, what do you want with me, Nibs?"

"About our rabbiting tomorrow night, Bitem. Of course, you can speak freely before Mr. Kay. . . . I rather think my cousin Blackmalkin has betrayed us to the keeper. I happened to see him come from the keeper's cottage—I was up in a tree among some ivy. He came out licking his lips, for he'd been having milk. He didn't see me. He passed just underneath me, but I heard him chuckle to himself and say 'Keeper will get the lot of them.' You see, Kay, my two cousins, Blackmalkin and Greymalkin, and myself have been in this midnight business together for quite a long time. Well, lately we've been helping Bitem in the game industry, on quiet nights, after new moon, and so on, and we had planned a big hunt for tomorrow, out Coneycop Spinney way. A really big hunt: ourselves, Bitem, and some of his relatives. . . . Now, Blackmalkin has not been dependable for a long time. This magic business is very bad for a fellow, and he is in it deeply, with a very bad set, all the Pouncer seven. You mark my words, he has been put up by the seven to betray us to the keeper.

"When he had gone, I crept down from my tree, got into Keeper's cottage, and upstairs under the bed. Presently Keeper came in with those nasty dogs of his and put his gun on the rack. 'I've got some news for you, my dear,' his wife said. 'Here's Blackmalkin just come in to say that there's a big rabbit drive arranged for Friday night in the spinney. That Bitem lot and his cousins are in it.'

" 'I'll rabbit 'em,' Keeper said. You know his coarse, red way. 'I'll rabbit 'em.'

" 'Yes, my dear,' his wife said. 'Blackmalkin said you'd get the lot of them. Of course, after what he'd told me, I gave him some milk and that bit of sardine that there was.'

" 'Quite right,' Keeper said. 'If I get the lot of them, he shall have more than milk and sardine. He shall have Long Tail's wing.'

" 'Oh, hush, my dear,' his wife said. 'Somebody might hear you.'

" 'Tut! Nobody can hear me,' Keeper said, blowing out his

big lips. 'But I'll rabbit 'em. Let 'em come on Friday, I'll ask no better.' Then he went out and began oiling his gun. I could hear him singing:

> " 'I'll get him oiled for Friday,
>   So it shall be their die-day,
>   And Satter-day
>   Shall be Batter-day,
>   And Sunday hot rabbit-pie day.'

"I had to wait in the room for hours, because his nasty dogs were in the room below. But at last I could stand it no longer: I made a dart for the chimney and was over the roof and into the pines before the dogs were upstairs. I heard Keeper ask 'What's the matter with the dogs?' and his wife said, 'It sounded like a young jackdaw got down the chimney again.' 'I'll jackdaw them jackdaws one of these days,' he said, 'if they keep on jackdawing me.' 'That's that,' she said. So that was that, and here I am."

"Ha," Bitem said, "so that's that for tomorrow's hunt. Now what can we do for Blackmalkin? Of all the traitors I ever did hear of! But we'll pretend we're going, up to the last. Keeper and the beaters will all be at Coneycop, waiting for us. And we'll send Blackmalkin there. But we ourselves will go off and draw out Brady Ride way: there's pretty toothing in the rabbit there, especially in the south warren. And Keeper and beaters will wait all night for us at Coneycop, and when they learn that we've been at Brady, they'll pretty well have it out of Blackmalkin for misleading them. They'll toss him in a game bag, and serve him right."

"I say, you have got a brain, Bitem," Nibbins said. "I knew you'd have a plan at once. That's the advantage of working with you—never at a loss. I never saw such a fellow."

"A fellow had need to be never at a loss," Bitem said. "The huntsmen are bad enough, in their red coats, but at least you do expect a keeper to stand your friend."

"If you wouldn't mind just moving to the door, Kay," Nibbins said, "Bitem and I could plan out our hunt a bit, using the floor as a map."

Kay moved to the door. He watched them as they put rabbit skins and feathers on the ground to mark places in the wood. He listened to them for a few minutes.

"This hen's head is the big yew. That rabbit skin is the boggy patch—you know the place. Then here is where we got the partridge chicks. I'll put this pheasant's tail to mark the end of the south warren. Hob Ferret'll join in here, and Jill will come if we want her. Then you will steal up here . . . and I will steal up there. . . . Yes, and then Greymalkin is awfully good at a drop-pounce. Then we'll all go over the down to the north warren. . . ."

Kay grew weary of all this talk, because he had never been to Brady Ride Wood. He strolled quietly along the passage towards its mouth in the quarry face. He put back the glowworm on the ledge and peeped out of the entrance.

He drew back at once, because there, in the quarry, not far from the cave, was a man at work among the stones. He was kneeling in a patch of shadow, but his face came up into the moonlight from time to time. Kay saw from his velveteen coat that it was the keeper. "What on earth is he doing?" Kay wondered.

Presently the keeper stood up to stretch his back. He was wearing gloves. He drew from a sack a big iron snap trap, which he opened and set among the stones in the middle of the path leading to Bitem's earth. When it was set, he very cleverly and cautiously strewed it over with moss, dead grass, leaves, and earth.

"That will catch your light feet, Mr. Lightfoot," he said. "And then, with my good gun, I'll put an end to your snibbing of my rabbits. Many a young hunter will give a pound for that mask of yourn, and your brush shall be a cobweb cleaner before you're a week older. I'll get up my tree, my master, and watch till you walk click into it. You'll be coming home within an hour. I know your ways."

Kay saw him move into the wood above the quarry, where he began to climb a tree. As soon as he was climbing, Kay hurried back to tell the others what he had seen.

"A trap?" Bitem said. "And Keeper watching from a tree? I am very much obliged to you, Mr. Kay. I must be gone from here by the secret door. I'll move off to my place Wicked Hill way."

"There's something on at Wicked Hill, the owls said," Nibbins said. "Do you think it would be safe?"

"A lot safer than this," Bitem said.

"Yes, for you," Nibbins said. "But I meant for us."

"They don't harm anyone who keeps outside the magic circle."

"I'd love to go, just to look on," Nibbins said. "It's probably a big magic night, Kay, when they have a bonfire, and oh, I do love to see them at magic. It's terrifying, but I can't resist it."

"Well, come along," Bitem said.

"We can steal round to our horses and give you a lift, Bitem."

The fox led the way out of his study into a narrow passage, where Kay had to crawl on hands and knees. This led into a biggish room from which several passages branched. Water was dripping in one of them.

"Very convenient in here," Bitem said. "Lots of ways out and plenty of water, but this is the way we'll take tonight."

In a few minutes they scrambled out among some gorse roots (at least a hundred yards from the keeper) near the spindle trees where the brooms were tethered.

"You mount with me, Bitem," Nibbins said, "and you, Kay, just follow us. There are spindles where we can tether, lots of them."

In a moment the brooms were sweeping through the air over the treetops. Kay saw a few white houses here and there below him, and many gleaming ponds and brooks. Far ahead, among the hills, was the glow of a bonfire. Soon they could see people dancing round it. Kay came to ground with Nibbins and Bitem beside a spinney on the hill. There were many spindle bushes in the spinney, but to many of them brooms were already tethered.

"I'll be off to my place," Bitem said, "over there among the Old Ones. You'll find the Night Folk up at the top. Good night."

*W*icked Hill was a big round lump with a hollow top. The lower slopes grew bracken and bramble, but near the top nothing grew except a short-bladed grass. The stump of an old gibbet stood at one end of it. An earthwork with two gates ringed the top of the hill. On the top of this earthwork the magic circle was burning in a narrow line of blue fire, which was being fed by little black cats who walked round the ring dropping herbs on it.

"That used to be my job when I did this kind of thing," Nibbins whispered.

The bonfire, which had now sunk to a glow, was in the midst of the circle. The people who had danced about it were now drawn together in a group. They were listening to a wizard, in a long scarlet gown, who seemed to be their king or chief.

"That's Abner Brown," Nibbins whispered. "He's always the head of these big parties."

"Hush," Kay said. "Let's hear what he's saying."

"So, my brothers and sisters," Abner was saying, "we have had our evening's frolic; now let us come to our evening's business. The great task before us is to find the Harker treasure." (Here there were cries of *"Hear, hear!"*) "We all know what that was: it was the treasure of the great South American cathedral of Santa Barbara. It was a bargeload of gold, silver, and precious stones, wrought and unwrought, but worth, so the records prove, at least one million seven hundred thousand pounds. There are seven times seven of us. If we find it, the share of each one of us will be some thirty-five thousand pounds. I ask you, is it worth trying to find?"

There were loud cries of *"Yes!"*

"You say 'yes,' and you may mean 'yes,' but will you all work for 'yes'?"

There were shouts of *"Yes, to the death!"*

"Very well, then," he said. "I am glad that we are all resolved. We will now break up our party. Let all the sevens leave the hill except the Pouncer seven."

When most of the party had gone, Kay saw that Mrs. Pouncer, Sister Nightshade, and the rest of the seven drew near to Abner.

"Sister Pouncer," Abner said, "why are you vexed?"

"Enemies are at work," she said. "They took my broom and Nightshade's broom, so that we had to walk."

"Do not be vexed, my Pouncer," Abner said, "because I am far from vexed. I have discovered something very important about the treasure."

"Oh! What, dear Abner?"

"You are quite wrong about it. It is not in the Harker home, but somewhere near here."

At this there came cries of "No! It cannot be. How can it be? Where do you suppose it is? Why is it not in the Harker house? Where is it?"

"We will find out that presently," he said, "of WHERE it is. Listen to what I have to say of WHEREABOUTS it is."

The seven drew nearer, intently listening.

"You know," Abner went on, "that when I was little, I helped my father and grandfather (both of them Abner Browns like myself) to look for the treasure. I might say I was at this quest from birth." (Here there were remarks of *"Hear, hear!"*)

"As you know, my grandfather once had the treasure, but

lost it. For more than twenty years he and my father dug for it where they thought it would be. One of my earliest recollections is of helping them to dig for it in a hot country of very red mud.

"Then my grandpop disappeared, and within a week my pop died of the yellow fever. I had the harsh world to wrestle with before I could take up the quest.

"When I took it up, just thirty years after those two laid it down, it wasn't easy to pick up the threads at that place in the red mud. The yellow fever had killed 'most everyone who had lived there when my pop and grandpop dug there. But I met an old Negro who knew just why my grandpop gave up digging and disappeared.

"He gave up digging *because someone found the treasure and carried it off to sea.*

"He disappeared *so as to settle matters with that finder.* The finder was an Englishman, named Benito Trigger.

"That is not much to go upon, is it? Thirty-five years ago an Englishman gets to sea with the stuff three thousand miles away and disappears. My grandpop goes after him and disappears. At first I thought that this Benito Trigger might be Captain Harker himself, for as we know, he lived for many years in quest of the treasure."

"Or pretended to, so as to lull suspicion, while he lived on it," Mrs. Pouncer said under her breath.

"But it was not Captain Harker," Abner continued. "For when I came here to make inquiries, I found that Captain Harker was at that time upon his deathbed.

"I need not tell you how interesting it was to see the very house in which old Captain Harker lived, and to see his tomb, and to stand within just a few feet of those bones which, when they were alive, had started all this treasure hunt.

"For the moment I ruled him out. 'You didn't get the treasure, brother,' I said. 'You were in your tomb before it could have reached England, if it ever did reach England.' "

"It was in his secret den before he ever sickened," Mrs. Pouncer muttered. "Of course he had it. Had it all the time."

"But," Abner continued, "I fell right plumb in love with this green countryside, so full of real old buildings, so I just didn't rest till I'd taken Russell's Dene, that Queen Anne mansion, in the oak wood, where tradition says the Druids once practiced their rites. There, as you know, we have been able to establish our magic circle, for the quest of the treasure, upon the lines of the ancient knowledge.

"And there are red birds that come out of the wilderness with knowledge. One of them came to me this spring, just after I was settled in Russell's Dene. He led me to visit a certain church, not many miles from here. And what did I find there?"

Here some of the seven said, "The treasure? Some of the candlesticks? The church vessels in use again?"

"No, none of those things," he answered. "I found the tomb of my long-lost grandpop, Abner Brown. He had been drowned in the Great Flood here in February 1850: February Fill-Dyke, as you call it.

"Was not that wonderful?

"I have now raked out something of his end. He was last seen alive at the Condicote inn, the Ring of Bells, on the last night of January 1850. He was then heard quarreling, with whom?

"With Sir Piney Trigger, a rich Honduras merchant, who had just returned from two years' absence in the West. That Piney Trigger was the Trigger who had found the treasure and carried it off to sea: my grandpop had run him down.

"That night, after their quarrel, both my grandpop and Sir Piney disappeared. What happened, do you suppose? Many asked that at the time. I answer it. I say that Sir Piney had the treasure here, that my grandpop had discovered so much and asked for a share. They quarreled. I say that Sir Piney flung my grandpop into the flood and then fled the country. Left the country, left the treasure, and never dared come back for it because of blood-guiltiness.

"The case is reported in the *Condicote Remembrancer* for

February 1850. They knew nothing of any treasure, of course, only inquired into the disappearance. The coroner's jury supposed him to have been washed out to sea by the Great Flood.

"Now, Sir Piney was a well-known sportsman, mixed up in many shady matters. His daughter is still alive. I have seen her. There's no getting anything out of her.

"What I have tried to find out is, what brought him to Condicote that night? In the coroner's notes I found this: that it was supposed that he had come to look after a big barge of his which had come up the river some days before. It was a seagoing barge, fitted like a yacht. He had been in her in the West.

"I say that he brought the treasure in her. He hid it somewhere not far from Condicote and had come to see to it, or to remove it, when my grandpop interfered."

Here, as Abner paused as though for applause, Sister Nightshade asked, "May he not have taken all the treasure away in the barge when he took himself away?"

"No," Abner said. "Because the barge (dead empty) had been washed ashore and stove in in the floods two days before he disappeared.

"No, my sweet seven. Depend upon it, the treasure is near here, and somewhere here, probably near the river, we'll find it."

Here there was a sensation among the company. All were much impressed and excited. Sister Pouncer said, "Was there ever such a mind as our Abner's? Like crystal from the spring." But after saying this, she moved nearer to Kay and muttered, "This is all pure surmise. You have a bee in your bonnet, my good sir. I, too, have my views of where the treasure is, and we shall see who is right. Magic is a surer guide than a grandpop or a little-pop. For all your Tingo and Tango, Sister Pouncer holds the silken clue."

"And now, my dear seven," Abner continued, "we will have one short dance more, and then away, for the stars are dim and the cocks are stirring on their perches. Join hands and dance."

A strange music began from somewhere in the air. The witches and wizards at once swept into a dance.

Nibbins was very uneasy. "I can't keep out of a dance like this," he said. "Oh, it goes right through my marrow, and then in a minute they will all join hands and swing round and round, till they see all sorts of things."

"You come away," Kay said, pulling him down the hill. "You always were one for getting into scrapes. Let's get back home, before they all come hurrying for their horses. If Mrs. Pouncer catches us at the spindle trees, we shall be in a mess."

He made Nibbins run, keeping one hand on the scruff of his neck all the way lest the sound of the dance should prove too exciting. In a few minutes they were high in the air again upon their horses, sailing far from the hill.

"It's just as well we started when we did," Nibbins said, "for there's the dawn beginning."

Sure enough, the sky behind them was showing color. The two horses began to droop down towards the ground. Presently they were dragging along the ground, and at last they collapsed.

"We left it till too late," Nibbins said. "However, we're almost at home. Come along. The gate's locked, but we can get over the wall by the ivy."

They left their horses in the road, scrambled up the ivy, over the wall, and then along behind the laurustinus till they were near the house.

"This is the place," Nibbins said. They were within thirty yards of the house, in a thick shrubbery, but Nibbins must have touched a spring, for the ground gave way beneath them, and down they went into a secret passage. In another minute Nibbins was gone and Kay was in his own room.

"What a night I have had," he thought. His slippers were muddy from the soil in the garden. "I shall catch it," he thought.

The cuckoo clock struck five. The room was quite light. He popped into bed at once. He did not stay long awake, you may be sure. Just before he fell asleep, however, he heard a curious noise on the wall of the house, not far away, as though the jasmine had broken away and were scraping as the wind blew it. "I suppose it's the jasmine," he muttered drowsily, "but it may be Ellen up already, sweeping the stairs."

When he came downstairs to breakfast the governess was not down. She entered just as he was at the sideboard, helping himself to pork pie. She looked a little cross, as though she had not slept very well.

"You know," she said, "that you're never allowed to help yourself to pork pie. It's a very bilious, rich food, and then you won't be able to do your French. You must have an egg like any other boy. And you don't mean to say, Kay, after all the many times that I've spoken to you, that you've been in the garden again in your slippers, and on the beds too! And then you wonder if you catch your death of cold!"

"But I haven't caught a cold," he said.

"Don't answer me back, sir," she said. "You're a very naughty, disobedient little boy, and I have a very good mind not to let you have an egg. I wouldn't let you have an egg, only I had to stop your supper last night. Take off one of those slippers and let me feel it. Come here."

Kay went up rather gingerly, having been caught in this way more than once. He took off one slipper and tendered it for inspection.

"Just as I thought," she said. "The damp has come right through the lining, and that's the way your stockings get worn out."

In a very pouncing way she spanked at his knuckles with the slipper. He had expected a blow of the sort, and by drawing his hands swiftly aside, the slipper struck the spoons on the table and made them dance.

"Now, you naughty boy, put that slipper on, and you'll learn the whole of *pouvoir* before you go out this morning. What were you muttering under your breath, Kay?"

"I was just wondering if this was a duck egg or a hen egg."

"Use the subjunctive and the genitive," she said. "*Were* a

duck's egg, not *was* a *duck* egg. And it's a hen's egg. Ducks' eggs
are a great deal too rich." At any other time Kay would have
boasted that it was a double-yolker, but refrained, thinking that
this would probably lead to confiscation, as too much for a
young stomach. He ate his egg, but his mind was intent upon
many other things.

Ellen came in.

"If you please, ma'am," Ellen said, "would you mind speaking
to Jane."

Jane was at the door behind her.

"If you please, ma'am," Jane said, "would you please to look
at this."

This was the dish on which the cold goose had lain, but
alas, now nothing remained but a few picked bones and a
skeleton almost bare.

"The cats have been in again, ma'am. I don't know how they
get in. And the chine's gone the same way, and there's two
more brooms gone."

"Did you lock the larder door, Jane?"

"Yes, ma'am, and I took the key and had it under my pillow.
And if it isn't cats—and I don't know how cats get in—then
somebody must have a key and come in in the night, and I
don't like it."

"I'll look into this after breakfast, Jane," the governess said,
"and I'll speak to Wiggins."

Kay stared at the bones of the goose. He knew how that
goose and chine had disappeared. Almost immediately Jane
reappeared.

"If you please, ma'am, Wiggins has found the two brooms,
the besom and the broom broom. They were in the road
outside, near the spring."

"Well, how on earth could they have got there?" the governess said.

"I don't know how they got there," Jane said, "but I don't
like it."

The governess did not talk during breakfast, but seemed to be considering this question of the brooms and the goose. Kay's thoughts were far away with Nibbins, Mr. Bitem, and that gathering of witches on the hill.

"Of all the dreamy boys," the governess said suddenly, "going off into daydreams. It's my belief that you need a dose. It's my belief you eat too much. You'll put on your boots before you come to lessons, and ask Ellen to dry those shoes in the oven."

"Please can't I wear my slippers during lessons?"

"No, you won't wear your slippers during lessons. For one thing, they're not dry and you'll catch your death wearing them, and for another, you fidget me distracted by rubbing one slipper off and then the other, just as though you were playing a game with them."

This was a cruel thrust, because Kay did play games with them. When he had scraped off a slipper, he could push it about with his toes and imagine that it was a canoe full of redskins on the warpath, going down the rapids; or a diving bell at Tobermory, bringing up treasure from one of the ships of the Armada; or Great-grandpapa Harker's ship, the *Plunderer*, engaging seven French privateers; or that famous horse Lottery, at various stages of the steeplechase, the prints of which hung in the study. But the boots were laced-up things that gave no solace. There they were, and there you were.

The governess stalked out of the room to investigate the larder door. Ellen came in to clear away. Kay looked up at the portrait of Great-grandmama Siskin. Her eyes seemed all right. "This is the loveliest time that I've ever had," Kay thought, "and anything may happen." He walked slowly round the room, tapping the paneling.

"What are you doing, Master Kay?" Ellen asked.

"I was just seeing if there were any secret passages," he said.

"Oh, there's no secret passages in here, Master Kay. What should there be secret passages for?"

"Oh," Kay said, "when people were doing murders, they always used to have them. And then smugglers had them."

"The smugglers were never here," Ellen said. "Not in this

house. Down by the river the smugglers were, so my father said. They had the mill at Seven Hatches. Oh! And by Drowned Man's Copse way they'd a place, and at the Springs another. But they never could have come here—your great-grandfather would never have allowed them."

"No," Kay said. "But he would never have known. They could have crept in at night and made the passages."

"I don't think they could, Master Kay, not in stone walls."

*A*fter he had put on his boots Kay went out among the laurustinus to look for that secret place where the trapdoor had opened beneath his feet. Ten o'clock struck while he was still searching, but by great good fortune he got to the schoolroom before the governess arrived. It was French morning. He struggled through an exercise in Ollendorf and a little translation from Chardenal. Unfortunately, the governess would not let him translate what had seemed (at private readings) a very promising passage about an ax and skull, with a war cry of "Hailulli." She said that it was not fit for a little boy to read. Then came the dreaded moment.

"And now, Kay, since you were a very naughty little boy last night, and were most disobedient and dreamy this morning, you will learn *pouvoir*, while I go to look at the larder again, now that Wiggins is there."

"What do you think it was that did it in the larder?" he asked.

"You learn your lessons," she said. "Never mind about what I think it was."

She left him with *pouvoir*. Kay had a special prejudice against *pouvoir*. It wasn't a good, straightforward word like *aimer*. It was a mean and ugly word, which went into *peux* and *pu*. It didn't

seem to have any sense in it. He wrestled with it with each
boot twisted round a leg of his chair, scraping up and down.
Then, looking up, he saw Great-grandpapa Harker looking
down at him from his portrait over the mantelpiece.

The portrait was one that he had looked at during lessons
ever since lessons began. It was just "Great-grandpapa Harker's
portrait," though it was labeled Baxter. When people were
shown the schoolroom, the governess always said "That is a
Baxter," and then people said "Really!" or "Fancy that!" or
"How interesting!" It was the full-length portrait of a man in
old-fashioned clothes. There was a sort of shrubbery behind
him and a sort of blueness behind the shrubbery. It was said to
be the only full-length Baxter, as generally Baxter only did
down to the knees. But now, as Kay looked, Great-grandpapa
Harker distinctly took a step forward, and as he did so, the
wind ruffled the skirt of his coat and shook the shrubs behind
him. A couple of blue butterflies which had been upon the
shrubs for seventy-odd years flew out into the room. Great-
grandpapa Harker took another step forward and smiled. Now
Kay could see into the shrubbery: it was just where Kay's fort
now was, but the box trees had grown enormously since then,
although the bullfinches were already there. Great-grandpapa
Harker held out his hand and smiled again. His face, which had
seemed such an old-portrait kind of a face, became alive and
full of welcome. He seemed a fine fellow, not at all old, and
very kind and good.

"Well, Great-grandson Kay," he said, "*ne pouvez-vous pas*
come into the *jardin avec moi?*"

Kay thought it odd, but it was a perfect excuse for not doing
pouvoir. "I would have learned it, but Great-grandpapa Harker
asked me to come into the *jardin avec* him, so of course I
thought you wouldn't mind." He smiled back at Great-grandpapa
Harker and said, "*Oui, Grand-grand-père,* thank you. *Je serai* very
glad."

Great-grandpapa Harker held out both hands, and Kay jumped
onto the table. From there, with a step of run, he leaped onto

the top of the fender and caught the mantelpiece. Great-grandpapa Harker caught him and helped him up into the picture. Instantly the schoolroom disappeared. Kay was out of doors standing beside his great-grandfather, looking at the house as it was in the pencil drawing in the study, with cows in the field close to the house on what was now the lawn, the church, unchanged, beyond, and nearby some standard yellow roses, long since vanished, but now seemingly in full bloom.

Kay did not know quite what to say, so he said, "Did the cows really come so close to the house?"

"Yes, indeed. This is Sweetlips, that one is Rosemary, and the brindle is Colinette."

Kay was looking at the cows, who were all in the rich grass, grazing and swishing away the flies. An amiable-looking man, with a fat, pale face, a sun hat, and big green spectacles rose up from behind an easel among the roses. "That will be all that I can do for today, Harker," he said as he packed his things. "Come to think of it, you're the first full-length I've done."

Kay knew somehow that this was Baxter. He watched him move off across the grass to the gate, which was not a drive gate, as now, but a farm field gate, overshadowed by trees long since cut down. Kay was alone with Great-grandpapa Harker in a place that was his home but yet strangely different—so much of it was not there at all, not yet built.

"Is that all the house?" he asked.

"Yes. Come in, Great-grandson, and see it."

He led the way along a cobblestone path to a door— "somewhere near where the dining-room door is," as Kay thought. Pear trees grew up the house here. The porch was supported by the snouts of two carven wooden dolphins standing on their tails. "I brought those from Sainte Eustasie," Great-grandpapa Harker said. "They came off the stern of a Dutch ship that was wrecked there in the great storm of 1782, the year I was born. They must have blunted some chisels to carve them. Feel how tough the wood is."

Kay felt the hard, dark wood, as close-grained as African

oak. Great-grandpapa Harker opened the door into a long, rather dark-paneled room, now completely gone. There were some portraits on the wall: the man in the blue coat, with white stockings, now in the best bedroom; the man in the long brown coat with the red belt, now in the hall; and the lady that looked so like a camel. As they entered, a white cockatoo, which had been sitting quietly upon her perch, rose in excitement, with an open bill. An old, old lady was asleep in a chair. Something told Kay that when she had been younger she had looked like a camel. The only other things that Kay recognized were the arms in colored glass. These were in a window, whereas Kay saw them daily now in the fanlight of a door: three oreilles couped, for Harker; two siskins proper, for Siskin; seven abeilles grommelees or, for Colway; and three alms spirty, for Mynd.

Great-grandpapa Harker led the way out of the dining room, which was dark, into the study, which was still darker—too dark, as Kay thought, for anybody to read in comfort in it. It was paneled up to the ceiling and lined with books, nearly all of them little volumes bound in calfskin. They had been arranged according to size. When he looked round, having entered the room, he found that there were folios behind him.

"You see, Great-grandson," he said, "these books are not really books, but a shutter."

He moved something in the wall and a shelf of books swung away and let in a flood of light. Over the mantel was the portrait of the man in the puce coat, who was now in the hall. There was a blunderbuss up in one corner, wired to some nails, and an old harpsichord, which was now up in the boxroom with so many other moldering wrecks.

"Now, my little great-grandson," Great-grandpapa Harker said, "let me look at you and talk with you. Do they still think that I stole the treasure?"

"I'm sure you didn't," Kay said.

"Many thought that I did, and that I hid it somewhere— perhaps in the floor above this room. For years I had letters from people (who dared not sign their names) accusing me of stealing it. I lost it. It was trusted to me and I lost it. And what became of it, no one knows, though I think it must be sunk or scattered."

A black cat, with white throat and paws, which had been ashes for forty years, rubbed up against Great-grandpapa Harker's legs, and then, springing on the arm of his chair, watched the long-dead sparrows in the plum tree which had been firewood a quarter of a century ago.

"You ought to know about the treasure, Kay," Great-grandpapa Harker said, "for until it is restored or traced, no man of our name ought to rest. Your grandfather would not move in the matter, your father could not, there is only you."

"I'd love to hear all about it, if you'd tell me," Kay said.

"It was in the year 1811," Captain Harker began. "I was then in the *Plunderer*, West Indiaman, which I commanded and partly owned, in the port of Santa Barbara, loading sugar. War was raging all over the world. We in the *Plunderer* were very shorthanded. The admiral on the station had impressed all our best men, and we had lost some by fever. We had a crew of twenty-one, all told, to load, sail, and defend the ship, and of all of them only Hollings, my mate, was a man to trust in trouble.

"Nearly all the South American states were then breaking loose from Spain. A revolution broke out in Santa Barbara. The rebels marched up on the capital, which had only a hundred soldiers in the garrison. The people expected the city to be sacked.

"The archbishop with his priors came off to the *Plunderer* to ask me if they might lodge the treasures of the churches on board my ship for safety. I said that I had a very weak crew, that I was in an undefended port, and that French privateers were known to be on the coast. They said that as the rebels were in sight, they had no other chance of saving the things. So at this, I consented.

"They brought it aboard at once, and I had it stricken down

into the after hold. It consisted of church ornaments, images, lamps, candlesticks, reliquaries, chalices, and crosses, of gold, silver, and precious stones. Most of it was packed in grass matting, but in the hurry some were bare. I had never seen such wealth. Certainly my crew never had.

"In a way I saved it, for two hours later the rebels entered the city and sacked every church within the walls.

"Then my troubles began, but not from the rebels. Seven ships were seen approaching the port. From the whiteness of their sails I judged them to be French. Hollings, my mate, agreed with me. Roper Bilges, my gunner, a drunken and careless man, thought that they were Brazilians. Twiney Pricker, my sailmaker, a sinister person, with a great deal in him, said that they were French privateers. I gave the word to lower the boats and tow the ship out to sea, there being then a dead calm in shore.

"By the time that we were clear of the headland, the squadron was within shot. They were four French corvettes, two brigs, and a schooner, all full of men and well armed. In the first shots exchanged between us they wounded poor Hollings. They continued in chase till dark, driving us to the westward, but not gaining on us.

"I was more than anxious, having now only eighteen unwounded men on board, to sail the ship and defend this great wealth.

"After seeking guidance, I determined to make for our naval station at Puerto Recife, to hand over the treasure to the British admiral commanding there, and ask him to rereturn it in a ship of war when the civil troubles had ceased.

"Having set down this determination in writing, I read it to poor Hollings, to the gunner, Roper Bilges, and to the sailmaker, who all approved it. Going on deck, I read it to the ship's company.

"It was then dark, but the enemy ships' signals were still visible astern, perhaps two miles away. The wind was freshening from the north, which made the land a lee coast to us. Our rigging had been somewhat cut by shot, and with poor Hollings dying, the enemy near, the rocks close, night upon us, two wounded men to dress, and the whole navigation of the ship depending on me, I had my hands full. I have blamed myself bitterly for being taken unawares. I had no thought that what afterwards happened would occur.

"Poor Hollings died at midnight. With the wind freshening, I could not be present to minister to him. I stayed on deck till about three o'clock in the morning, when it was light enough to see the enemy ships far astern. That danger being past for the moment, and the ship holding her course well, I left the deck in charge of the sailmaker, intending to lie down in my clothes for an hour. I was gravely uneasy at my position, but did not doubt that I had decided rightly, both in receiving the treasure on board and in making for our squadron at Puerto Recife.

"I had not been long asleep when I was awakened by Roper Bilges bursting into my cabin with some of the crew, who seized me and bound me, threatening to kill me with their pistols, etc., and saying that the ship was now theirs. On my trying to reason with them, they put a gag in my mouth and gave three cheers 'for Roper Bilges and the bishop's treasure.' They said that they were now going to be gentlemen and 'on the account' —that is, pirates. Whether the first thought of this came from Bilges or the sailmaker, I cannot say. Certainly Bilges was now their captain.

"After five days of standing to the west, they put me ashore on the coast three hundred miles from any settlement of white men, with no weapon but a knife and no means of livelihood but that and a fishing line, which my Negro seaman had the humanity to slip into my hand. They left me on the coast and sailed away upon a northwesterly course, as though for the Gulf. What became of them, no man knows.

"I was made prisoner by the Indians, who took me with them far into the forest, to their camp by the falls. I was with the

Indians, as a slave, for more than five years. Being a slave is bad. It makes a man think too much of his own misery.

"Still, in the end I escaped, which few slaves do, and returned to a home of love and beauty, such as few slaves have ever had. I had been given up for dead by many—some supposed that I had run away with the treasure. I am glad to say that the archbishop, who knew me, never thought that. He had caused the ships of our navy to search for us. The admiral in his report said that the *Plunderer* had left Santa Barbara fighting an enemy squadron, and that although she had not been captured (as the men of the squadron confessed, when they were afterwards taken), she had probably received grave injuries and had sunk.

"When I made the truth known, the members of the crew were described and posted as pirates throughout the western seaports. I visited all the possible ports myself, and sought among the receivers of stolen goods for some trace of the treasure. I searched among hospitals, prisons, hulks, and galleys for some of the crew. I found no trace whatever, nor could I find any ship, lighthouse keeper, or signalman who had seen the *Plunderer* after me, when I saw her heading northwest as though for the Gulf. I do not know what became of her. Sometimes I think that she sank with all on board. Sometimes I think that she reached some port in the Gulf, where the crew settled and lived at ease. The treasure was trusted to me, my little great-grandson; I cannot tell you how the loss of it weighed upon me. I could not go back to my profession of merchant trader. My remaining days were passed in hunting for clues of it. For months I would say to myself, 'No, the *Plunderer* sank with all on board.' Then I would read that pirates had been captured in such and such a place, and after that I would know no rest till I had examined the confessions of the crew, what ships they had taken, and whether any could have been the *Plunderer*. Then after more months of thinking that she had sunk, I would say to myself, 'No. Roper Bilges probably sailed her to Europe, to a port of France or Spain. He may now be a great man in either land.' When such thoughts came, away I would go for months, to either land, or to Holland or Denmark, or further still to Italy and the Levant, to ask in the ports, till my heart sickened. I was known in many ports as 'the mad Englishman.' No one had ever seen the *Plunderer* except an Italian in Genoa, who had been my steward in her for a year.

"One of my griefs was this: that my wife and son (your grandfather) longed for me to give up the quest. They were sure that the *Plunderer* had sunk, and thought me mad to persist.

"Another grief was the knowledge that many people here believed that I had run away with the ship and stolen the treasure. It is said that listeners hear no good of themselves. I sometimes heard people say 'Ah, old Harker! They do say that he was a pirate and ran away with all the cathedral money.' Or 'Yes, he says that they took the ship from him with all that treasure on board. I daresay he wasn't very unwilling. Why didn't he shoot them? He had his pistols.' Or 'A very likely tale, that he was among the Indians for five years. Much more likely he was spending the treasure somewhere.' Once I heard a man say 'It's my belief he's got the treasure hidden in his house. Everybody says so. Besides, if he hasn't, what is it that he's got hidden under the hearthstone in his bedroom?'

"My bedroom is now yours, Kay, the room over this."

"What is underneath that big hearthstone?" Kay asked.

"Underneath that big hearthstone," Great-grandpapa Harker repeated. "Of course, some say the treasure. Then some think that somebody has been murdered and hidden there."

"And what is there?" Kay asked.

"Would you like to see, my little great-grandson?" Great-grandpapa Harker answered. "There is not much to see. What is it, Rover?"

As he spoke, the door of the library was thrust open, a pointer came shambling, wagging, and cringing all at once to his master's feet. The library changed and blurred at his coming. He seemed to have let a lot of light into the room. Indeed, even as Kay looked, it was not a room, but the field where the cows were grazing. But the cows were blurring all together, into one. They were, in fact, not cows, they were bushes, browner than bushes ought to be, with a blueness above them which he knew was meant to be the sky. He saw Great-grandpapa Harker standing there, but something dark and oblong surrounded him and shut him away. "Why, he's gone back into the picture," Kay thought. The glass of the picture shut the old man still further away. The picture was over the mantelpiece, and there was he, Kay, on the other side of the table, bent over the French verb *pouvoir*. Baxter's portrait of Great-grandpapa Harker was staring down unmoving.

The governess entered.

"Put away your *pouvoir* now, Kay," she said. "It's time for writing lesson. Take a piece of paper and write a nice letter to yourself while I do my books."

Kay began his letter.

My dear Kay,
    I hop you are quite well.
    I hop your friends, the cats, are quite well.
    I am quite well.
    Please give my love to Ellen. I hop she is quite well.
We have a nice dog here, but he is norty.

He sucked the end of his pen for a long time, but could think of nothing more to say, except that the norty dog was quite well.

"Haven't you finished yet?" the governess said. "How many more times am I to tell you not to suck your pen like that? You are a disobedient child. Let me see what you have written. Really, Kay," she said, having read the letter, "I forbid you to mention the words *quite well* in any other letter that you write. You learn a phrase and then repeat it just like a little parrot. And then how do you spell *naughty*? N-A-U-G-H-T spells naught. N-A-U-G-H-T-Y spells—what does it spell?"

"I don't know quite what it would spell."

"Yes, you do, sir. Think. Now what does it spell?"

"Think."

"No, it doesn't spell think. It spells what you are, naughty. Now you'll write out N-A-U-G-H-T-Y twenty-five times. And look at your writing, all slopping and sliding. You will not put both your fingers on the pen. You never see me with my finger under the pen in that way. You'll never be able to write unless you get both your fingers onto the pen. Now put them on the proper way."

*U*sually after lessons he played by himself in the garden—in the shrubberies if it were dry, and on the paths if it were wet. Today he went out of the garden, to walk by the brook which ran beside it, to watch the minnows in the shallows, and to see his friend the water rat coming from his cool swim to nibble a cress.

The water was clear, with green weeds swaying in it like fishes' tails. The water rat slid into it with a little fall of earth and swam downstream to his hole.

"I do wish I could be a water rat," he thought.

He wandered into a lane and then away across the fields to the church, where he found old Bert the sexton going up the tower to wind the clock.

"Mr. Bert," he said, "did you ever know my great-grandfather Harker?"

"Why, Master Kay, I've known all of you. I've known your father, Mr. Harker, and your grandfather, old Mr. Harker, afore him. And yes, I knew old, old Mr. Harker, but he was an old man when I came on to be a boy. That is, he wasn't an old man, but he seemed old. And he *was* old, beside old Mr. Harker."

"Will you tell me about him?"

"Why, I don't know that I can. Let me see, now: old, old Mr.

Harker. He'd been a savage Indian, so they did use to say. Ah! Old, old Mr. Harker. Yes, things were very different in those days. They'd no railways in those days, nothing but the coach up and down. And they'd the old gallows up on the hill. Let me see about old, old Mr. Harker, then, whether I can tell you anything. He lived where you live, only it wasn't built on to then, the new part. That was your grandfather built that, old Mr. George. I remember old, old Mr. Harker had a stick he used to walk with, a foreign stick all carved by the savages. They used to say he had a lot of foreign treasures all buried away, all gold and that, but I never believed that, for my father once heard him say to old Mr. Robert, that used to live in the Dingles' old place—but they made him bishop after—'Robert,' he said, 'if I could only find that treasure, it would be a load off my mind.' So I never believed he had treasure.

"But about him, Master Kay. I used to see him stumping about with his stick: he had the rheumatic complaint from being wet through so often. He gave me some of these foreign fruits once, done up in sugar, because I took a letter for him. They did say he oughtn't to have died when he did, for he wasn't what you would call old, but they did use to say that he had something on his mind, if you understand me. He had his tomb done out very pretty in the south aisle, though it seems old-fashioned now. There it is, by the pew where the Pengas sit, just this side of where they put your grandfather."

Kay stood upon the stone which covered Great-grandpapa Harker. On the wall, above the pews near it, was a memorial tablet carved with a small lady in high relief mourning beside a very big urn. A ship showed in the distance, part of an anchor stuck out of the urn. Underneath the design was an inscription:

Beside this Stone
Lie the mortal remains of
ASTON TIRROLD HARKER,
son of Charles Tirrold Harker, Esquire,
late of Seekings House, in this Parish.
Born 17th August, 1782. Died 13th January, 1850.

He was constant in Affection, spotless in Integrity, a useful Magistrate, eminent in his Calling, manly in Fortitude, womanly in Tenderness. He combined the graces of a Scholar with the Virtues of a good Citizen. Reader, canst thou say as much? If not, forbear to judge.

This Stone was erected 1850 by his sorrowing Widow, Jemima Siskin Harker, eldest daughter of Sir Brambling Siskin, of Siskin Hall, whom he married in 1811.

A stone to Jemima Siskin Harker, erected by her sorrowing son, George Tirrold Siskin Harker, lay a little to the east of this tablet on the same south wall.

Kay spent some few minutes looking at these and other tablets in the aisle. He then tried to make out the subject of a stained glass window, which he had puzzled over at a distance during many a dreary sermon. He could not get it clear: there were bits of heads, glories, horses and old writing; what he had decided was a yellow, half-lop rabbit seemed to be a hat with spikes. This was a blow, for the rabbit, named Bunkin, had beguiled even the litany.

"Mr. Bert," he said, "could you tell me the name of the gamekeeper who looks after Coneycop Spinney?"

"Why, yes," the sexton said. "That's the squire's covert. His keeper lives by the pine trees, out by Rye Meadows. Roper Bilges is his name, and Bilges is his nature, they do say."

"Roper Bilges!" Kay cried. "Roper Bilges? Were his ancestors gunners?"

"No," Bert answered, "not so far as I know, unless shotgunners."

"Did they come from these parts, do you know?"

"No, they came from up Salop way somewhere, not so long since. That Roper's brother is footman to Sir Hassle."

"Were there ever many smugglers here when you were a boy, Mr. Bert?" Kay asked.

"You mean what they used to call the nighthawks? Why, no, those were done before I began. They took to killing people. No, but there was something like them going on, bringing brandy and tea and that, not so very many years ago. I knew some who were concerned in it, though it's best not to speak of it. Only it was a blessing to poor folk in those dear times. Dreadful the prices were. I don't know who the head of it was, except that he was a gentleman, and he worked it very cleverly, no one quite knew how. No, they never caught him, but it came to an end."

"Was there anyone called Brown, or Trigger, doing it, do you know?" Kay asked.

Mr. Bert's face changed at the two names. He looked hard at Kay.

"The name I always heard tell was Mr. Galloway," he said. "But it may not have been his real name."

"I suppose all the things were brought up the river?"

"Yes, all these fellows, the nighthawks as well, brought their things up the river. And a very queer thing, now that we're talking of this, was what happened at the time of the Great Flood. There were some barges that had come up with corn to the old mill that was. It's gone now, but you can see where the wheels used to be—Condicote Old Mill, they called it. A very big mill he used to be—you'll have been to the place."

"Yes," Kay said. "I went there to a picnic once, and afterwards we all fished but never caught anything."

"Well, that's where Condicote Old Mill was," Mr. Bert said. "And about these barges that had come up: they'd come to what they called the wharf just below the lock in very rough rainy weather. You'll remember the wharf, maybe—it is just at the mill. Then there came the Great Flood, when all those barges were washed away and stove in about Cold Comfort Bridge. My father was a carpenter and builder, and as the barges were stove, he offered for the wood, to break up the wrecks and carry them away. Now when he came to break up those barges, he found that every one had a false bottom; there was a secret place in each one, where quite a lot of things could be put. And in two of them he found packs of tobacco, only the flood had got at it. So that shows you, doesn't it, how the stuff came and where it came to. My father never mentioned it to people, but it was queer, come to think of it, wasn't it?"

"Yes, indeed," Kay said. "And do you remember the Great Flood?"

"Why, yes, Master Kay. No people who saw it will forget it. There was a week of storm in January after a very wet season—oh, dreadful it had been, with the corn all lying out as late as October, all sprouting in the stooks. Then in this week it rained very hard, and the river rose, and then at full moon the spring tides came up and stopped the head of water from getting out. So it was like a sea all the way from Upwaters to Seven Hatches and beyond; bridges broken, all except the old one; cows, pigs, and sheep carried away: no getting across the river anywhere for days and days; and the weirs—oh, they were terrible, they would turn a man's mind to look at them, with all bits of cow byres, haystacks, pig troughs, trees, hencoops, bee skeps, everything just going tumbling down. I saw a cradle go over at Condicote Old Mill, and if there had been even twins in it, no man could have saved them. And nearly all the boats were gone too. It was all like a big sea as far as one could see, with hedges and trees standing out of it, and sometimes a sort of island, with a few cows on it mooing to be milked, poor things, or a poor horse running round half starved."

"Did you ever hear of a Mr. Brown who was drowned in the flood?"

Again Mr. Bert's face changed. "You mentioned that name before," he said, "as well as another name. There was a lot of talk about those two: that that Sir Trigger—for he was a Sir—murdered Mr. Brown, and flung him in the water and then fled."

"Do you think he did?" Kay asked.

"No, Master Kay, I don't. It's my belief that they both fell into the flood at Condicote Old Mill, and were drowned, only the Sir Trigger was washed into a mudbank and buried, whereas Mr. Brown was carried to Seven Hatches and found. Three or four people disappeared in the flood and were never heard of again. I believe Sir Trigger was one of them. If not, Master

Kay, I would say that it was the other way about: that the Brown man murdered *him* and was drowned while escaping."

"What makes you think that, Mr. Bert?"

"It's a long while ago," Mr. Bert said, "and everybody concerned is dead. But that Pimply Whatto's father, who was a bad one, when he was dying, told my father that on the last night those two were seen, he saw them both at the Ring of Bells, so as to know them. And at midnight that night he saw them both again, near the mill, and the Brown man was threatening the Trigger man, saying 'I've warned you twice: you'll get no third time." And the Trigger man said, 'If I lay hands on you again, I'll mark you. Get out!' And the Brown man did get out, but when the Trigger man moved on, Whatto saw the Brown man creep after him and take out a pistol, and no man ever saw them again alive. They both went on towards the flood. Whatto never came forward with this story at the inquiry, because he was afraid he might be charged with murdering them himself. Besides, he wasn't there himself for any good, you may be sure. And maybe his story isn't true, for he wasn't always quite the one for the truth. It's best to give them both the benefit. The Great Flood was more than enough to drown them without either of them doing murder. Still, that was the tale he told.

"They put a tablet to that Brown in Little Zennor Church, if ever you go there: 'To the memory of Abner Brown, Esq., a stranger. A victim of the Great Flood.' But there, I'm rambling on past dinnertime."

He had moved away, after dusting the knees of his trousers, when he stopped.

"That Mr. Brown was a western gentleman, it was thought," he said. "No one knew where he came from. He had twenty-five pounds in his bag at the inn, and no clue to where his home and people were. A white-haired man, he was. I've often thought of his people, far away, never knowing. Though they'll have done sorrowing by now, poor souls."

*T*hat night Kay had not been long asleep before he woke up to find the room brightly lit as before, although it was dark night outside. In the passages near his room there were whisperings and footsteps, as though people were pausing at his door to mutter some password. He sat up, expecting them to come in, but they passed on. When they had gone, he quietly opened his door an inch or two and peeped out. Some people in scarlet cloaks were just passing through a door at the end of the corridor, but one of them had paused. She was a young, very handsome witch, with long earrings. "Come along, sweet Belladonna," her companion said. "We shall be late for our chapter."

"Wait," Belladonna said. "I must just see what is in here."

"No, come along. We must not keep Abner Brown waiting."

Saying this, the witch pulled Belladonna away, and in a moment the door closed behind them. Whether it was the closing of the door or the sudden movement Kay could not tell, but at the instant something fell onto the carpet from Belladonna's sleeve or pocket. Kay crept out to see what it was. It was a little red glass bottle, with a cut-glass stopper.

"I expect it's her scent bottle," he thought. He tried to open the door through which she had gone, so that he could give it back to her, but the door was fast closed, and what was worse, the handle gave him pins and needles when he touched it. And another strange thing was that all this part of the house was unlit, while his own room was brighter than a summer day. The cuckoo clock, inside the closed room, cuckooed for eleven o'clock.

When he was back in his room, he looked at the little glass bottle. "Witches' scent," he thought. "I wonder what it smells like." But it was not scent. It was labeled like a physic bottle.

INVISIBLE MIXTURE
Take 3 drops upon a lump of sugar.   Night Dose.
  6   ”   ”   ”   Day Dose.
Repeat dose if necessary.

"I believe it's the stuff they take to make themselves invisible," he thought. "I'll try it, and then I'll go out to the gamekeeper's cottage to see how they behave when they find that the hunters aren't at Coneycop Spinney at all."

He had some old lumps of sugar put away under the carpet. He took out one of these and carefully opened the bottle. The mixture had a warm, rich smell, like the smell of green bracken on a very hot day. "I must be very careful of this," he thought. He dropped three drops onto a lump, popped it into his mouth, and restoppered the vial. A glow went through him, as though he were sucking the loveliest peppermint ever made. He hid the vial in a mouse hole in the skirting board behind the valance, and then stood up. He felt a pepperminty feeling go tingling along his toes, and lo, he looked at his toes and could not see them, nor his legs, nor his pajamas. And though he looked at himself in the glass, he was not there; he was invisible. "I say, what fun," he said. He put on his slippers and went down into the hall, where a mouse was eating a crumb in the center of a patch of moonlight. The mouse did not see him but went on grinding and nibbling at the crumb till it was finished. He pushed the chair against the garden door, clambered up it,

drew the bolts, turned the key, undid the chain, took off the
burglar alarm bell, and opened a way for himself. In a minute
he was over the wall and away to the pinewood out by Rye
Meadows.

It was thrilling to walk up to rabbits in the grassy places, and
to stroke them, while they thought that his touch was either a
grassblade or the wind. An owl blundered right into him,
bounced off, hovered, tried to make out what it was that it had
hit, and then sheered off, much puzzled. At Peter's Patch the
keeper's dogs came out barking at him, with the keeper after
them.

"What are Sol and Jo barking at?" his wife asked.

"Sounded like a footstep to me, but there's no one here."

"I expect it was only a rabbit."

"I'll rabbit them rabbits. Come in, dogs."

When they had gone into the cottage, Kay crept a little
nearer. Some friends of Mr. Bilges were there. Kay peeped in at
the open door. The dogs snarled, and their hair stood on end
with terror.

"Quiet, dogs, will you?" Mr. Bilges said, kicking them in the
ribs. "Now we'll have a little drop of our nice spirit, which
nobody knows about." He produced a bottle, some sugar, and a
lemon, while his wife brought a kettle of hot water and a bowl.
Then they began to brew a punch. Kay could see the keeper's
friends: they were Brassy Cop and the Pimply Whatto, as they
were called, the two worst poachers and fighters in the district.
The other was the young Bilges, who was footman to Sir Hassle
Gassle. They drank the punch when it was made; then they
began to boast.

"It must be nearly time to move off to the spinney," Brassy
said. "I heard the clock go one."

"They'll not be finished before two or three, we hear," the
keeper said. "What I want to do is to come in among them with
my good gun, just as they're packing up my rabbits. I'll soon
settle their hunting."

"Ah!" his brother said. "What I want is to get their rabbits and get the money for them. I reckon to get four times drunk out of what we get tonight."

"What I'm for," Whatto said, "is to bang them black and blue with my knoppy blackthorn."

"Ah!" Brassy said. "A few good bangs on the heads with that, and they'll not poach so gamesome another time. But I've got my nice brass knuckle-dusters. That's what I'll dust them with."

"Why, mercy me," the keeper's wife said, "if we haven't left the game bags down at the hall! Whatever shall we bring their rabbits home in, when we've beaten them?"

"Ah!" the keeper said. "Why, whatever shall we?"

"We shall want a big thing. There'll be a hundred rabbits, they said."

"A hundred rabbits," Brassy said. "They'll kill and we'll eat, and bang 'em into the bargain."

"But what shall we bring the rabbits home in?"

"I don't know. Except we each carry twenty."

"I know what we can pack the rabbits in," the keeper cried. "My old grandfather's sea trunk, or chest, as he called it. That will hold the rabbits. I'll fetch it down."

Kay heard him go upstairs. Soon he came down, trundling the chest after him. It was a big black wooden chest, bound with iron at the corners. It had the name "R. Bilges" painted in dirty white letters on the side. There were rope beckets or shackles curiously wrought, instead of the usual handles, to lift it by.

"He might be your grandfather's coffin," Brassy said.

"He was a seaman gunner, my grandfather was," the keeper said, "and a fine old drunken boy he was. It's my belief he had something on his conscience. There's some of his things still in here."

On opening the box to empty it, he pulled out some old bottles covered with wickerwork, an old leather kneeboot, a patched pair of shoes from which the buckles had been cut, and some books. "That's my old grandfather to the life," the keeper said. "Just some empty bottles that you can't drink, and old leather that you can't wear. Into the woods with you!"

Kay had just time to slip aside before bottles, boots, and books were flung out past him into the wood.

"Now, Brassy," the keeper said, "if you'll take that end, I'll take this, and we'll move off to the spinney. We won't take the dogs."

"Come on, then."

The three men moved off towards the spinney.

"Make an end of them all, my Bilges," the keeper's wife cried.

"Never you fear," the keeper answered, beginning to sing:

> "My name it is Roper and Willem,
> And I do intend for to killem
>   With my good gun-and-cartridging
>   I'll finish their partridging,
> For I'll shootem and deadem and stillem."

As they moved into the pinewood, Kay saw the black figure of Blackmalkin step from the hedge to join them. "They'll be at work in the spinney now," he said. "You'll catch them just as they're packing up the spoils and planning what they'll do with them. Oh, what fun it will be to see their faces! But I say, Keeper, what is that by the gate that your dogs are barking at?"

The dogs had come out to bark at Kay, whom they could scent but not see.

"I'll dog those dogs," the keeper said, turning back a little. "Get you back into kennel, or I'll give you one. Keep the dogs in. Don't let 'em make that outlandish row, as though a basket of wildcats was turned loose."

The keeper's wife called in the dogs and shut the door on them.

"Now, Blackmalkin," Keeper said, "and what are *you* gawping at there? Are you going to bark too?"

"No," Blackmalkin said. "I suppose it is all right."

"Suppose what is all right?"

"That path there, from your house to the wood."

"What could be wrong with it?"

"Look at it," Blackmalkin said. "Didn't you see the twigs stir on the path, just as though somebody trod on them?"

"Can't you see that nobody trod on them?"

"Yes," Blackmalkin said. "But they moved as though someone trod on them."

"It was the wind," Brassy said.

"Or a mouse running across."

"I know when a mouse runs across," Blackmalkin said. "This wasn't a mouse."

"Well, then, it was the shadow of a leaf or a moth, or a bat."

"It looked like a person's footstep."

"Well, there isn't a person, so it can't have been."

"Look here," Pimply Whatto said. "How much more time are we to waste? Nice fools we'll look if they've gone with the rabbits before ever we get there."

"Yes, come on," the keeper said. "You go in front, Blackmalkin, and forget all about what you thought you saw."

They all moved off after this, growling at Blackmalkin, who kept looking back suspiciously at where Kay stood. He had seen the earth and twigs displaced by Kay's feet. Kay saw him looking back until the party was so far downhill that he could look no more.

When they were all out of sight, Kay looked at the things which the keeper ·had flung away. The bottles and leather seemed useless to him, but he looked at the books with interest. They were:

Mother Shipton's Prophecies Explained
Zimmerman on Solitude
The Execrable Life and Death of Scarlet Blackbones, the Barbados Pirate
A Book to Reckon Tides
The Sea Gunner's Reckoner

Tom Maggot's Fifty Merry Jests
The Sea Gunner's Practice

All of these books, except the last, were dirty, tattered, dog-eared pamphlets without covers. Kay left them where they lay but took *The Sea Gunner's Practice* to look at later. He did not think that this could be wrong, since the keeper had flung it away.

He was not sure of the way to Coneycop Spinney. He went down the hill as the others had gone. The path led over a brook into the valley below two rolls of down. He went on till he came in sight of Coneycop Hill, which there was no mistaking. A strip of wood in a bottom below the hill seemed likely to be the spinney. It was a still, moonlit night, with nothing stirring except himself. He could not see the keeper's party. He went cautiously. Soon he caught sight of Brassy Cop staring into the spinney from behind a tree. Blackmalkin was beside him. Coneycop church clock, which was just beyond Coneycop, struck four. Kay marveled that the time had gone so quickly, but every instant had been lovely, being out there alone in the moonlight, seeing everything but not being seen. Suddenly, quite silently, two figures crept past him, peering at the spinney. They were so intent on what they were doing that they never scented him. Both were very muddy and shaking with excitement. One was Nibbins, the other was Bitem.

"There's the keeper," Nibbins whispered. "He's got no dogs now, hush!"

Kay saw the two Bilgeses, followed by Pimply, come up to Brassy.

"Not much good waiting any longer," the keeper growled. "Here it is beginning to be light. Not a sign of any hunt, nor of any rabbit."

"I suppose they got the alarm and didn't come," Pimply said.

"How could they have got the alarm? And here we've waited hours in the cold and have to drag that empty trunk back."

"Where's the hundred rabbits you promised?" Brassy asked.

"I'll hundred rabbits you if you ask that again," the keeper said. "Of all the withering watches I've ever watched, this has been the witheringest and the watchiest. Here, you Blackmalkin, if that's your name, where's your friends that were to come, eh? Where are they?"

"Well, they *said* they were going to come," Blackmalkin said.

"Ah, they *said*, did they? And on what you said we've suffered."

"Are you sure you didn't get the night wrong?" Pimply asked.

"I'll bet they said Friday next week and he mistook it," Brassy said.

"No, I didn't mistake it."

"Well, if you didn't mistake it, where are they, then?" young Bilges asked.

"I don't know."

"Nor we don't know."

"Wait a minute," Pimply said. "Here's people coming. Perhaps it's them, after all."

Kay saw a woman and a man coming hurriedly towards them.

"It's your wife, Bilges," Brassy said. "With that young Artful Artie."

"Is Bilges there?" Mrs. Bilges asked.

"Yes, I'm here, of course I'm here. What is it?"

"It's about Brady Ride Wood, Bilges. Here's Artful just come from there. While you've been watching here, that Bitem and his friends have cleaned out all the rabbits from the whole south warren."

"Not a scut left white in the whole boiling," Artie said.

"They've been and cleaned out the south warren?"

"Yes."

"That's why they never came here, then. The whole thing was a blind to bring us here, so that they could hunt in peace."

"Seems like it."

"How many rabbits would there be in the south warren?"

"A hundred and fifty, if there was one."

"You've been made a fool of, Bilges."

"Yes," Bilges said, "I've been made a fool of. We've all been made fools of. And this sneaking, prying Blackmalkin that told us all the story, is the one that made us the fools. Don't you try to sneak away, you black, sneakin' sneak, for I've got you by the scruff."

"I didn't make you a fool. I told you the truth. Oh, please let me go, you're almost choking me," Blackmalkin said.

"I've a very good mind to quite choke you. You were in the plot with them. You knew they were going to Brady Ride Wood."

"Oh, please, sir, I didn't, sir!"

"Yes, you did," Pimply said. "Don't you dare deny it."

"Of course he knew it," Brassy said.

"And we gave you milk and the bit of sardine," Mrs. Bilges said.

"Oh, please, ma'am, they disagreed, ma'am, indeed, indeed, they disagreed."

"Yes, and we're going to disagree," Bilges said, swinging him up by the scruff. "He's led us all here for the whole night, and his friends have robbed our rabbits. I vote we fling him into Sousepig Pond."

"Yes, with a stone round his neck."

"Oh, no, please! Not into a pond: I shall catch my death. I can't stand water, indeed I can't."

"Who's going to put you into water, to poison what's good drink (when mixed with gin)? No. Sousepig Pond is mud, and mud is what you're fittest for. Take his tail, Pimply, and twist it if he tries to escape."

Kay saw them carry Blackmalkin away down the hill. He followed them at a little distance to see what they would do. Not very far from the end of the spinney was a big shallow pan fed by a spring, and full of water in the winter, but now full of soft pale mud in which Farmer Fattenham's pigs loved to wallow as a protection against the flies. It was a most filthy, messy place.

At the brink of this hollow the party paused.

"Now, Blackmalkin," the keeper said. "This is Sousepig Pond, and as you're a dirty little pig, you're going to souse in it: once for sneaking and once for squeaking and once for telling us lies, oh." As he sang these lines he swung Blackmalkin round his head and pitched him SWOOSH into the mud. They all laughed at him and mocked him as he tried to clamber out.

"There. Now we'll go home," the keeper said. "Another time perhaps he'll be careful who he tries to make an April fool of."

*T*he party moved off for home in a very bad temper. Kay heard them growl as they passed.

"And we've got to drag that sea chest up the hill!" "And all those rabbits, which we could have got sixpence apiece for, let alone the soup and the skins." "If I'd shot that Blackmalkin with my good gun, I'd only have given him some of what he deserved," etc., etc.

Kay saw Nibbins and Bitem peering from behind the hedge, both of them shaking with laughter. When the keeper's party had passed out of sight, Nibbins and Bitem hopped over the hedge to the brink of the pond. Kay heard them call out:

"I say, I say! How did . . . how on earth . . . Here, there's someone in the mud. Get a stick, quick. Here, give us a paw. Stick out your brush, Bitem. Poor fellow, he's pretty nearly smothered. Catch hold, now. Pull now, Bitem, pull. He's coming. . . . I say, he's nearly stuck past saving. Heave together now. There he comes! Why, if it isn't poor old Blackmalkin! Why, Blackmalkin, whatever brings you here?"

"Whatever brings you here?" Blackmalkin growled. "This is a pretty sort of time to come hunting, just as it's getting light. You're nice people to arrange to go hunting with. I turned up, according to the plan. Keeper catches me and souses me in the mud. You two silly asses go gallivanting somewhere, and turn up grinning, hours too late to do anything. Oh, for pity's sake stop grinning in that insane way. It's nothing to laugh at, that I can see."

"No, we're really ever so sorry," Bitem said. "But we'd better be off to our beds. It's too late to do any hunting now."

"Perhaps at least you'll explain where you two grinning idiots have been passing the night, while I've been waiting for you."

"We got into a bit of fun out Brady Ride Wood way," Bitem said, "and the time slipped away just like magic. We'd no idea it was so late. But we mustn't keep you talking here, old man—you'll be taking cold."

"Yes," Nibbins said, "you must hop off home, old man. Have a good rub in the bracken shed—nothing like bracken for mud—and then have a good stiff bowl of hot milk, with a sardine to it, if you can get one."

With this they set off to their homes.

Kay followed at a little distance and let himself in just as the blackbirds were stirring. He was visible by this time, but very dim and blurred. As he climbed into bed, the thought occurred to him, "Suppose I'm invisible at breakfast time. What on earth shall I do then? I'll give Ellen a jolly good scare, that's one good thing." At this he fell fast asleep, till Ellen called him for the second time, by shaking him hard.

"You'll be late again, Master Kay, and then you'll be punished."

He sat up in bed, blinking, not knowing quite where he was. He stayed there blinking long after Ellen had gone. He was not quite sure that he had not dreamed all his adventures. He was no longer invisible, that was very sure. Then as he sat blinking, a nibbling, scrunching noise came from the dressing table. Something there was grinding and eating one of his lumps of sugar. He sat very still, staring at it. He could see nothing, but the lump was being turned about and becoming smaller. Presently it was all gone, and the scrunching ceased. Then a queer thing happened. There was a little odd flickering sort of a noise upon the dressing table. One of the other lumps of sugar moved in a most odd way to the edge and toppled over to the floor. After lying there for a few seconds, it began to move again, along the edge of the skirting board, behind the dressing table, where he could no longer see it. Soon after this the scrunching noise sounded from somewhere in the wainscot. "I know what it is," he thought, "the mice have been licking the invisible mixture."

He hopped out of bed and pulled the vial from the mouse hole. Alas, they had been more than licking it. They had contrived to pull or to knock out the stopper, or perhaps he had not fixed it in properly, and the precious mixture was gone, either drunken by the mice or evaporated. Even the smell of green bracken and the flavor of peppermint had gone from it. It was just a tiny empty vial of red cut glass. In his grief and disappointment he flung it through the open window into the bushes. "I'll never be able to be invisible again," he thought. "Just as I'd set my heart on it!"

As he entered the dining room he noticed Nibbins curled up on his chair with his chin twisted up underneath his paw, sound asleep. The governess asked for Blackmalkin.

"Oh, I can't let him in, ma'am," Ellen said, "he's in such a pickle. He's plastered with mud or something, just as if he'd been down a rabbit hole."

Blackmalkin was brought in plastered with the mud of the hog wallow.

"He'd better be bathed," Kay said, "because that mud is like tarring and feathering. It closes all the pores of the skin, and he may die."

A big pan of hot water was brought, and although Blackmalkin objected very strongly, he was soaked, scrubbed, rinsed, and dried.

"Another time," Ellen said, "you keep out of those rabbit holes, you foolish thing. You get enough food here without crawling down rabbit holes which don't belong to you. Another time the rabbit hole will fall right in on you, and then where will you be?"

After lessons that morning Kay went to his bedroom to the cool, pink secret cave made by the valance of his bed. "I don't suppose the book will be here," he thought. "That was probably only a dream, though it was a jolly one."

When he turned back the flap of rappy carpet, the book *was* there. He turned over on his stomach with a sigh of pleasure, to examine it in peace.

"*The Sea Gunner's Practice,*" he read to himself, "With a Description of Captain Shotgun's Murdering Piece with the improved Breech Action for use upon Savage Coasts. Together with Tables and Proportions for all Pieces usual to that Service, by B. Blastem, Master Gunner." On the flyleaf, in a neat handwriting, with a clove-hitch flourish below it, was the name of the owner: "Aston Harker, Seekings House, 1804."

"Why," he said to himself, "it is my great-grandfather's book. How very strange!" The book had been the property of other men before it had come to Captain Harker, for other names and earlier dates were written in it. He settled to read.

The Sea Gunner's Practice was stiff reading for a little boy, though there were thrilling pages in it. One page was labeled: "To Make Fine-grained Gunpowder, for Priming." Another had the heading: "To Make Coarse-grained Gunpowder." Another began, "To Make Colored Flares and Other Artificial Fire Works."

"Some day," he thought, "I'll make gunpowder by the help of this. Then I'll fire off Great-grandpapa's pistols that are on the wall, and I'll have fireworks every night."

At the end of the book some twenty blank pages had been left by the publishers so that sea gunners might make notes and accounts of their stores according to the tables printed for their guidance. Captain Harker had made notes upon the first of these pages. The rest had been scrawled upon in a clumsy, coarse, untidy writing by someone who did not know how to spell. In the cover of the book, at the end, was a pocket, which had once contained an engraving of Captain Shotgun's murdering piece. The engraving was gone; in its stead was a very old brittle yellow piece of newspaper, headed:

—EW YORK, December 1811
Strange Rescue in Gulf

He read on. "Great interest was roused in West Street last evening by the arrival of the ship *Seamen's Rights*, Captain Isaac Winterbourne, with a cargo of logwood from Campeachy. Captain Winterbourne reports that while in the Gulf he saw smoke rising apparently from the sea. Thinking that some ship might be on fire or assailed by pirates, he stood towards the smoke, and was soon rewarded by raising the Cranes Reefs, or rocky islets mentioned by Narvaez in his *Gulf Pilot*. The smoke proceeded from a fire of driftwood kindled by a solitary castaway, whom they found to be too crazed by his misfortunes to give a clear account of himself. No doubt he was the survivor of some merchantman wrecked in one of the great hurricanes, of which the last season was so fruitful. He seemed accustomed to a seafaring life, but neither his clothing nor his speech gave any clue as to who or what he was, the hardships to which he had been subject having destroyed his reason.

"On arrival in West Street, Captain Winterbourne sent him to a well-known doctor in Bleecker Street, from whose house he escaped in the course of last evening. Though he is certainly harmless, his manner may perplex or even frighten people, and the following description of him is issued to the public:

"A strong-built man of five foot seven or eight inches in height, brown hair and eyes, short sandy beard, nose broken as though by a blow, and the lips somewhat slobber. When found on the rocks, he was dressed only in a suit of threadbare cottons. He left the *Seamen's Rights* in a costume supplied by Captain Winterbourne, tarred trousers, a tarred hat, blue shirt and jacket. He had no property but an old Bible, a prayer book, and a pamphlet on gunnery, to all of which the demented creature appeared equally attached. All these volumes had had several possessors and gave no clue to his identity.

"Captain Winterbourne in his passage home was twice assailed by the tyrants of the waves, but by his vessel's speed was on both occasions able to uphold the challenge of her name."

Kay wondered if the story could refer to some survivor of the *Plunderer*. Captain Harker had said that the *Plunderer* was last seen sailing towards the Gulf. Here was Captain Harker's book taken from a rock in the Gulf at about the time of the *Plunderer*'s disappearance. And then the strange thing was that the book had been in the possession of this gamekeeper, whose name was Roper Bilges.

"Yes," Kay thought, "the gamekeeper is the descendant of my great-grandfather's Roper Bilges, and probably the man taken off the reef was Roper Bilges himself. I'm jolly glad that he did have some hardships. But wait a minute. There's all this writing at the end. Perhaps that will tell me more."

Turning to the writing at the end, he read as follows:

"The true statement of Roper Bilges, gunner in the ship *Plunderer*, Captain Harker, master.

"Since I have been spared to see that honesty is the best policy, I, Roper Bilges, set down the truth, so that justice may be done on villains. After I took charge of the *Plunderer*, to prevent her falling into bad hands, I had words with Twiney Pricker, the sailmaker, as he called himself, though he was nothing better than a pirate, having been one often, as I will swear. On my giving him orders as captain, he gave me low words, which I passed by, thinking that they would wait till we was ashore. In the night he came to my cot with three others, with Jake and the coffin-maker (having been such in Bristol), and English Joe, that deserted the *Blanche* frigate and had her on his stomach in blue. They said, '— —, we'll no more Bilges for captain. Get down into the boat!'

"They put me ashore on some rocks, where there was nothing but birds and a kind of rat what lived on shellfish and the rain. They give me nothing but Bible and Prayer and one about gunnery. Pricker was against giving me fire, but the men stood out for me to have that. When they pulled back to the ship, she filled and stood off, and I never heard of her again. She was going, as they said, to the French settlements.

"On being left alone, I collected driftwood for a dozen fires which I always kept well heaped up so as not to lose my fire. I ate on rats, shellfish, and seabirds, and the fish in the pools. At first I thought the crew was doing it for a pretend and would come back and take me off, but my fine scoundrel Pricker saw to that.

"I reflected what my lot would be when the rains ceased on those hot rocks, with no shade, and whether I would go mad, etc.

"My main fear was of a hurricane which might whelm me out of this wicked world, which is but a snare. My one hope was, I had good books by me.

"On the eleventh day, or it may be the twelfth, for my mind was not very correct, being crazed with horror at T. Pricker's monstrous ingratitude, I was took off by the ship *Seamen's Rights*, Captain Winterbourne, master, with whom I returned to New York, tho' not recovered in my brains. So fearing to be had into the madhouse to be cut open by the doctors, I thought it best to avoid into the country parts, where little by little my reason, which parts me from the brutes, came back as good as ever it was, tho' no thanks to T. Pricker, the madhouse being my dread as well he knew.

"Coming back to England, I see in the newspapers that Captain Harker is not dead, of which I am heartily glad, for I never meant him harm, and I am glad not to have his blood on my soul, it lying all on Twiney Pricker, who, I doubt not, has reaped his judgment according. It was he had the treasure. Whether it profited him I leave all to judge, for from that day to this no one has ever heard what came to him and them. One thing is sure, the ship is sank, for else we'd have heard of their folly, spending their ill-gotten gains, etc.

"If she was not sunk in a squall, she was cast away, and her crew and fine sailmaker captain made examples of as pirates, as I heartily hope. But having suffered according to his deserts, I forgive him the dirty turn he done me, but if this should come after my death into the hands of the police, let them know that Twiney Pricker was from the northern parts, a sailmaker by profession, and speaks in the northern way, lobster-eyed and blue of both eyes, wears his beard in the Newgate fringe fashion, has two teeth missing from the upper jaw on left side, being hit with a pot in a dispute about the victuals. He has also a lady's heart transfixed with arrow on chest in gunpowder, also the fat ox of Bedford on his right arm. He speaks somewhat thick, owing to the teeth being gone, stands a short fellow but very thick. His hair, which we call twiney, is of a fair color, like sea twine. Anyone laying such by the heels would be entitled to the reward against pirates, though for my part, not being wishful to testify against an old shipmate, as well as being of a Xtian turn and having forgiven him, would like to be kept out of it, not to come into court, if I could have the half reward for him, my one wish in this being for justice on bloody-minded villains. If he be now dead (as I sadly fear) guvvanment should hang his bones up as a warning what comes to these fine sailmakers that puts their betters upon rocks and would not give them even fire until forced to by some as would have shot them if they'd refused, it being only bullets as such dogs have brains to understand, being very ignorant fellows, for all they sit so high, as these northern parts men do.

"But I have now done with these wicked men, and took back my own name of R.B., and no harm can come now, Capt. H. being now dead. So I live at peace, only write this so as truth may prevail and justice be done. The half reward might be left for Roper Bilges, at the post office, Shrewsbury, and would consent to a third. R.B."

Kay read this story through three times. "It served him jolly well right," he thought, "to be served as he served my great-grandfather. I'm jolly glad that he was put ashore. It is hard luck that all the treasure was lost, but anyhow I'd rather that than for Twiney Pricker and the others to have the benefit of it. It is exciting fun, piecing out the story."

He went to the library, where with some trouble he pulled out the atlas, which had belonged to his grandfather. It was a big, heavy book. He lugged it to the table, turned up the western maps, and tried to find the Cranes Reefs. After some time he found them, as little black specks in the midst of the pale blue Gulf, not very far from the lagoons of the French settlements. "That is where they left Roper Bilges," Kay thought. "And somewhere between those specks and the coast is where the *Plunderer* sank. I expect she is all covered with coral now, or fallen all to bits."

He left the atlas open on the library table and returned to his lair above. When he had read the tale again, he left *The Sea Gunner's Practice* on his dressing table.

"That is what happened to the treasure," he thought. "Pricker took it from Bilges and then it was sunk. I wish that I could tell Great-grandpapa Harker, for that would be a load off his mind. No one could call that his fault."

*T*hat afternoon the governess took him into the village, where he had to wait in the milliner's shop while she matched a reel of silk; to wait outside the butcher's (and not to play in the water of the gutter there, because there was blood in it) while she complained of last Sunday's joint, which had been tough even when minced; then to wait outside the stationer's, and not to go staring at the sweets next door because she would only be a minute, whereas she took eleven, because she met Mrs. Gossip there changing her novel; then in the last torment to wait in the sitting room of Mrs. Tattle, looking at her case of wax fruits while "they" talked about Mr. Holyport's sermon, and the sermon before that, and whether bugles were going to be much worn that year. The mention of bugles roused him for an instant, but it was soon plain that it wasn't his kind of bugle, and that neither the governess nor Mrs. Tattle would come rousing the forest like Robin Hood: far from it. Then there was talk of the butcher, whose meat was so tough, and of the new butcher, down in the River Road, who had supplied a piece of veal that really, Mrs. Tattle was usually afraid of veal, because Dr. Gubbins says that you must be careful about veal, especially at night, but that this piece of veal, really it wasn't like veal at all, but just like young lamb, so crisp when hot and delicious cold. Then there was all this talk about this and that in the newspapers that it was really dreadful what people were coming to, especially young people. . . . Here there came a home thrust at Kay, who wasn't at all "what we were when we were girls," which was very likely true.

However, this visit, like so many others, came to an end at last. He was walked home to tea with a lecture about not fidgeting when he was paying a call, and especially of not twisting his hat elastic round and round, and then letting it untwist, just as he'd been told not to at the swing, because it made everybody sick.

He was undressing for bed that night when the governess, who was preparing to play the piano, called to him from the study, "Kay, was it you who had out the big atlas and left it open here?"

"Yes, it was, please."

"What did you have it out for?"

"Please, I wanted to look out a place."

"Yes, but why didn't you ask me or Ellen to put it back when you had done with it? You must get into the way of being tidy and not leave great books about when other people want to use the table."

It was just this interruption which kept him from putting *The Sea Gunner's Practice* into the secret nook. It was lying there on the dressing table, just as he had left it. He had almost picked it up to put it away when she asked that question, then it went out of his mind. He got into bed, making up his mind to keep awake. He was quite sure that he would not go to sleep. He half thought that he would get out of bed to hide away the book, but he did not see the use of it. One of the mice was scrunching away at the wainscot—he wondered if it were still invisible. It went scrunch and scrunch, as though grinding at the wood sideways. The scrunching mingled with the singing of the governess at last in a very drowsy noise which made the room dimmer, dimmer, and dimmer, until . . .

He woke up suddenly, wide awake and still with terror from

the knowledge that someone was in the room. He rolled under the clothes at once, waited terrified there for a minute, and then peeped out.

The room was brightly lit, as before, by no apparent light. It was dark night out of doors still, as he could see. An old woman in a poke bonnet was standing close to his bed looking about her. "Our young friend is fast asleep, Blackmalkin," she said, "but tread quietly. I must have a look about here."

He knew that sharp voice at once, and the next instant saw her face. It was Mrs. Pouncer.

"Yes," Mrs. Pouncer said, moving to the book upon the dressing table, "what have we here? Aha, a very interesting book, very interesting. No wonder, Blackmalkin, that we pull down big atlases, to see where gulfs and places are. A very interesting pretty little book, Blackmalkin dear, but not at all the sort of reading for a nice young gentleman who ought to be giving his mind to *pouvoir*. I think, my dear Blackmalkin, I will remove this little book."

At this she put it into her handbag, which shut with a snap. The odious Blackmalkin sidled against her ankles, purring.

When she had taken the little book, she said, "I will just look round the room, Blackmalkin dear, in case there should be any other things of interest." She lifted up a pair of glasses upon a handle, and began her search. She looked under the valance of the dressing table. "Sugar, I see," she said. "Our young friend's private lunch, I presume. Rather dirty sugar. Unwholesome, I should say. Something of a smell of peppermint, too, isn't there. Or am I wrong about the peppermint. Not quite peppermint, either, though, but I've lost the scent now." She stared at the prints and at the model of the *Plunderer*. "The sports of our dear fathers," she said, "and the toy . . . ah . . . *Plunderer*, I see. . . . Ah, *Plunderer*. The name of the ship . . ."

She paused for a minute over the ship. Then she pulled a chair to the wall, stood upon it, fixed a magic lens upon the handle of her glasses, and stared through the model fixedly. "Nothing there," she said. "Nothing hidden there. No clue."

She carried the chair across the room, again stood upon it, and examined the pistols in the same way. "Useless," she said. "No clue there. But let us now look at the hearthstone."

She rolled back the carpet so as to expose the slab. It was a big, clean block, six feet by four, apparently mortared and leaded into brickwork. She knelt down upon it, tried several magic lenses in her glasses, but seemed unable to see through it with any. She tapped it with a little hammer which she had in her bag. She pressed the knobs in the planks near it, as though hoping to press a secret spring. Nothing happened.

"I don't think that there is anything there," she said. "But there may be a hollow space. . . . It is a very big stone for an upstairs fireplace. There seems to be nothing more to examine here." She tapped the window seats and the wainscotings, looked under the bed, pulled the sofa to one side.

"I think, my dear Blackmalkin," she said, "we might go. There is nothing of any interest. We will go back to the library, where books like this seem to be found." As she moved past the dressing table on her way to the door, she paused again. "It is odd," she said. "I really distinctly caught that smell of peppermint, or not quite peppermint. Perhaps it is a little the smell of mice, my dear young friend. You really ought between the three of you to be able to control the mice."

The odious Blackmalkin sidled against her ankles, purring.

"He's a regular little sucking-up sneak," Kay thought. "I'm jolly glad the keeper soused him."

Mrs. Pouncer looked at Kay for a moment. He rolled slowly over drowsily. "How soundly our young friend sleeps," she said. "Well, the sounder the better—we don't want young friends prying about the house while we're at work."

Saying this, she moved out of the room, followed by Blackmalkin. When the door was closed upon her, Kay sat up to make sure that she had gone.

"I'll know her again if ever I see her," he said to himself. "She has a hooky nose, a hooky chin, very bright black eyes, long dingle-dangle earrings which click, a poke bonnet, a red cloak, a stick with a hooky handle, and pointy, black shiny shoes. And although in a way she looks old, in another way she looks very young. And she has bagged my book. . . . I'll see if I can't follow her, to get it back."

It was all very well to make this resolve from a warm bed, but when out of bed, and about to open the door onto what might be a dark passage full of witches, it did not seem so wise. "And yet," he thought, "Roper Bilges's name is in the book. If she finds out, somehow, that I got it from the keeper instead of from the library, she'll probably tell the governess, I shall be asked how I got it, and then there'll be a row. It will all be discovered then: my going out and everything. I must get the book."

He looked out into the passage, which was now all dark and still. The house was asleep. He could not see Mrs. Pouncer nor her cat. "They'll be in the magic room," he thought, "and the magic room is in this direction. It's in the wall, here."

But although it was in the wall he could not find it, nor any door nor window to it. There was nothing but the bare wall, papered over. "I believe I'm only dreaming this," he said.

He was about to go back to his room, when he heard a door open in the northern corridor. A light appeared. He shrank back into the powdering chamber, as it was called, near which he was standing. Lying down on the floor he could see fairly well.

Blackmalkin appeared, bearing a red light. After him came Mrs. Pouncer, crowned and wearing a long robe covered with magic signs. She bore a staff or wand. After her came Greymalkin, bearing a smoking dish. They did not see him. They went straight down the stairs into the hall. The smoke from Greymalkin's dish was sweet to smell and gave one an excited feeling.

"I do believe," Kay said to himself, "that they are going to practice magic in the hall. I'll jolly well watch what they do, and see if I can't do it myself."

He gave up the thought of the book. That did not seem nearly so interesting as watching magic.

Unfortunately, although he climbed to a place from which he could see into the hall, he could not see where Mrs. Pouncer stood, nor what she did. He saw Greymalkin coming round from time to time with the smoking dish, and he could hear Mrs. Pouncer's voice making the incantation.

"I know what she is doing," Kay thought. "Witches make incantations to call their familiar friends, who tell them all that they want to know. I do wish that I could hear what she said. . . . And I wonder what Blackmalkin is doing all this time."

He tried creeping down the stairs, so as to see, but the old stairs creaked, and the noise of the incantation, growing louder, frightened him. There came a rushing noise. The hall door opened with a clang. Kay felt the cool night air in a blast about him. Looking down at the hall, he saw a glittering child enter from the garden. The child strode up to the circle in which Greymalkin had been moving.

"I am here," he said. "Why have you called me?"

Mrs. Pouncer's voice replied, "Tell me, if you know, what became of the ship *Plunderer* after Roper Bilges was put on the island."

"I do not know," the child answered. He moved back to the door, growing less bright as he receded. He seemed to fade away. The incantation went on for a minute, then there came another rushing noise. A glittering girl came into the hall and strode up to the circle.

"I am here," she said. "Why have you called me?"

Mrs. Pouncer repeated her command, but the girl did not know what had become of the ship. When she, too, had faded away, other figures appeared one by one, as the incantation went on: an old man, an old woman, a youth crowned with ivy leaves, and a woman riding a black mare. Mrs. Pouncer ordered the old man, the old woman, and the youth, each in turn, to tell what became of the *Plunderer*. Each said "I do not know" and faded away. But when the woman on the black mare rode in, Mr. Pouncer did not mention the ship. Instead of that she strode up to the circle and said in an angry voice, "Why do you come? You are not called."

"I am here," the woman said, "and I will not go without reason."

"I charge you to be begone," Mrs. Pouncer cried.

Kay saw Blackmalkin and Greymalkin run up beside Mrs. Pouncer. Blackmalkin shook his red light, Greymalkin his dish of burning guns. Mrs. Pouncer uttered charms and threatened with her wand. The woman seemed angry, but backed her black mare out of the door, out of sight.

"The bold-faced thing, to front me so," Mrs. Pouncer said, as she went back to her incantation. Somehow, the woman's riding in had upset the spells. It was a long time before another person appeared. When he did appear, he was a stern-looking man all dressed in red.

"I am here," he said. "Why have you called me?"

"Tell me, if you know, what became of the ship *Plunderer* after Roper Bilges was put on the island."

"She sank."

"With all the treasure on board?"

"Yes."

"With all her crew on board?"

"Yes."

"Can I get at the wreck, or where the wreck was?"

"No."

"Nor take the treasure from her?"

"No."

"Where is the wreck, then?"

"Where you cannot find her."

"Answer me, where is she?"

"Gone."

"Where was the wreck? I charge you, tell me."

"I will not be charged. Beware, you, how you order me."

He spoke these last words angrily, so that Kay, who was frightened, slipped back into his bedroom. He heard them talk angrily at each other for some minutes, making more and more noise, till Kay wondered that the governess did not wake. Mrs. Pouncer seemed to be getting rather the worst of it.

"Kay," said a sweet voice at the window.

Kay hopped round with a start. A light was shining in at the window—someone had opened it. It was the woman on the black mare. They were floating there beside the window, while she looked in to call him. There were golden wings on the mare's shoulders and hooves. He had not noticed these before. The hooves were treading the air much as a swimmer will tread water.

"Will you come to ride with me?" she asked. She was a somewhat fierce but smiling lady, with keen gray eyes full of courage, and a face tanned by the wind. Her cheeks were a rosy brown and her smile most winning.

"There's room on the saddle in front of me," she said. Indeed there was, a most lovely little blue saddle with golden stirrups and a bar in front to hold on by.

"Won't you come?" she said.

"May I, really?"

She held out her hands to him and helped him into the saddle. One thing troubled him. "Suppose Mrs. Pouncer comes back into my room and finds me gone?" he said.

"That will be arranged for," she said. "Look. There's Nibbins in your bed, so curled up that anybody would think it was you."

Indeed, there was Nibbins wrapped in the bedclothes, curled well down into the pillow. It was great cheek of him, Kay thought, not asking leave.

"How do you know about Nibbins?" he asked.

"Oh, I know about a great many things."

He heard the quarrel downstairs in the hall become very noisy indeed, as though Mrs. Pouncer and the man were flinging things at each other.

"We will come away from all that," the woman said, as she touched up the mare. Instantly she had swung away from the house towards the hills, flying high and very swiftly through the cool summer night, so warm in patches above bare ground.

They passed quite close to the church tower with its four gold weathercocks.

"Oh, do let me look at the weathercocks close to," Kay said.

"You shall give them some golden oats out of my mare's nosebag," the woman said. And then, lo, the mare sidled up to each weathercock in turn, and Kay was able to offer golden oats from the nosebag to each. The weathercocks were old-fashioned and somewhat battered birds, rather stiff upon their perches and blind from the weather. Each, on eating the oats, flapped his heavy golden wings and crowed a little. When all had been fed, they went on with their song, which they hummed together to pass the time.

The northwest cock sang:

> "I watch the common people live and die
> Between the hard earth and the windy sky."

The northeast cock sang:

> "I watch the great ones ruling, in their pride,
> That cannot last, the life that cannot bide."

The southeast cock sang:

> "I watch the wildlife stirring in the wood
> The green sap and the hungering for blood."

The southwest cock sang:

> "I watch the mind that seeks and will declare
> The meaning and the purpose everywhere."

Then they all sang together:

> "We keep the watch and face the wind that blows,
> While under us the heavy hour goes."

The wind shifted a little as they sang, so that each of the four creaked a little as they came round to face it.

"Good-bye, weathercocks," Kay called as the mare galloped away. "I should think they loved it up there, up in the wind, with the jackdaws and the pigeons, and the bells chiming every third hour."

"You wonder what became of the *Plunderer*," the woman said.

"The man said that she sank, with all the treasure on board, and all her crew."

"Well, perhaps we shall know more about that presently. . . . Come up, mare."

They were now going so fast that the rivers and ponds streaked away far beneath them like flashes of light.

"It is true," the woman said, "that the *Plunderer* sank with all her treasure, as well as with all of her crew who were in her at the time. But one of her crew was not in her at the time—he had been put ashore on an island before the ship was wrecked."

"Yes, I know," Kay said. "Roper Bilges, the mutineer, who put Great-grandpapa Harker on shore."

"Ah, how clever we are!" the woman said with a strange smile. "But we will not talk now, for we have to come down here."

"Where are we?" Kay asked. "How far have we come?"

"We are in the North," she said, "at Trigger Court. We have come some hundreds of miles."

*T*he mare slackened pace as she glided gently down to the end of a lake, from which a grass slope led to a big house. It was still dark night everywhere. Owls were cruising along the woods near the water, fish were leaping in the lake, and rabbits hopping about on the lawn. The mare steadied near the front of the house, which had many blank windows and one wide-open French window, brightly lit, on the second floor.

The woman stopped the mare beside this window. "We get down here, Kay," she said. She leaped from the saddle into the balcony, and then taking Kay's hands, she jumped him down beside her and at once drew him with her into the lighted room.

It was a big, bright, pretty bedroom, hung with white chintzes which were patterned with pink roses tied with pale blue ribbon. The furniture was old and very shiny from polish, lacquer, and brass. A fire was burning in the grate, although it was a summer night. To their left, as they entered, about fifteen feet from the window, was a big double bed, hung with chintz like the rest of the room. In this bed, propped up by pillows, a wicked old woman in a very gay dressing gown was reading a sprightly story, at which she was laughing. Beside her, on a table, was a bottle of champagne. She sipped a glass of the wine from time to time. In her mouth was a long cigarette holder containing a lighted cigarette.

"He, he," she chuckled, over one of the jests. "He, he. Oh, dear, if I read any more of this, I shall crack my ribs to matchsticks!"

"Miss Susan Pricker," the woman called.

The old lady sat up fiercely in her bed. "Deuce take your impudence, ma'am," she said, "I'm not Miss Susan Pricker. My name is Piney Trigger, of Trigger Hall. And what are you doing, coming in at the window at this time of night?"

"Miss Twiney Pricker," the woman said, "don't think to bluster me, ma'am. Your name is not Trigger, but Pricker."

"If I ring for my medical attendant," the old lady said, "you will be removed in custody."

"You may ring for your medical attendant, ma'am, but he will not hear, because in the first place the bell will not ring, and in the second place he has gone to a dance and will not be here until dawn."

"Look at that boy," the old lady replied, "catching his mortal end in pajamas."

"His mortal grandmother!"

The old lady put down her cigarette. She clenched her fist at them, pulled off her cap and wig and hurled it at them.

"Take that for your impudence," she said. "If I rise from this bed, I'll make you eat it."

"Miss Pricker," the woman said, "a great many years ago your father helped to do this child's great-grandfather a cruel wrong, which altered his life for him. Your father was swiftly punished for his share in the wrong, and got no benefit from it, but you can at least tell this child what became of the ship *Plunderer*, and how your father came to change his name. In the meantime, won't you put on your headdress. The night air may otherwise strike chill."

"Thank you, Miss Whoever-you-are. The night air certainly makes you sufficiently cool. I will put on my cap. And how do you know about Sir Piney Trigger?"

"He was not Piney Trigger, but Twiney Pricker."

"Prove it," the old lady said. "As they say in the law courts, prove it."

The young woman pointed at the wall. "There, Kay," she said, "is a portrait of this lady's father, the Twiney Pricker about whom you have read. See if he be like the description."

Kay looked as he was bid. The man in the picture had cold blue eyes which stuck out like lobster's eyes. He had a wide mouth, which suddenly opened to show two teeth gone on the left side. The hair was just the color of twine; it was twiney hair. The man looked "sinister," as Captain Harker had said, but with "a great deal in him," mostly evil, but not all—he was like the old lady in the bed. He wore gold black broadcloth, a white stock, and a blue necktie about the stock. The portrait had a label beneath it: "Sir Piney Trigger, Honduras Merchant. d. 1850."

"Twiney Pricker had that sort of hair," Kay said, "and those kind of lobster eyes, and two teeth gone on the left."

"A great many thousands have all those marks," the old lady said. "Think again, child. And then perhaps you will remove yourselves."

"He had a woman's heart transfixed with an arrow, done in gunpowder on his chest," Kay said, "and the fat ox of Bedford in the same on his right arm."

"He had nothing of the kind," the old lady said.

"Yes, he had," the woman answered. "Look there. Look at the portrait."

As they looked at the portrait, Sir Piney Trigger, Honduras Merchant, stirred in his canvas. His hands, which were coarse, blunt, and square-fingered, unbuttoned his waistcoat and rolled back his costly frilled shirt. There was the transfixed heart upon his chest, and the greater part of the ox of Bedford, fat beyond belief. He could not well show the beast as far as the tail without tearing his shirt.

The old lady poured herself a large glass of the champagne and drank it quickly.

"Very well," she said, "he was Twiney Pricker. What of it? He is not going to be bothered by that at this time of day, I think. I like to think that he was Twiney Pricker, and had a bit of go and a bit of fun as a young man. He did put his captain ashore, he, he! And ran away with the ship, with all the bishop's candlesticks . . . ho, ho, ho! How we used to roar with laughter over it! . . . And then he rounded on the gunner who was giving himself airs . . . and put him ashore too. Let me see, what was his name? It was one of these marine names, Squilges or Dirges."

"Bilges," Kay said.

"Just as I was saying, Bilges. He put Squilges ashore. But the others did not like that so well, for the next night, or almost the next night, they put *him* ashore on a sandbank. But my father marked some of them first—pinked, they called it then. 'Pinked them in the plexus' was the phrase. All these fine old phrases are gone out, since pinafores and temperance became the rage. My father pinked them to purpose, but they were too many for him.

"My father said that being on the sandbank was easily the hottest time he ever had, there being nothing whatever to drink, except the dew that collected at nights upon his tarpaulin hat. He used to lick this as it collected, and in the day he bathed in the sea. Food he had largely to do without, except a kind of marine worm which he found buried in the sand. Pa used to say that he never put in so much sleep as upon that sandbank. That, and thinking what he would have to eat and drink when he returned to civilization was how he passed the time. That and bathing, and getting into wet sand to avoid the hottest of the sun, and of course digging for these worms. Quite the early bird.

"A man like my pa is not easily to be quenched, any more than I am. My heart is no more use than a shifting backstay, but I can take my wine, I hope, and begone dull care. I'll sing till I die.

"I'll live to the age of a hundred and eight
And then I'll go courting to find me a mate;
I'll live to the age of a hundred and nine,
And finish my bottle whenever I dine;
I'll live to the age of a hundred and ten,
When I'll mount on my horse and go courting agen.

"Deuce take these lily-livered times! I'll have a deviled bone to my breakfast as long as I've a gum in my mouth. Cheer up, my lads, there's shot in the locker still.

"What was I saying about my father? Oh yes . . . he was on the sandbank, wasn't he? How did he get off? Why, a chasse-marée came by, not looking where she was going. He saw someone on board her striking a light with a flint and steel, so he hailed her to keep off or she'd be ashore, and then begged them to take him off, which they did, though most of them thought he was a ghost.

"Who were they? Well, everybody is young at some time, I suppose, and I suppose everybody has to live. One may as well have one's fling. Besides, the rich of that time used to flaunt their wealth: it was the greatest temptation to the poor to come to take it. I suppose they cracked people's crowns to take it. Some crowns are exceedingly easily cracked; and a lot, which are cracked already, are better cracked. Deuce take me, I'd have been a pirate myself if I'd had the chance. Besides, these people who rescued my father weren't pirates, they were only on a pleasure cruise. Besides, it was legal in a sense, for they were at war at the time, or just had been, or would have been, or soon would be again. Besides, although my father said they had a lot of watches and necklaces in the chasse-marée, that proved nothing, rather the reverse, for one of the party, a very gentle-manly fellow, was a jeweler by profession, and another, who was said to have been a titled person, was a collector of such things, what they call a connoisseur. Lots of people do collect them. What more natural than that he should acquire some on a pleasure cruise? I should call it quite remarkable if he didn't.

"However, I find a lot of these squeamish, mealymouthed people of the pleasant present day, who live on pap and poppycock, are always ready to condemn anybody who lives in a way that is not their own way. Nothing shows a narrow mind like that. I'm glad to say I'm without prejudice. If a man says to me 'I'm a pirate, madam,' I say to him, 'I admire your pluck, sir. Do you want a mate, sir?' That is my opinion of pirates. But then I take after my father. Burn my wig and bonnet if this bottle isn't empty!

"These people, whoever they were, lived on the shores of one of the lagoons near there. I daresay they do still. Some were French, some Spanish, some American, a few of all sorts. They'd rather lost their way. My pa directed them how to steer.

"That very evening, as they sailed, they sighted the masts of a wreck sticking out of the water, with the sails still set. My father knew the sails at once, from having made them and mended them. The wreck was the *Plunderer* lying in six or seven fathoms of water. She had been caught in a squall when the men were drunk. You see what came of getting rid of my father, the one man who could have saved them.

"There wasn't a sign of the crew, my pa said, but the sharks there had a well-fed sort of a look. Near by were the two boats floating bottom up. That was the end of them. Those that hadn't been drowned the sharks had eaten.

" 'That's my old ship,' my pa said, 'that I fell overboard from the other night.'

" 'She's fallen overboard herself now,' they said. 'What was in her? Anything worth diving for?'

" 'No, only sugar; it will all be spoilt.'

"So they left her there and sailed on, but my pa took a very careful reckoning of where she was.

"If you will oblige me with a light to my cigarette, instead of gawping at me in that South Country fashion, it will be a comfort and a change. Tobacco isn't ladylike, they say. Don't talk about these pinafore things to me, ladies, quotha!

"About my father. . . . He landed with the chasse-marée

people in a very pleasant French city—I name no names. Nice ironwork on the balconies, he said there was, altogether a change from the sandbank and the worms. But he was destitute. He could not set off at once by himself to fetch the treasure from the *Plunderer*, and for a long time he could not find anyone to be his partner. That is where respectable people fail—they won't gamble.

"My pa had a hard year of it, and all the time that treasure was sinking deeper into the coral. Believe me, he was there a year before he met a sportsman."

"Was the sportsman's name Abner Brown?" Kay asked.

"Yes, child, it was. Who was Abner Brown? He was a local gentleman who received things—that is, bought things from peddlers and people. My father dealt with him and at last persuaded him to come to look for the *Plunderer*. My pa had no money. Abner had. Abner fitted out a yawl, then he and my pa set out in her to whereabouts the *Plunderer* had been, and spent a month there dragging the bottom with grapnels, hoping to find the wreck. They sailed to and fro, to and fro. They found coral and seaweeds and squids with parrot heads, but no *Plunderer*. Of course a year had passed. There had been storms, and sandbanks form quickly there. Then she might have been struck by lightning and broken apart. Still, it was sad not to find any trace of her.

"After a month Abner said he would search no more—it was no good looking any longer. My pa was all for searching for another month, but of course it was Abner's yawl, and then the stormy season was at hand, so there was nothing for it but to turn. My pa spoke his mind though: he called Abner a lily-livered papgoose. He said Abner bore no malice for this, but on their coming ashore, gave him a sum of money and sent him along the coast to a seaport where he could go into the hotel trade.

"You might think that this was handsome in Abner Brown, my mouselike miss and sir. Judge by results, I say.

"What was he like, this Abner Brown? He was like a white,

sweet, sanctified horsedealer, or a hymn-singing cutthroat, or any cherry-lipped poisoner who will drop a tear at your pain and put ratsbane in your beer at the same breath. Talk? He would talk the hind legs off a mule. Weep? He would weep at a word. He wept when my pa called him a papgoose. He was always weeping. A crocodile was a drought to him.

"But how you two can expect me to speak of a man like that without rinsing my mouth to clear the taste away is more than I can comprehend.

"What did my pa do? He went into the refreshment trade, selling liquor to seamen. Then he did a little crimping, which is either needlework or keeping a sailors' home. With the profits of this he went into the industry business, getting Negro servants from savage parts to places where they could go to school and wear proper trousers, instead of the fans and things—sometimes only pieces of sealing wax, my pa said—which they were accustomed to where they lived in their heathendom. He did very well in the industry business and brought many heathen savages into the advantages of civilization. Sometimes they died, of course, but that was due to the fevers—that wasn't my pa's doing. My pa always gave them what he gave to a seaman, fifteen inches broad to lie upon, and always the very best plank and chain. He spared no expense in those ways, never. Penny wise, pound foolish, was one of his mottoes.

"However, there were so many anxieties in the industry business, my pa gave it up and went to Honduras, where he became a merchant under the name of Trigger. Until then he had usually called himself Suarez—Benito Suarez—which means Blessed Suarez. Now that he was Trigger he prospered so that he gave up thinking of the *Plunderer*—put her out of his mind as lost, in fact.

"When he was very rich he came to these parts, where nobody knew him except as the rich Honduras merchant. He was knighted, too, Sir Piney. Very jovial we were. When people saw a yellow turn-out tooling down to Epsom behind two bits of blood, they sometimes asked, 'By Jove, who is that extraordinarily handsome woman in the scarlet and fur, with the geraniums in her hat?' The answer always was 'That's Miss Trigger, the beautiful Miss Trigger, that the begum offered a cool million for. That is she and her pa.' Then the duke or the earl (and once it was a foreign prince) would say, 'By Jove, Badger, that's a woman to die for! How could I meet her pa, do you think?'

"Oh, the songs we used to sing coming back from the races, all those good old songs with choruses:

> "As we came from the races,
>   At our tandem's best paces,
> We rivalled the graces, we outshone the queen;
>   With our satins and laces
>   And the smiles on our faces,
> We wiped out the traces where sorrow had been.

> "Singing tooral li ooral li oddity,
>   Polly tooral li ooral li Een;
> Since sorrow is death to a boddity,
>   We wiped out where sorrow had been.

"O tooral, it goes on. There's another verse of chorus.

"My pa was rich, but what is that to a man who has energy? He found life quiet here. Who wouldn't, after all the stir of the West? He organized a business to bring moonlight into cheerless homes. You pretend that you don't know what that is, young woman and sir. Moonlight is what comes by moonlight, French brandy and tea and this burgundy; that none but the English are strong enough to drink. That's what I mean by moonlight—and many an ounce of tobacco that never paid threepence to the queen. They told my pa that the moonlight trade was dead, but they little knew my pa. Nothing is dead when there's somebody alive to do it. Seven barges with false bottoms he had, and he saw them go, all full of moonlight, right through a lock that the queen herself was opening. That was a triumph for my pa.

"But it was the beginning of the end in one way. If he'd not taken to the moonlight business, he might never have known that Captain Harker was still alive. The best place for his moonlight was on a river not five miles from where that Captain Harker lived, or moaned rather, for that Captain H. was a morbid man, mealyfaced, always mourning about the treasure. My pa was doing his moonlight business right close to that man's home, and saw him again.

"When I consider the change that seeing that man made in Pa, I feel that I must open another bottle.

"Some of the change was due to liver, no doubt, but the rest was remorse. 'It was I,' he said, 'made poor Captain Harker as he is. Oh, woe, woe!'

"I did what I could to change his heart, but who can change the heart when the liver's all wrong? No one.

" 'Piney,' he used to say. 'Piney, I have been a great sinner.'

" 'Nonsense, my pa,' I used to say. 'And if you have, you ought to be proud of it.'

" 'No,' he said, 'I am not proud of it. It weighs in here,' and then he would beat where his liver was.

"At last he said, 'One thing I can do. I can get that treasure back to Captain Harker before I die, if two marks of the five are still above water.'

" 'Why, rubbish,' I said. 'What stuff and rubbish! I never heard the like.' For I didn't want my pa at his age, and with his liver, to go wandering about in all sorts of mud and climates, dredging in the sea and diving. Still he would go, and without me. There was nothing for it but to let my pa have his own way, and he was away two years.

"And do you know what he found at the end of twenty months? Oh, the deceitfulness of false companions! Never shall I forget my sweet pa's letter about it. My pa found that one whom I sullied my lips over by calling him a gentleman had robbed him and deceived him. He found that Abner Brown had taken the treasure years before. This was how he discovered it: listen.

"After he had searched for twenty months and more, my pa had to change his divers: he was advised to hire some Indian divers from the pearl fisheries, because they stood the heat better. They were very nice men, these Indians—they always called him Massa. When he brought them to dive where the *Plunderer* had been, they said, 'O Massa, him no good. Mr. Blown he get the tleasure here long, long time ago. He take him all away, boxy and bundley and big piecee tandletick.'

"That was what Abner Brown had done in return for my pa's trusting him with the secret.

"When he took my father to look for the *Plunderer*'s wreck that first time, long, long ago, he sighted the wreck, as it chanced, when Pa was asleep. Did he tell my pa? No. Like a false knave he made a note of where she was, and told my pa it was no good looking any longer. So back he sailed, waited till my pa had moved elsewhere, then came back with his divers and took everything.

"But the divers were able to tell my pa what had happened next, though."

"Abner lost it," Kay said.

"Yes, my little lovebird, he lost it. He was taking it back to that French city that I mentioned. He had it all, and he was only five miles from home. All seemed to favor his false heart. But lo, when he got near, the army and the navy were there, rooting out all the settlement and hanging a lot of them. Abner had to leave his boat full of treasure and fly for his life, and even so, though he was not hung, he had seven years in a chain gang.

"But it is my pa that I want to talk of, not Abners and treasures. When my pa came home at the end of those two years, he did not talk about them but about his liver. 'Piney,' he said, 'my liver's like a shifting backstay. It takes me across the brisket instead of supporting my vital organs.'

"He was a broken man on his return, my pa. First he would say that about his liver. Then, once, he flashed out, just like his old self, 'By goom, Piney, yon Abner was theer, digging and digging for t' brass and finding nowt.' But that was only a rally. He told me nothing more than that about his last four months of search—only that yon Abner was there. What could one make of that?

"Then once, in a dreadful voice, he said, 'Captain Harker is dead, Piney. After all, Captain Harker is dead. But I have been beside his tomb, Piney, and told him I did my best.' Ah! After all my longing for him, to have him like that!"

Here the poor old lady shed a few tears, tried to fill her glass from the bottle, and finding it empty, sucked its neck instead. After a few puffs at her cigarette she went on:

"And he was only at home for two days. He went off again. No harm in that—he was always going off in the old days to see about his moonlight. But this time he went off muttering about the tomb. And this time he never came back to his poor little Tiney Piney. Never, never, never, never, never—Shakespeare.

"Do you ask me 'Was it liver?' No, I say, it wasn't liver. He went off in the fly, muttering about the tomb, and what became of him nobody knows."

Here she sat up in bed and gripped the bottle by the neck as though it were a club.

"Ah! What happened? What happened?" she said. "What happened in those last four months in the West? What happened when he went from here to Condicote? And what happened on that midnight after he left the Ring of Bells Inn? I ask what, and I ask why, and nobody answers.

"But if you ask me, I say that Abner Brown was at the bottom of it. However hard he was digging when Pa saw him, he certainly followed Pa here. Why?

"To try to get money from him, probably, by blackmail. He came to this house and my pa kicked him out. Next day, my sweet pa went away, forever and forever farewell, Cassius. He was traced to Condicote, and there he was seen talking to Abner Brown, for Abner followed him. 'The gents were having words,' the potboy said. 'Sir Trigger kicked him out and told him to do his worst.' It was the wettest season ever known, and the great floods were out. No one has ever learned what happened next. He went out very late, after dinner, to which he drank only barley water, and he never came back, though the maid had put out his nightgown and laid the warming pan in his bed. He was never seen by mortal eye from that day to this.

"Abner Brown was seen. They found my fine papgoose partly eaten by fish, but identified by his linen, at Seven Hatches Weir, having been drowned, the medical men said. Some said that my pa had killed Abner, but with a liver like a shifting backstay my poor pa was deprived of manly pleasures. To be killed by a man like my pa, let him lay not that flattering unction to what he called his soul—Shakespeare. That he had a tooth knocked out by my pa's hand is glory enough for him.

"Some said that Abner had killed my pa. I say, bosh, both miss and sir. It was thought that my pa fell into the floods while in a spasm from his backstay.

"What took him to Condicote? Did I mention the word moonlight ever?"

"You did," Kay said.

"Then don't repeat it," she said. "Moonlight is a thing of the night, all these things beginning with M are: there's Moonlight, and Murder, and Mystery, and Missing the Midnight Train, and Mourning and Much-loved Pa; all dark, sorrowful things.

"However, a long life and a merry one is Piney Trigger's motto, and a very good one too.

"Miss Piney Tricker is a girl whose wisdom is most weighty,
She never went to bed till three till she was over eighty.
When claret red is in her head, she carols from her throttle,
Hurray, hurray, my jolly lads, let's have another bottle!
  Tooral-loo.

"At ninety-five her chief delight was going out to dances,
At ninety-nine she dazzled men by fire from her glances;
And now that she's a hundred odd, she fills her glass with
   liquor
And says hurray, my jolly lads, hurray for Piney Tricker!
   Tooral-loo.

"I call myself Tricker in poetry, because Trigger has so few rhymes. There's bigger, and digger, and figger, and jigger, and nigger, and pigger, and rigger, and wigger, and the man who goes zag-zig is a zagger-zigger. If he isn't, I don't know what he is, and I'm sure you don't. Where is that electric light switch?"

For some minutes Kay had been longing to speak, but the old lady had talked with such energy that he had had no chance. As she paused to grope for the light switch, he broke in.

"Miss Trigger-Pricker," he said, "your father found the treasure and I believe he brought it to somewhere near Condicote. And some think it may be there still. And Pimply Whatto's father said he saw Abner Brown, with a pistol in his hand, following your father towards the floods on the night they both disappeared."

"I shall most certainly give Sophronia a piece of my mind," the old lady answered. "Not only is the stitching giving way in the seams, but the stuff itself shows signs of wear, which is not the wear for Piney Tricker, Man's True Blue TOAST."

She said this very rapidly and at the same time seemed to recede. He could not see her so clearly, nor could he see the lobster eyes of Sir Piney staring out of the portrait. The fire in the grate had burned dim, all the room was dim and far away, though he could hear Miss Piney's voice going on still like a millwheel. He felt the young woman with her fierce and smiling face pluck him towards the window, where the horse was, but he was so very, very sleepy that he really could not keep his eyes open. He managed to say, "Do let's stop at the weather-cocks," but they were already rushing and rushing through miles of wind.

"Weathercocks, Master Kay," Ellen said, as she shook him awake from his bed. "Do wake up, there's a good boy. Such a boy to wake I never did see. Now, don't be late for breakfast, but get up at once, like a little mortal. Why, you sleep like one of them things that curl up all winter! Now don't go to sleep again, or I don't know what she'll say."

*A*s it was Sunday, he had no lessons that morning, except the collect for the day, which had to be learnt by heart. After this he was taken to church to a pew in the forward part of the nave, from which he could see the chancel through the hollow of the tower. He was much too young to understand or follow the service. He liked some of the hymns, and adored Miss Holyport, who played the organ. Apart from these joys, church had few solaces. Often in the summer a swallow would flit about. When there was no swallow, the only thing to do was to look at the walls, which were full of queer things. For instance, if you looked at the lines of mortar which held in the irregular stones on the walls, you could sometimes imagine that they made pictures. Close to him there was a very good portrait of Henry VIII, thus:

and a picture of a boat, thus:

which filled in a lot of time. Then, in some of the walls were the moldings of windows and arches long since filled in. It was quite good fun to imagine the windows and arches as still there, and to go through them into some jollier place than church. He knew all the memorial tablets within sight by heart, from Captain Porkins, late of the 91st (Duke of Cumberland's) Light Horse, who was slain while doing staff duty at Hougomont on the Field of Waterloo, to

> Annabel Bethesda Mee, Spinster of this Parish.
> She rests in peace till Wars and Tumults end,
> We an Example mourn, the Poor a Friend.

But the chief pleasure in church was to look at the carved and painted figures arranged along the wallpieces of the chancel roof. There were sixteen of these on each side. They had been put there, with the chancel roof, somewhere about the year 1500. No one knew quite what they represented, for only a few of them were winged. They were "the busts and heads of men and angels," so the guide book said. Some tried to make up the sum of 32 thus:

$$
\begin{array}{ll}
12 & \text{Apostles} \\
7 & \text{Virtues} \\
9 & \text{Worthies} \\
\underline{4} & \text{Archangels} \\
32 &
\end{array}
$$

To Kay they were all sorts of things at different times. Now they would be the Condicote and Muck Zennor rugby football teams (with an umpire each) all lined up for kickoff. Anon they would be the Australian eleven, 1882, facing the team of Cambridge University, which beat them. Then on another Sunday one side of them would be A False Start for the Derby, from a well-known print, while the other side would be the start for the Grand National Steeplechase, 1839, with Mr. Mason on Lottery, and Mr. Martin, in his pink sleeves, on Paulina. Sometimes they would be Britons and Romans, and sometimes they would be the House of Parliament, with the east window coming in on them as Oliver Cromwell.

After the service people gathered outside the church in the broad walk near the porch. The governess was stopped by Mrs. Gossip, who had something to discuss with her. The two of them walked together deep in talk through the churchyard. A man whom Kay did not know, but who seemed to know him, clapped him on the shoulder and began conversation with "Well, Kay, have you found the Harker treasure yet?"

He started, because how could this man know how much the Harker treasure had been in his thoughts for these last few days?

"Oh, don't look so startled," the man said. "I won't peach if you've found it, but I'm afraid that there's no hope of that. But there is a treasure that I wonder you don't seek for."

"What treasure is that?" Kay asked.

"Well, did you ever hear of Bendigo the highwayman? Benjamin, as people called him."

"I should think I had," Kay answered. "He used to live in our stable when it was a house. But had he any treasure?"

"Oh, I expect that he had a great deal of treasure," the man said, "from robbing the stagecoaches. I was reading an account of him in the Annual Register. He kept his mare Dowsabel, which is a French name, *Douce et belle* (meaning 'gentle and lovely'), at the Cock and Pye, the inn where you go to see the hounds meet. They searched for his property when they caught him, but they never found anything. You ought to look in your stable for it."

"What sort of treasure would it be, please?" Kay asked.

"Oh, purses of guineas, and repeater watches (that is, watches which will *repeat*, that is, restrike, the last hour that struck whenever you press a spring). Then I expect he took gold rings and pocketbooks full of bank notes. Those were more worth having, don't you think, than pieces of eight, which were only worth four shillings when all is said?"

At this point the governess claimed Kay and led him back to dinner.

After dinner Kay thought, "Well, why shouldn't I explore for Benjamin's treasure?" The governess always passed her Sunday afternoons in her study, which she called "having some letters to write," but he judged from her bitterness when he had been noisy in the garden on these occasions that she really took a long nap.

All through his life he had dreaded exploring that side of the garden, where the stables, that had once been Benjamin's home, stood. In some undated past a man called the Tailor had been found killed in one of the outhouses there, "stabbed right through the skull," as Ellen said, "which shows you the force that must have been used." Today the Tailor seemed very far away and treasure very much in the air. "I'll go," he said.

The stables (they were no longer used as stables) stood at the end of a long chain of buildings or ruins, which shut the garden from the road on that side. First was the barn, the thatch of which was green with moss and sunken into pits, which would presently be holes. Next to this was the dangerous brewhouse, where cavernous old barrels stood falling asunder, as their hoops rusted through. The rotten floor was full of holes, through some of which you could hear the murmur of running water. Indeed the brewhouse was a terrible place, which made one remember the worst that one had ever heard of Sweeney Todd.

When he entered it this afternoon, another tale came back to him, that one of his grandfather's workmen, who had worked in the brewhouse, had so soaked himself with spirits that at last, as Ellen said, "he took fire and burned all blue. There was nothing left of him but some black oil on the floor." However, Dr. Gubbins had thrown doubts on this tale.

Beyond the brewhouse was an open space, which had once been covered by the malting house. It was now a jungle of giant heraclea, nettles, plantains, burdock, and dandelion. Beyond this jungle was the pigeon house built out like an apse from the wall of the stable. Both pigeon house and stable were swathed more than a foot thick in ivy.

As Kay came into this wilderness, a big gray cat, which he had learned to call the Phantom from the swiftness with which he fled, leaped from his sleep in the sun and disappeared. This time Kay saw that he had darted into a hole below a projecting stone, which looked like a paving stone. After poking and digging at the hole for half an hour, he found that there was a hollow beyond and below it. He fetched a trowel from the toolshed, cleared out the entrance, and groveled on the ground, trying to see. Yes, there was a room or cave.

Creeping into the house, he took some candle ends and a box of matches from the pantry mantelshelf. By candle-end light he could make out masonry, slug tracks, and specks of quartz in the stone.

"It must be Benjamin's secret den," he thought. "I'll get down it to make sure."

He fetched a newspaper, in which Joe the gardener, who came once a week, had wrapped his lunch. He lit this, dropped it into the hollow, and saw it flame down, lighting up a little cellar about five feet deep. Within a minute he had squirmed down feet foremost into this cellar, to explore. The phantom cat had long since gone by another hole between the stones, through which he could see into the garden. He could find no other opening. Roots of ivy thrust into the ground among the masonry; tendrils of ivy with bright, pale leaves had trailed in through the holes. There were slug tracks on the floor and walls. A dead centipede was phosphorescent in a corner.

"What a lovely place," Kay thought. "I shall be able to come here always and have it for my cave. I'll bring bread and ham here. I'll keep a catapult here. Perhaps I'll run away some evening and sleep here. I wish I could get one of those lanterns with colored lights; that would be just the thing for here."

He lit two more candle ends. By their light he found a recess in the wall, where the stones had been removed. In this lay a padlock with the key rusted into it, half a dozen links of rusty chain, the heel grip and rowels of a spur, and part of a horse's headstall.

"These must be relics of Benjamin," he thought. "The spur that he spurred Dowsabel with. I shall call this place Benjamin's Lair."

Footsteps sounded outside. He saw Mrs. Scatternews coming down the path within a few feet of him on her way to call on the governess. He could hear her muttering, as was her way, "The bombazine, ninepence three farthings; two pennyworth of tape, eleven-three; a penny reel, a shilling-three; two packets of best assorted—but they're gone up: how much did Sarah say they came to?"

"I can be here," Kay thought, "and no one will ever suspect where I am. It's the loveliest place that I've ever found, and I'll spend all my time here always and have books and a clothes brush, so that the dust won't show."

He made another careful examination of the walls and then "Terang, terang, terang!" it was the bell for tea.

When he came indoors he found that Mrs. Scatternews was more fun than Mrs. Tattle. She had been to Mr. Holyport's lecture, the night before, on "my predecessors in this parish."

"Imagine the things that went on here," she said. "The parish was honeycombed with crime. No sooner was the smuggling stopped than the highwaymen broke out and stole Sir Hassle Gassle's repeater watch worth five hundred guineas. No sooner were the highwaymen hanged than out came the rickburners, holding meetings and setting fire to property. Oh, it was dreadful! And all in red nightcaps, too, just as in the Reign of Terror. No sooner were *they* all sent to transportation than back came the smugglers, only this time they came secretly, and left the brandy and wines at the doors, just as though they were the milk, and so cheap. . . . Mr. Holyport read from the journal of the reverend gentleman who was rector here in the forties. He said that 'although wages were lower than he had ever known them, hardly a man in the parish failed to find means for a Saturday intoxication.' Then he went on to say how the parish now remembered only its criminals, Benjamin the highwayman and Mr. Galloway, the nickname of the smuggler, whereas in former times it remembered its saints, St. Alpig of St. Alpig's well—who is thought to have had a hermitage near the river—and St. Conda, to whom the church was dedicated. He said that this was because courageous energy is always valued and remembered, and that though the highwaymen and the others often used their energy wickedly, they still used it, and risked their lives to use it. We shall have half the boys in the parish tomorrow playing at highwayman and knocking people's eyes out. I wonder that he did not tell the girls that they had better all take to being witches!"

"Do you mind," the governess said, in her very sweetest voice, "do you mind if we do not talk of witches? I am sure that we ought not to talk of them, because of course, well . . . really."

This ended the talk of witches.

After tea Kay went back to the garden, thinking to explore the stable for some other relic of Benjamin. Usually the stable was locked, there being now no horses, but today, to his surprise, the door was open.

The reason for its being open lay within on the wheelbarrow. There, on some straw, with a crimson, drunken face, lay Joe the gardener, fast asleep, breathing heavily. He was a very drunken man, who had been in the Afghan War. When sober, he could set wires for rats (which never failed) and sing "As I was a-walking by the light of the moon." He could also dance two or three steps of the step dance.

Kay was afraid of him when he was drunk, because Ellen and Jane were. He edged away from him cautiously.

Two stalls further down the line was the harness room, which Kay could just remember, or thought that he could remember, in the warmth and glitter of use. A memory, so early that it might have been a dream, showed him that room all bright with a blazing fire, gleaming with bits, curb chains, buckles, and stirrups, and comfortable with the smell of saddle soap and metal polish. Two men, called Bob and Jay, had been there then, singing Twankydillo as they worked, and Bob had opened the marvelous carven corner cupboard, which had the arms of the Harkers, three oreilles couped proper, done above it between supporters. Inside there had been a blaze of shining things, the coach lamps, and the silver turrets that old Mr. Harker had used when he drove four-in-hand.

The corner cupboard was still there, but frowsy and cobwebby. Rusty bits of harness still hung on the nails; the grate was broken. Starlings in the chimney had knocked soot, mortar, and scalings down into the room. Cobwebs containing bits of fly, bluebottle, gnat, cleg, bee, wasp, and moth covered the window. There was a broken carriage clock still on the mantelpiece.

Kay pulled the rusty key of the corner cupboard so that the door swung slowly open to show its blackness of decay. Dry rot was at work upon it; spiders, earwigs, woodlice, and centipedes all had their dwelling there. There was nothing within except a scrubbing brush and a horse picker. Kay took the scrubbing brush to serve as a clothes brush in Benjamin's lair. On second thoughts he took the horse picker too.

In the next stall he found another treasure. Two years before, in the winter of the great frost, Joe had made him a toboggan by nailing battens across two runners. The toboggan had disappeared at the thaw. Kay had not seen it since, but now here it was, shoved aside, propped up against the manger, even the rope still on it. "The very thing I've been panting for," Kay thought. "This will make a ladder down into the lair."

Outside the stable, on the walls which seemed to be directly over his lair, he noticed the toadflax. It had little, mouthed flowers of palest purple touched with gold, which reminded him of snapdragons, violets, and sweet peas. It had vivid green leaves and thrusters of purple. Noticing it for the first time on this exciting day in that place, he remembered it always, as something even more strangely beautiful than most flowers.

A solitary mushroom grew on the site of the manure heap. He seemed to remember that Bob, in the old days, had grown many baskets full of mushrooms there. Now the giant burdock and the overgrown laurels had taken charge. All the garden was like that—weeded up.

As he was clambering down the toboggan rungs into his den, the runners gave way beneath him so that he fell. He found that one of the runners had sunk into the floor, through the run of some rat, into what looked like the lid of a box. On groping with the horse picker, he pulled out the remains of a wooden box, long rotted into touch in the ground. Within its shell was moldy stuff, which may once have been cloth. Underneath the moldy stuff was something hard, done up in what felt like a mummy rabbit, which had been tied with strips of leather now broken. The wrappings unrolled to display a tin box rather more than a foot long, also tied with leather. The hinges were decayed through. The lid came off as he opened it. Inside was a bundle tied with oilskin, which contained a rather heavy net purse and a decaying mahogany box with battered metal corners. Kay opened the mahogany box first. It contained a pair of dueling pistols, by Turner, Milsom Street, Bath, 1803, so an engraved brass plate said. With these pistols, in little beds in the green baize, were wads, caps, a rammer and picker, and a neat carven horn with a stopper at the end. They were the real dueling pistols with the saw handles which he had read of in books. Rust had eaten deeply into their cocks and barrels, but they were still pistols, perhaps the very pistols with which Benjamin had made people stand and deliver. The purse, which was secured by sliding rings, contained six heavy bullets, a broken shilling of George III with a cross cut on it, a cameo ring, a monogram seal, and a small pewter snuffbox embossed with a fox's mask. He knew that the broken shilling had been cut with a cross for use against ghosts. Ellen had told him of a farmer who had shot a ghost with such a bullet at the Wantways, where the suicides were buried. "No ghost," she said, "can stand silver marked with a cross."

In the bottom of the purse was a paper pulp, which seemed to be rotting Scottish bank notes. On the inside of the lid of the pewter snuffbox someone had scratched with a sharp nail the following inscription:

S 100 yds frm. S.S.S.
_____

J.G.Z. R.P.C.

What that meant Kay could not tell.

"It's where Benjamin's treasure is hidden," he said to himself. "South a hundred yards from S.S.S. What would S.S.S. be? Might it be," he thought, "South of Seekings Stable? This may have been called Seekings Stable then. J.G.Z. and R.P.C.—I suppose that those are the initials of his gang. Now, a hundred yards south from here would take me into the Crowmarsh estate."

Going out from the lair, he began to measure. Eleven yards took him from his lair to the garden wall. Beyond the wall was the road, roughly eleven yards across, counting in the grassy strips. Beyond the road was a higher wall, topped with broken glass; beyond that was the Crowmarsh estate. Twenty-two yards from a hundred left seventy-eight yards. Seventy-eight yards into the estate would bring him across a piece of orchard into a spinney of scrub, in which some tall fir trees grew. "It must be somewhere there," he thought, "but I shall catch it if I'm caught trespassing there."

The bells began their lin-lan-lone to call people to the evening service. It was time for him to go indoors. The governess had walked off with Mrs. Scatternews. Ellen gave him his cup of bread and milk.

"Ellen," he asked, "how long ago did Benjamin live?"

"Oh, a long, long time ago," Ellen said. "In my grandfather's time, in the French wars."

"Do you know if he had a gang who went about with him?"

"Why, no, Master Kay. I think he was all by himself. They do say that the man who had the Cock in those days, a man named Morgan, was in with him. The Cock was a coach inn, where the coaches stopped. They do say that Morgan kept a spy on the people who came by coach, to see if they had money or necklaces. If they had, he used to tell Benjamin, or send out a little girl to him to say dinner was ready. And he used to water the guard's gun, too, so they said. And then Benjamin used to lie in wait for the coach and rob the people. He robbed Sir Hassle Gassle once as he was coming home from the races, near Gassle Court, and took his gold repeater watch worth ever so much that was given him by the hunters. That wasn't this Sir Hassle Gassle, but his grandfather.

"Benjamin had a mare called Dowsabel, that was trained to stop coach horses. She would go right across the leaders and turn them into a ditch. They do say the coachmen were in with him."

"Do you know any of their names?"

"Why, no. It was all so long ago."

"Is it all written down in a book about him?"

"Why, no, Master Kay, who would write a book about him?"

"I don't know, I thought they might."

"Why, he was only a poor thief, Master Kay, who took what didn't belong to him by frightening people."

"And he did really live up in the stables here?"

"Yes, that was like a house, then, opening on the road. He used to lodge there and let out he was a traveler for malt—or so they say. It may be only old tales."

"Did your grandfather ever see him?"

"Why, yes, Master Kay, many a time, and he was at his

taking. You see, he stopped a carriage out Rugby way, and took some rings and a watch from a gentleman. The gentleman said nothing while he was being robbed, but he recognized the mare, because he'd seen her, as it happened, just in the last day or two in the Cock stable. So the gentleman thought, 'Probably you belong near there,' so he had a watch set.

"By and by Benjamin came back to these parts. The watchers saw him riding to the Cock by the brook where they dip the sheep, so as to come to the back of the stable. They were all ready for him, in about the stables, and some were in the road hidden among the trees. Well, as he came down to the brook to jump it, he saw these people, for one of them raised his head to see the mare take the jump. Others say it wasn't that, but the little girl who used to say dinner was ready waved a red handkerchief, which was their danger signal. Anyway, he saw it wasn't safe, so he turned the mare and rode for here. But some of them were in the road, so that couldn't be either, and they all gave him chase across the Tump, and then past Barbara's, and along the Long Lane there, down past Hollings' Quarry, all shooting and shouting out 'Stop, Thief,' and lots of new people joining in. Oh, they'd more than a hundred persons out.

"My grandfather was working then for old Mr. Pullean that lived at Ley Cop. He was digging in the flowerbed, he said, when Benjamin came over the hedge. He said the mare was nearly down, for she was a little thing, he said, and not fresh when she started, and she'd come five miles best pace and been hit, too, for she was bleeding from the side, poor thing. So Benjamin said, 'Come up, old girl. Tell them I went along the road,' he said to grandfather. But they were too close on him for anything of that.

"So then Benjamin put the mare at the fence out of the garden. It was a big blind place with a stank of water the far side. The mare got over clear, but she didn't land clean, she fell back, and she couldn't get up. My grandfather said Benjamin gave a little cry, like he'd been shot through the heart. But he picked up his pistols and ran down the field along the stream to the little spinney. You will know the place well, Master Kay: it's the big foxes' lie where we saw what we called the shrike's larder. It was all full of scrub and stubbed stuff, and deep, on this side, from a fall of earth. Well, Benjamin got in there and tried to load his pistols, and they all came riding up shooting at him, shouting out to surrender, and young Mr. Dogface, as they always called him, who was afterwards sent to Botany himself, shot him in the arm and broke it. So then they got a cord of old Mr. Pullean's, what had the washing on it, and tied poor Benjamin with that.

"My grandfather said he was all trembling from the fall and the ride, and the fight and from pain, but not at all from fear. He was not a big man, but middlesize, and slight rather. Very active, though: ran just like a hare. He'd black hair and eyes, altogether very black, yet clean-shaved, as people were then. Rather a slight, quick man, with a nice face, nothing bad in it, only bold. So then he was taken off and that was the end of him."

"Did they ever find his treasure?"

"How you do run on about treasure. I believe it's all you ever think of. He never made much by it, to leave treasure. Just barely enough to pay his horsemeat, my grandfather said."

"What happened to the mare?"

"Oh, she'd broken her back. She was taken to the kennels. Old Sir Hassle had the hounds then. He used to come in all hungry from hunting and take like a ladleful of the hounds' broth, all dead horse and pony. But there, some men you can't make particular. And you'll be one of them, to judge from your stocking. Whatever have you been doing to get your stocking into that state?"

"I say, Ellen, thank you for telling me all about Benjamin. Did you ever go into the Crowmarsh estate? Is it very dangerous?"

"Now don't you go going there, Master Kay—it's not allowed. It's preserved, and apart from the keepers it's full of mantraps and spring guns; the one will blow your head off and the other will nip your ankles half in two, like they did to my

cousin Bob. He went in there, against the notice, and got
caught in a mantrap; he didn't walk the same in a twelvemonth
after. Then they've got their bloodhounds loose there some
days, able to tear a child's head off, and always they've got their
watchers just now, so soon before the shooting. You run off to
bed now, like a good boy, and let me be sure you say your
prayers. Don't gibble-gabble them, but think what you're saying."

*W*hen he got into bed, the sun was nearly down. A glow from it lit the wall opposite, so that the hunting men riding at the brook in "Full Cry" were made most vivid. A ray touched the model of the *Plunderer*, so that she glowed, too, and the green stripe upon her forecastle and the scarlet rims of her tops looked beautiful against her brown and black. "I have had a jolly day," he thought. "And tomorrow I'll jolly well go into the Crowmarsh estate to see if I can't find the J.G.Z."

Just before he fell asleep he was almost sure that the water in the brook in "Full Cry" had eddies in it—eddies and those little clouds of dissolving earth which the water rat makes when scared from a bank. "He must have been a jolly good painter," he thought, "to be able to do all that." He fell asleep soon after this, thinking that if he were a painter, he would paint—well, he did not know what he would paint, so very much was happening.

As before, he woke up into what seemed like broad daylight, although he could see the stars through the window. He was aware at once that something very odd was happening in the print of "Full Cry": the hunting men, whose red coats were flapping, were turning from the brook. And what was the matter with the brook? It was very, very full of water, and coming with such a strong current that it swished against the loose alder root. He could see not only eddies but bright, hurrying, gleaming ripples which ran into bubbles, and yes, yes, it was coming into the room, it was running on both sides of the bed, clear, swift, rushing water, carrying down petals and leaves and bits of twig. Then there came the water rats, who dived with a phlumphing noise when they caught sight of him. He was in an island in the midst of the stream, and the stream was so crystal clear that he could see the fish in the shallows, flapping like water-plant leaves, and filmy as dead weeds.

But what on earth was happening to the morel of the *Plunderer?* He could see that the water had reached her on the wall: she was afloat. She seemed to be alive with little tiny men, all busy with ropes. No, they were not men, they were little mice. "Water mice, I suppose," he thought. Now she was coming across the stream to him, and how big she was. Or no, how little he was—he was no bigger than the water mice. There she came slowly to the edge of the bed. She had flags flying, a Blue Peter at the fore, a house flag, with three oreilles couped proper, on the main, and a red ensign at the peak. But lovelier than the flags were the decks, with the little doors, each with a shiny brass handle and real lifeboats ready for use. He could see the barrels and lockers in them marked "Best Preserved Milk," "Corned Beef," "Ship's Bread," "Pemmican," "Raisins," "Chocolate Cream," "Turkish Delight," "Split Peas," "Currants," "Hundreds and Thousands," "Mixed Biscuits," "Dry Ginger Beer," etc., etc. No fear of starving in lifeboats like those. Then all the little brass cannon were shining in the sun, ready for use, with the little powder tubs all handy, and little men standing by them ready to fire them off in salute. Then as the ship came alongside the bed, each little gunner blew puff upon his match, to make it glow (some of them had red-hot pokers instead of match), just as *The Sea Gunner's Practice* described, and popped the glowing end on the touchholes. All the little brass cannon went bang together in salute.

Then Kay saw that the captain of the ship was his friend the water rat. He was standing on the poop, with his telescope in his hand, telling the mate to put the gangway over for Mr. Kay. Some of the little seamen at once thrust out a gangway onto the bed.

"Step on board, Mr. Kay," the captain said.

"May I really and truly?"

"Yes, we're waiting for you."

Kay walked from his bed to the deck. He was amazed at the neatness of everything: all the rows of buckets, the sponges and rammers for the cannon, the capstans that worked, the compasses that pointed, the cask, painted red, for salt meat, and the other cask, painted blue, for fresh water, and all the rigging, with little ladders on it for going aloft. Then there was a ship's kitchen on the deck close to him, with a real little cook, with a wooden leg, making plum duff for dinner at a real fire.

"Welcome on board, Mr. Kay," the captain said. "I thought we might stand over to the westward to see what we can find of the old *Plunderer*. We've got a cabin prepared for you, with a hammock slung in it, and here are some nice long seaboots to pull over your pajamas, and a double-breasted pea jacket to keep out the seas and keep in the plum duff. And now, my hearties, cast loose forward, let go aft. The tug has got her. Hurray, lads, for the westward."

Kay noticed now, what he had not noticed before, that on the other side of the *Plunderer* was a tugboat under steam. Long before, he had had a beautiful tugboat with a scarlet funnel. She had gone by real steam made by methylated spirit, which you lit under the boiler in a little lamp. But after two voyages she set forth across the squire's pond on a windy day, and in the draught of the gale she caught fire, blazed for a few minutes from stem to stern, and then went down head first in deep water. Yet now here she was, repainted, and with powerful new engines in her, which were threshing the water as they towed the *Plunderer* clear of the bed.

Soon they had swung round clear of the sofa and headed to the west, through the open window, into the night. Sidelights and towing lights were lit. She plunged on beside her tug, casting streaks of colored light upon the water. Soon she was in the stream where Kay had so often seen the water rat. Someone in the *Plunderer* turned a strong searchlight onto the water ahead. Lookout men went aloft to watch the water. They called to the helmsman from time to time to do this or that to dodge the rocks. "A bit anxious, this reach of the stream," the water rat said, "but there's lots of water tonight."

The ship went faster and faster over rapids and shallows. Soon she was in the big, quiet pool where the stream entered the river. An otter looked out at them and wished them good luck. A moorhen came out and swam ahead of them to show them the best passage. Dawn was now breaking, but all the world of men was asleep. Kay saw the deserted quay of the riverbank where he had so often watched people coming to hire skiffs. A light was burning there, although morning was growing everywhere. Kay saw the tug stand away from the *Plunderer*'s side and cast loose the tow ropes. The *Plunderer*'s men ran aloft and cast loose the sails. When Kay next looked back, the river wharf was far astern; the ship was running swiftly down the river under a press of sail.

"But come, Master Kay," the captain said. "Breakfast is on the table. Step down the ladder with me to the cabin."

He led the way down to a passage where there were a great many doors labeled First Mate, Second Mate, Third Mate, Captain's Stores, Instrument Room, Chart Room, Steward's Pantry, Bullion Room, warranted iron-lined, Captain's Bath, Mates' Bath, Jam Room, Sardine Room, etc., as well as one big open door leading to the cabin, where the table was set for breakfast. They had for breakfast all the things that Kay was fondest of: very hot little round loaves of new white bread baked in the embers of a wood fire, very salt butter, a sardine with a lot of olive oil, some minced kidneys, a poached egg and frizzled bacon, a very fat sausage all bursting out of its skin, a homemade pork pie, with cold jelly and yolk of egg beneath the crust, a bowl of strawberries and cream with sifted sugar, a bowl of raspberries and cream with blobs of sugar-candyish brown sugar that you could scrunch, some nice new mushrooms and chicken, part of a honeycomb with cream, a cup of coffee with crystals of white sugar candy for a change, a yellow plum, a greengage, and then a ripe blue plum of Pershore to finish off with.

"That's the way, Master Kay," the captain said. "I always believe in a good breakfast: something to do your work on and start the day with. And now, if you've finished, as you haven't had much sleep lately, perhaps you'd like to keep the next watch in your hammock. Come up on the deck for a moment first, though—we are now in the open sea."

The wonder of it was that they *were* in the open sea, out of sight of land, with the ship under full sail flying westward. One or two of the water mice were at work far aloft. Others on deck were washing their clothes and hanging them out to dry on clotheslines, or fishing with hooks and lines, or feeding the sparrows (which they kept for the eggs) in the hencoops, or polishing the brass on the ship's bells and railings. The sea was all blue and bright, the hot sun was shining, not a cloud could be seen. The ship was flying faster and faster.

Kay's cabin was a charming room, with mahogany lockers and a porthole covered with red curtains. A telescope hung on a rack ready for use. A canvas hammock swung from hooks in the wall; it had a pillow, mattress, sheets, and blankets. The captain showed him how to get in and tuck himself up. In a minute he was fast asleep.

He was wakened half an hour later by the ship anchoring in calm water. On going on deck he found that she was not far from a low, tropical shore, blindingly white from the surf bursting on it. Palm trees grew here and there on the shore. There was no sign of man. The water, bright blue to seaward, with vivid green streaks, was clear as crystal.

"Now Master Kay," the captain said, "we will get into the diving bell and go down to see what we can see. We are now just over the wreck of the old *Plunderer*."

"How do you know?" Kay asked.

"We can always get directions about wrecks, we underwater folk," the captain said. "We ask the otters, and they get into touch with all sorts of seafolk, mermaids and sirens, not to speak of dolphins and these other fellows. Some of them are very old and have astonishing memories. It was a mermaid who told Tom Otter about the *Plunderer*, and he told me."

The diving bell was a tight little room, just big enough for two nice comfortable armchairs. It was built of iron framing, with floor and side windows of strong clear glass. Airpipes and speaking tubes were let into the walls and through the roof. When Kay and the captain had taken their seats in the armchairs, the crew closed the door very carefully so that no water could possibly squeeze in. Then they hoisted the bell up and began to lower it carefully into the water. Kay found that he could see quite clearly through the glass of the sides and the floor. The fish came to the windows and sucked at them with their mouths. Presently, when the captain called through the speaking tube to stop lowering, he turned on a searchlight which pointed through the floor. Kay could see the bottom of the sea, growing like a garden with white and red coral, weeds, anemones, and sponges, all seeming to dilate in the light. Some gaily colored fish came poking to the light, to find if it were good to eat; a few big fish, some of them like shadows, others like round collapsing bags with suckers waving from them, drifted or finned by, all noiseless. There was no whisper of sound, except a drumming in the ears. "There's what is left of the *Plunderer*," the captain said.

Lying on the bottom, partly on white sand, partly among coral and weed, was the wreck of an old wooden ship. All that remained in sight of her was her stern post, her nameplate, marked *Plunderer*, a part of her keel, and a few ribs fallen out of place. All these timbers had been blackened by years under the sea. White and blue barnacles were growing on them; sprays of red and white coral had thrust up among them. The sunlight made all these things so glorious suddenly that the captain turned out the light. Kay could see even the eyes of the lobsters peering into the crannies of the coral.

A mermaid floated to the side of the diving bell. She was young and merry-looking, with bright, big brown eyes and very white teeth. She wore a gold crown over her long brown hair. Her cheeks and lips were full of color. She put her mouth to the glass and smiled at them. "That's Seaflower," the captain said. "Say good morning to her."

"Good morning, Miss Seaflower," Kay said. "Can you tell us how this ship came here?"

"Yes," she said. "She was upset in a squall, long ago, and all her men were drowned. They were making merry at the time. You can still see one of them: that scarlet coral is he. But open the door and come with me."

The three other mermaids had swum to the diving bell. Together they opened the door. In an instant, Kay was swimming with them in the warm water that was so like green light. All the floor of the sea shone. Here and there were patches of a green plant which had flowers like flames, they were so bright. At first he thought that everything there was dead, but when he had been twenty seconds in that tingling water he knew that it was full of life. The white sand of the sea floor was alive with tiny, scurrying, glittering creatures, little beings looked at him from the branches of the coral, flowers poked out eyes at him upon stalks like snails' horns, he could see the leaves of the seaweeds shine with joy at every good suck-in of light. All these living forms were swaying gently as the swell lifted and fell. All were glistening and tingling with joy: A kind of drowsy song of delight moved through the water. Everything was singing, or murmuring, or sighing because life was so good.

Kay went up to a big scarlet fish that had pale goggle-eyes and a collapsing mouth. He tickled its throat, and others knew that he was liking it, because they, too, came to have their throats tickled, till he was surrounded by fish of all colors and shapes, scaled and slimy, finned, or legged, or feelered, all noiseless, most of them strange, many of them most beautiful.

"Come away, Kay," the mermaids said. "But first look at the lovely golden lad."

Lying among the coral, as though he were resting upon a bank of flowers, was a golden image of Saint George, still holding a white shield with a scarlet cross.

"We used to sing to him at first," Seaflower said, "hoping that he would wake. The ship was full of golden and silver people at one time. We loved them, they were so very beautiful, but they never answered when we spoke to them. Men came here searching for them in the old days, dragging anchors for them along the sea floor. At last some Indian divers came down and carried them all away to a yacht, all except this one, which they would not touch, because we had so decked it with flowers.

"I see that you know who it was who took those lovely things. He was going to take them to a city of evil men near here. We followed his yacht on his way hither, for we were sad to lose our lovely people. But come, Kay, you shall come with us as far as we can go on the way those golden people went."

They all set out together, Kay between Seaflower and Foam Blossom, each of whom held one of his hands. Foam Blossom was a golden-haired mermaid with bright blue eyes and lovely rosy cheeks: She was always laughing. "Is not this lovely?" she said, as they went swimming along.

"Oh, it *is* lovely," Kay said. Every stroke of their arms took them over some new kind of shellfish, or past some new anemone or waving weed.

"Come," Seaflower said, "let us go in on the tide, at the surface."

They rose up together to the air. There, on the shallow shore, long lines of rollers were always advancing to the beach, toppling as they went and at last shattering. A little river came out to the sea there. Its little waves seemed to enjoy meeting the big waves.

"Come," Foam Blossom said, "let us ride on this big roller that is just going in."

Together they sat on the neck of the wave, with Kay between them. Kay felt the wave begin to run like a horse, and to
gather speed and to lift. Soon the toppling water began to hiss
and foam all about them. The shore seemed to rush nearer, and
then they all rolled over and over in boiling bubbles into the
cool pool of the river, where the seashells looked as though
they were all made of pearl.

Soon they were swimming up a river which flowed between
ranks of reed and bulrush. Some of the reeds had flowers like
the plumes of pampas grass, but pale blue; others had delicate,
dangling, yellow tassels. All over these flowers the butterflies
were hovering and settling. Giant flags grew among the reeds,
with heavy blue, white, and golden flowers. Little speckled
birds with scarlet crests clung to these flowers while they pecked
something within them. Waterfowl as big as swans, with orange
bills and big black and white plumes on their heads, swam to
them to be stroked. In the gloom and zebra striping of the light
and shade of the reeds Kay saw long-legged water birds standing
ankle-deep, fishing. Here and there, when they passed mudbanks,
he saw the turtles enjoying themselves in the cool ooze.

Presently they left the river and swam up a backwater, where
the reeds on both sides gave place to quince trees, which smelt
like Arabia from the ripe fruit. At the end of the backwater
there was a patch of red mud much poached by the feet of cows
that had come to drink there. Beyond the cows was a little roll of
grassland.

"The man took the gold and silver things this way," Seaflower
said. "In those days the river ran this way, through all that
grassy piece and for miles beyond it. We often used to swim
there. We followed his yacht for a long way, further than we
can see from here. He was a rosy-faced man, not old, but his
hair was already gray. His eyes were very bright, and his mouth,
when one could see it through the beard, was most cruel and
evil. He had three Indians with him, who were his divers and
sailors, whom he used to beat.

"When he was in a narrow part of the river, he heard guns,

for his city of wickedness was being destroyed. He poled his yacht far into the reeds against the mud and sent one of his Indians to find out what was happening. As the Indian did not come back, he sent a second Indian, and when the second did not come back he sent a third, but the third did not come back either."

"What happened to the Indians?" Kay asked.

"They all went home to their village in the sea. They have houses there, built upon piles driven into the water. In the rainy seasons they keep very snug in their hammocks and tell each other stories."

"And what happened to Abner Brown, please?"

"He waited for the Indians to bring him news. When they did not come, he changed his yacht's hiding place, by driving her still further into the reeds, and then he set out by himself to find out what was happening. He was captured as a pirate that same night and sent far away.

"Nobody found his boat, she was too well hidden, but there came great changes which hid her further. At first we used to play in the water near her, hoping that she might soon fall to pieces, so that we might have her gold and silver people again, but then there came the earthquake, which raised the riverbed and buried the yacht in the mud. After the earthquake there came the great summer floods, which made a new channel for the river and altered all the coast. When the floods went down, the place where the yacht lay was five miles from the water and covered deep with flowers, so the birds told us.

"The man came back presently to look for his yacht, but with the land so changed he hardly knew where to begin. We used to see him digging sometimes, when we went up the streams. But he was evil, do not let us think of him. Let us go to the sea, to play in the rollers as they burst."

In a few minutes they were in the shining shallow water across which the breaking rollers were marching. At first Kay was frightened of the waves as they curled and toppled high over his head. Very soon he was wading to meet them, so that they could break all over him or carry him in to the sands.

"And now," the mermaids said, "let us all go down to look at the city under the sea."

They all swam for a few minutes, then Kay suddenly saw something very golden in the green of the underwater.

"Those are the walls," Foam Blossom said. "And if you listen, you will hear the bells. Let us wait here."

They had paused at what had been the harbor. Three or four little ships had sunken with the city; they were there, still secured to the walls. Sponges like big yellow mushrooms covered one, another was starred all over with tiny white shells, another was thickly grown with a weed like many-colored ribbons. The walls, which had once been of white marble, seemed golden in that dim light. As Kay looked he heard a sweet but muffled booming of the bells as the swell of the water surged and lapsed in the bell tower.

"Come, Kay," Seaflower said. "The city gates have fallen open. We can go in."

They passed through the gates, which now drooped upon their hinges from the weight of the shells which grew upon them. Inside the gates was a guardhouse, with a rack of spears still standing against the wall. Beyond that was a street, with shops open, and fish slowly finning from shop to shop. At the end of the street there was a temple with a bell tower. No one was in that city. Kay went into two of the houses. In one, the kitchen was set out with pots and pans for dinner; two eggs were in a bowl and the bone of a leg of mutton was on a dish. In the other, the beds in the nursery were turned down ready for the children, and in one of the beds a child had set a doll, on which the little shells were growing. There were gaily painted carvings on some of the walls, showing the racing of children and romps and tugs-of-war.

"What is this city, please?" Kay asked. "I would love to go all over it, into every house. What is it called?"

"We call it the Golden City. But look, here come the merchildren, playing touch and tag. Let us play with them."

At that instant about twenty little merchildren came darting down the street at full speed, with streaming hair, bright eyes, and laughter. They twisted about like eels, dived down chimneys and through windows, crying aloud from joy in the fun.

"I wonder," Kay said, "if we might play hide and seek? This would be such a lovely place for it."

"Yes," Foam Blossom said, "let us all play hide and seek. Seaflower shall be He. And Kay, you come with me, for I know a lovely place to hide."

She took him through one of the houses into what had been a garden. The fruit trees still stood but were now crusted over with shells. Sponges, anemones, and corals, which were so covered with points of glitter that they seemed full of eyes, grew like mistletoe on the branches. There came a sort of cloud in swift movement across the golden light.

"Look," Foam Blossom said, "there's a ship passing overhead. If you look up, you may see one of the crew looking down."

"That reminds me," Kay said. "I meant to ask you before. Did you ever see another man taking away those golden and silver people? He may have taken them away in a big barge."

"Why, Kay," she answered, "that is the *Plunderer* passing. There is the water rat captain looking down. You must be quick. And oh, do look at the flying fish."

Kay felt a sort of swirl as he rushed past a lot of green bubbles into the light. The billows burst all about him suddenly and the sun made him blink. Foam Blossom, the lovely merchildren, the city and its gardens, among which the beaked fishes had flitted like birds, were gone. He was sitting on the end of the *Plunderer*'s jib boom in the clouds of spray flung up as she sailed. Sheets of spray, as bright as snow, soared and flashed all round him. Then he saw that it was not spray, but a flight of flying fish, skimming and falling like darts, all glittering and quivering. "O, how lovely," he cried.

As he cried, he heard his window creak. Somebody rolled him into bed and the *Plunderer* went back to the wall. As for the sea, it was not there. When he opened his eyes, Ellen was there, but no water at all.

"Where did it all run to?" he asked.

"Where did what all run to? Wake up," Ellen said. "You are such a one to sleep as I never did."

"Well, it was here a moment ago," he said.

"I declare, you're dreaming still," she said. "Now, don't go to sleep again. Breakfast will be in a quarter of an hour, and you're not to be late," she said. "I was to tell you specially."

*W*hen lessons were over, he went out to Benjamin's Lair with a little compass, which had been on the schoolroom shelves for years. With this he judged that a point a hundred yards south from the Seekings Stables would be in the Crowmarsh estate, somewhere near the fir tree in the spinney. All of the Crowmarsh estate was an unknown world to him, where spring guns banged, mantraps snapped, bloodhounds tore the heads of children and the Pimply Whatto had been shot in the leg. Yet it looked quiet enough in the hot summer morning—no bloodhounds and no keepers.

"I don't believe that anybody's there," he thought. "I'm sure that nobody's there." He hovered about, unable to make up his mind to it, until the bell rang for dinner.

After dinner he wanted to go, but the thought of the bloodhounds daunted him. Then he thought, "From the loft in the stables I may be able to see over into the estate beyond the spinney there."

He scrambled into the stable through the harness room window and then climbed the steps nailed to the wall. The loft was very dark. It was littered with musty straw, in which black walnutty things, which had once been apples, lay. Baskets, hives, a honey extractor, brood frames, comb foundation, saddletrees, decaying top boots and the catcher of a mowing machine lay in one corner. In the wall, showing light at the edges, was a big wooden shutter, through which the hay and straw had once been hoisted. Through just such a shutter, when he was drunk and wasn't minding what he was doing, Ellen's uncle had fallen at the Tuttocks, and broken his hucklebone. However, by being sober and very carefully minding what he was doing, Kay reached the little glazed window at the side without mishap. He looked through over the road and the orchard.

Old Jarge came by with a pair of steps and a bag of tools on his way to see to Mrs. Tattle's dovecote. He explained this to Mrs. Bucket, who was on her way to see her married daughter. They said that it was lovely weather for the crops, though a nice drop of rain would freshen things up a bit. When they had gone, pretty Polly Colway drove past in her dogcart with a friend. When she had gone, Kay stared at the Crowmarsh estate. It was all peaceful. In the orchard the gray trees were growing barer of leaves, as the fruit ripened. The birds were moving without alarm, rabbits humped themselves about, nibbling grass at the spinney edge. Somewhere just a hundred yards away was

S.S.S.

J.G.Z. R.P.C.

"I'll try it," he said. "I believe it's safe."

Within a minute he was flat on his stomach in the Crowmarsh spinney. "It's all lies about the keepers being here," he said to himself. "Nobody ever comes into this spinney. The branches are all covered with that brittle stuff, which hasn't been brushed away."

He looked back at the ruins of barn, brewhouse, and stable. A hundred years before, Benjamin had lived there; two hundred years before, people had died of the plague there, so Ellen said. There was a mark on one of the doors, which had once been a red cross to show the dead-cart man that a corpse was inside.

He reckoned up his distance. "Two cricket pitches still to go," he thought. He crept through the spinney to look at the other side. There he saw that a hundred yards south from S.S.S. would take him to the middle of a pond in a cemented basin.

"That is where he put it," he thought. "People often buried their treasures in ponds. It's the safest place you can choose really, but I shan't be able to get it."

He looked out in peace at the Crowmarsh estate, which he had never before seen. Rabbits were nibbling the grass. Just beyond the pond was the old ruin of an elm tree swathed in ivy. Beyond that was a paddock, where hunters were being summered. Beyond the paddock was pasture, in which the Crowmarsh Guernseys were grazing. Beyond that was grass, where someone was lunging a chestnut colt. "Those young gentlemen care for nothing but horses," Ellen had said.

A pheasant walked out of the spinney close to him. "What lies people tell," Kay thought. "Of course, there can't be bloodhounds and spring guns. The rabbits and pheasants would set them off at once. I'm going down to look at the pond."

He crept to the water's edge to watch the insects and the spinning of grains of sand below the lip by which the water trickled away.

Looking up, his eyes were caught by a big hole in the ruined elm tree. It was a hole big enough for Kay to get into.

He was thrilled by holes in trees. Ellen had often told him how they had found the skeleton of a man inside a big hollow oak in Sir Hassle Gassle's wood. "He was supposed to be a murderer or something, who had got in to hide and didn't think that it would be hollow all the way down, but it was, so there he was and he didn't dare to cry out, people thought, for then he would have been taken and hanged, so he just starved to death. Father said that his coat was still on him, hanging by the buttons, and bits of shoes with buckles."

Then he had read of a skeleton in armor found inside an-other hollow tree near one of the battlefields of the Wars of the Roses. The man must have run away, climbed in, fallen down, and died there. And other things were found in oak trees. The rector had half a dozen black iron barbed arrowheads, which had been shot into an oak tree in the Butts in the reign of Henry VIII. He had found them when sawing up the logs for firewood. Old Mr. Colway had dug bullets from old trees at Naseby.

"Very likely," Kay thought, "Benjamin's treasure might be in the hollow of the tree, for of course I can't tell what S.S.S. is. It might be Stable's Southern Side. A hollow tree would be as good a place as a pond."

At that moment, as he stared upwards, a white dumpy figure sidled into the center of the hole, stared down at him with big fierce eyes, and then, closing both eyes, stood still like a stump of decayed wood. "A white owl," Kay said. "He's got a nest there. I'll climb up and peep in."

He was wondering how painful a peck from that hooked beak would be, when he heard the click of a gate latch. "It's the keepers," he said. "They've seen me."

Peeping round the tree trunk through the ivy, he found that it was worse than the keepers. It was young Mr. Crowmarsh and his mother, whom everybody called "the Tigress." They were about a hundred yards away, coming slowly toward him, deep in talk. If he ran for home, they would recognize him or run him down. And then there was that terrible notice, TRES-PASSERS WILL BE PROSECUTED. What was he to do?

"Get up into my house," the owl said. "Look alive or they'll catch you. Oh, my mouse and sparrow, take hold of the ivy and pull yourself up. That's better. Now the other foot. Now catch a good grip of my claw. Now, oh hoo, a long pull. Up you come. Now, here you are in my nice house. Just step aside behind the ivy till they've gone by."

Kay stepped aside behind the ivy as he was bidden. He found that he was in a snug room littered with moss, dead leaves, and soft, rotten wood. He heard the two companions come to the foot of the tree.

"I thought I heard a squirrel, then," young Mr. Crowmarsh said.

"I don't think it was a squirrel," his mother said. "I expect it was only Blinky flapping his wings. Our red squirrel has gone. I can't help thinking that that man Bilges shot him."

"A regular scoundrel, Bilges, and his brother at the Gassles' is as bad," the young man said. "But is this the old Blinky that used to roost in the ivy on the ruin?"

"It is," old Blinky growled.

"There he is growling," the young man said. "It *is* old Blinky. Well, I'm glad he's alive still. I've half a mind to climb up to look in on him."

He had clambered up a foot or two when his mother stopped him. "The tree really isn't safe," she said. "Besides, you will ruin your clothes."

Probably he would have climbed up, but at that moment some of the bark gave way beneath his feet, which brought him slithering down.

"There, you see, it isn't safe," his mother said. "You must come along now. Look in on old Blinky some other time."

When they had gone, old Blinky said, "Well, Kay, have you been riding the hoofless horse lately?"

"No, I haven't."

"Nor found the treasure yet?"

"No, not yet. But I found out where it went to, up to a point. It was swallowed up in an earthquake, and though some people say that it was afterwards dug up and taken away, others aren't so sure."

"Well, why don't you make sure?"

"Please, I don't know how to."

"Is it as good to eat as mouse and sparrow?" Blinky asked.

"It isn't good to eat at all."

Blinky blinked at this and gurgled in his throat. After a long time he said, "Do you want to find this stuff?"

"Yes, please, rather."

"Well, I might find out for you, perhaps, if you tell me just whereabouts to begin."

"The place was somewhere near the Golden City . . ."

"Not so loud, please," old Blinky said.

"Why? There's nobody listening."

"How do you know? There are a lot of these invisible people everywhere, and spies . . . well. It will be wiser to whisper."

Kay whispered into Blinky's ear directions which he thought could help.

"Right," Blinky said. "Now I'll tell you what I'll do. I'll call my friend the swift. He'll take the message to the stormy petrel, who is much the fastest bird there is. The petrel will be across ocean in no time . . . then he'll pass the word to a skua or something on the other side, and the skua or something will ask my cousins about it. I've a lot of cousins over there, very good sorts of creatures, but they have an odd habit of living in holes in the ground. I can't understand the habit myself, but each man to his taste. It will come in handy now, though, for of course they will know everything that is underground in those parts. By the way, here is Swift. He'll go at once—he'll have an answer by your bedtime. Hoo, there, Swift."

The swift paused on the ledge of Blinky's lair. He was a fine bird, bright-eyed and eager.

"I say, Swift," Blinky said, "this is our friend Kay. He wants to find out about some treasure, so will you pass the word along to my foreign cousins? Put your head up to mine, will you, it had better be whispered. There are reasons why this should be kept secret, if it can be."

As he whispered the directions to Swift, it seemed to Kay that something rustled in the ivy above them.

"Right," the swift said. "I'll take the message and wait for an answer. It should reach me before roosting time. If it doesn't, I'll send it by Bat. Anyhow, you will get it before you start your evening's hunting, and you can send it on to Kay. Good-bye, all."

He slipped into the air and was gone before Kay could thank him. As he sped away, Kay was quite certain that somebody or something rustled in the ivy above.

"What was that?" he asked.

"What was what?"

"That noise in the ivy."

"I didn't notice any noise."

"There was a noise like someone climbing in the ivy."

"I expect it was the wind," Blinky said. "The wind is always rustling this ivy. Time and again I keep thinking it's a mouse, but it never is. It's always the wind.

> "A very queer thing is the wind.
> I don't know how it beginn'd,
> And nobody knows where it goes.
> It is wind, it beginn'd, and it blows."

He uttered these last words very drowsily, and snapped out a snorey kind of grunt once or twice after he had finished. He blinked at Kay once or twice, then closed his eyes and fell fast asleep.

"It sounded liker someone climbing than the wind," Kay thought. "But he was so drowsy he probably did not hear it."

He would have climbed up to make sure, but at that moment the church bells began:

> Ding dong, ding dong,
> Dong, dong, ding dong,
> Ding dong, ding dong,
> Ding ding, dong dong.

And then struck the hour. He was sure that it would only be four o'clock. Alas, it was five. The tea bell must have gone long ago. He would be late again—he would catch it this time and very likely be sent to bed. And he was still up the tree in the Crowmarsh estate.

Despair made him reckless. He slithered down the tree, ran to the spinney, dashed across to the road, scrambled over the gate, and ran for home, not caring how many keepers caught him. He did not know who saw him—there were people in the road as he passed. He was ruined anyhow; what could one or two more witnesses add to his sentence? He tried to brush the green powder, dust, and ivy clips from his clothes as he ran—he was in a filthy mess. Then his right hand had one of those black resinous smears which you get from laurel or pine boughs. That would not come off, as he knew only too well, except with hot water, Ellen, and pumice stone. "Oh, I shall catch it this time," he moaned.

There was no question of making himself later by washing and brushing. He went straight in to the dining room, and there, oh horror, horror of horrors . . .

There was the governess in her icy-sweet society manner sitting at the horrid little society tea table, with the best tea service, which everybody called the Lowestoft, pouring out tea for Lady Crowmarsh.

"She saw me after all," he moaned to himself. "And now she's come over to sneak."

"Kay," the governess said, "you're very late. Say how do you do to Lady Crowmarsh, then come and have your tea."

He said how do you do to Lady Crowmarsh, and was expecting the sword to fall on him for trespass, when the governess noticed the state of his hands and clothes. "Where have you been, Kay," she asked, "to get yourself into that pickle? Go and wash your hands and brush your suit before you sit down."

"Oh, let me plead for him, won't you?" Lady Crowmarsh said. "I don't like a little boy to come in to tea too tidy. Come and sit by me, Kay, and tell me all about your fossil collection. Have you found any more nice fossils lately?"

He had given up collecting fossils for more than a year, under orders from the governess, who found that grubbing in the quarries brought him into meals too muddy. Lady Crowmarsh had once seen him grubbing for fossils and had remembered it.

He thought that it was nice of her to remember, but he still could not understand why she did not begin about the trespassing. Before he could answer, the governess broke in with "Oh, don't ask about fossils, Lady Crowmarsh. The very thought of those quarries in the rains, and the state of his clothes when he comes in, is enough . . . and then lumps of stone under all the taps, and the taps left running. . . ."

"I like men to get through the collection habit in childhood," Lady Crowmarsh said, thinking of her son, who was still a collector of things and something of a disappointment to her. "And now about the bazaar. Are you quite sure that you can take the Magic Peepshow?"

The words Magic Peepshow made Kay prick up his ears. He looked hard at the governess, who changed color at the words, as though she did not quite like them. "Oh, yes, lady Crowmarsh," she said, "I will do so gladly, but might it be called the Wonder Peepshow, as Magic Peepshow might give people such strange ideas. . . . Magic, you know . . . well really . . . in these days."

"We've always called it Magic Peepshow in the past," Lady Crowmarsh said. "I don't think that anyone has minded, as it is only to amuse the children. . . . Still, call it Wonder Peepshow if you would really rather."

"I think . . . perhaps . . . if you don't mind."

Kay thought her a silly ass to object to the word *magic*. "Ah," he thought, "if you knew what goes on at midnight in this very room you would be less particular."

Lady Crowmarsh was very nice to him during the rest of her stay. He could not think why she did not begin about the trespassing. His spirits began to rise as he thought, "She may not have seen me after all. And Sylvia Daisy hasn't found out yet either." But he knew that his black hands and dusty clothes would be inquired into later, when Lady Crowmarsh was gone. "I shall catch it then," he thought, so he ate as much at tea as he could, because his chance of supper was slight. "When Lady Crowmarsh goes," he thought, "as soon as she is outside the door, it will be 'Kay, how dare you come to tea in that state. You will scrub your face and hands and go straight to bed.' "

When Lady Crowmarsh rose to go, she said, "This young man shall come with me, if you will spare him, to open the gates for me." She clapped him on the shoulder and pinched his ear, but in such a kind way that he did not mind. "She can't know," he thought. "She can't have seen me."

As they walked to the gate togther, he felt that he could not let her be ignorant of how he had trespassed on her estate.

"Lady Crowmarsh," he said, "I'm very, very sorry, but I went into your estate today, in spite of the notice. I climbed the tree with the owl's nest, and I was hiding there while you were just below, with Mr. Crowmarsh, just before tea."

"Oh," she said. "Were you?"

"Yes, while you talked of old Blinky."

"Well, why do you tell me this?"

"At first I thought you knew, and now I feel I ought to tell you."

"Hm," she said, in a very tigerish way, "you are quite right to tell me. And what if I take you straight back to the governess and make you tell her?

"Don't look so lost, child. I'm not going to do any such thing. But tell me . . . had you climbed the tree after the cat?"

"No, Lady Crowmarsh. What cat?"

"There was a black cat in the ivy there. It is yours, I think. I have seen it go over your wall. A black cat with white paws and throat."

"Yes, that's Blackmalkin. I didn't know that he was in the tree, though I did hear something rustle."

"You'd better tell him not to touch old Blinky," Lady Crowmarsh said. "Blinky has been in that tree for years, and was in the ruin before that, until we pulled it down. Do you often come into my grounds, may I ask?"

"No. I never came before today."

"What made you come today?"

"Please, I wanted to see where a hundred yards south of a place would bring me."

"What a curious notion. And where did it bring you?"

"To the middle of your little pond. Could you tell me, please, when those little ponds were made?"

"They were made in 1782, when the formal garden was laid out. I suppose you are not interested in formal gardens."

"Please, I don't quite know what they are."

"Well, come in and see. Then, if you like them, you can come in to see them again whenever you like, as long as you don't disturb the birds. The gardens will bore you, but you may like to see my mice. I have a great many mice, for I'm interested in them."

Kay spent a most happy hour looking at the mice. When he was dismissed to his home he was given a big bunch of muscatel grapes for the governess. "Give her these from me, with my compliments," Lady Crowmarsh said. "And say that it was all my fault if I've kept you from preparation or bed."

Kay walked home with the grapes, fearing that he would catch it for being there so long, as well as for the other matters.

"Please," he said, "Lady Crowmarsh took me to see her mice, and she sends you these grapes, with her compliments."

"That is very kind of Lady Crowmarsh," the governess said, with a greedy gleam in her eyes. "Please put them on the sideboard, but let me be sure, first, that you haven't eaten any on the way. It was very kind of Lady Crowmarsh to take such notice of a dirty little boy who comes in late for tea, particularly as I hear you were seen climbing a tree in her estate this afternoon."

She said these last words with slow relish, knowing that they would surprise him. They did. How could she have known? Who could have been and told? Could it possibly have been Blackmalkin? There he was, curled up on the armchair, pretending to be asleep, but Kay could see that he was listening with all his might, and grinning too, although he kept his face down.

"Don't try to keep things from *me*, Kay," she said, "for you see I get to know. Now don't let me hear of you climbing trees there again, or woe betide you. Now it's past your bedtime, go to bed at once. I know all about owl's nests, remember."

*K*ay went up to his bedroom sorely perplexed. It was bad enough to be sneaked on. But supposing the sneak had heard the directions for finding the treasure? Supposing the treasure were still there under that red clay? Supposing the sneak lay in wait for Swift, Bat, or Blinky as he brought the news from over sea? Suppose the sneak tortured the messenger until he told where the treasure was? Perhaps he had done that already . . . it was time for the message to be there, and it wasn't there.

He stood at his open window for a long time, hoping that the message would come. Some swifts were flying about; none of them was his swift. Presently the sun went behind the wood, which at once became very black. It was said that in the camp in the wood, called King Arthur's Round Table, there was a door which led to the table itself. Now the brown owl, which had nested in the hollow bough of the ruined pippin, flew out to look at the twilight. "Perhaps he will have the message," Kay thought. No, the brown owl cried his tchakking cry and flew away.

Now that the swifts had gone to their roosts, the red in the west grew clearer. In the middle heaven this red merged into a green in which a planet glowed. Soon bats began to flitter here and there across the green sky—he could hear their little shrill cries. "Perhaps one of those is the bat with the message," he thought, so he called, "Bat, Mr. Bat. I am Kay, please." It seemed that he had made a mistake. None of those was his bat. He had no answer.

As it was now chilly near the window, Kay got into bed, where he sat up waiting for the message, which did not come. He heard the owls in the wood at their hunting. "That settles it," he thought. "The message has been stopped. Swift told Blinky that he would have an answer before he began his evening's hunting. They have laid in wait for the messenger and caught him."

Then, in his drowsiness, he began again to wonder. "How did she find out all about owl's nests, remember? Did Blackmalkin sneak, or could she have overheard me telling Lady Crowmarsh? If she heard it from Blackmalkin, she must be a friend of the witches. But of course she can't be, that's absurd. I must have been watched by someone in the road who sneaked. All the same, it was Blackmalkin who has made them catch poor Blinky."

He worried over this, wondering what he could do, until he fell asleep. He woke up, or half woke up, about an hour later, when Abner's voice (he thought it was) rang out in the hall, saying, "Well, if you won't speak, you shall very soon be made to speak. A little torture will soon change your mind. Down with him to the dungeons."

He thought that he heard this. He thought that it was followed by a scuffling and dragging noise, with calls of "Down you go." "Put him in the kennel." "We'll teach you." He thought that he heard Blinky's voice giving a little hoo of pain. He was so very sleepy that he could not be sure that all this happened. It sounded like voices in a dream in the dark night. He heard some chain jangle, then a door slammed. After that he slept very heavily.

Presently there came a noise in the wainscot, and shuffling of feet on the carpet, and someone clearing his throat. Kay sat up to see what this could be. He saw a strangely disreputable rat, who was wiping his mouth with the back of a dirty paw. "What is it?" Kay said. "Have you come with a message from Blinky?"

"I'm Rat, I am," the rat said. "I'm a cellarman, I am. I never done nothing against no young ducks, nor I didn't neither not against no chicks. I lives in a cellar, and I does a bit in the dustbin. But him as says I ducks and I chicks, he says what isn't it, because I never."

"And what do you want now, Mr. Rat?" Kay asked.

"I don't want nothing," Rat said. "Him as thinks as Rat wants anything for doing anything, he'd ought to have the cat after him, and he'd ought to have the dog after him."

"Yes, yes," Kay said, "I'm sure he should."

"Ah," Rat said, "that's what."

"Is there anything that I can do for you, Mr. Rat?" Kay asked.

"Ah," Rat said, "there's many might have asked that question before now, what didn't. Because a fellow is a cellarman and does a bit in the dustbin, and comes a bit close to a old bone now and then (though even that he don't often), people thinks, why, I don't know what they don't think. But what I says is, a fellow is a fellow. You have to come back to that in the end, for all your Tirritts and flurts, and then where are you?"

"Yes, where?" Kay asked, because he didn't know where he was.

"Well, that's what I said, ain't it?" Rat answered in a surly tone. "I thought I'd settled all that once for all."

Kay could not think of anything more to say. He was silent.

"Ah," Rat said, "it's a cruel life is being a cellarman. If I'd my time again, I'd be, I don't know what I'd be, but rather than be a cellarman again, I'd have the cat after me, and I'd have the dog after me, and I'd have . . . I don't know what I wouldn't have after me."

"Is it as bad as that?" Kay said.

"Ah, that's what," Rat said.

"Look here, Mr. Rat," Kay said, "will you have a lump of sugar? It's a bit grubby, but I haven't sucked any of it."

"Now there's talking," Rat said. "A lot of persons talks, and what good does it do? I ask you what, and echo answers where. I eats your very good health, Master Kay, and as good a bit of sugar"—he called it shugger—"as ever I grit my teeth on. That's Mr. Spiceman's sugar, that is . . . you won't tell me that that came from that old cove in the Jewry. He's a mean one, he is. He traps his basement . . . gah. He sic a terrier dog on me once; he's a regular mean one. I suppose, Mr. Kay, you haven't got such a thing as a seedless raisin about you?"

"Yes, I have," Kay said, "in my waistcoat pocket. Here you are. I'm afraid they're a bit stuck together."

"That don't matter, not for that," the rat said, taking the raisins. "It's wonderful how a bit of squash brings out the plumminess. It's a real treat to one what lives in a cellar to taste a bit of plumminess. It takes him at once right out into the vineyards and that; like what I saw once when I went marine cellarman. But it don't do, not being a marine cellarman, because they light a stuff what smokes, and the smoke it goes creepy and creepy. You don't want to breathe none of it, neither, for it lays you dead; ah, many and many a fine marine cellarman has it cut short afore he'd gnawed through the flour barrel."

"What a shame," Kay said.

"Ah," the rat said, "that's what."

There was a pause after this while the Rat smeared his mouth with the back of his paw. "I suppose," he said at last, "you don't carry no bit of bacon rind upon you?"

"No," Kay said. "I'm afraid I don't."

"Ah," the rat said. "A bit of bacon rind, what has been hung in the sun so as to take the crisp off, it's—why I don't rightly know what it's, but it's pretty picking of a morning, ah, and of a evening."

"I could get you some tomorrow, perhaps," Kay said.

"That's a fine day, tomorrow," the rat said. "I never did hold with no tomorrow, but as for 'tomorrow perhaps,' that's when it's going to rain soup and the grass is going to grow spoons."

"Here's a bit more sugar," Kay said. "It's a bit lead-pencilly, I'm afraid, from being in my pocket."

"I'll chanst the lead," the rat said, taking the sugar, "and I thank you kindly. But what I come here to see you about wasn't nothing to do with no sugar, what you're so fond of, nor about no raisins, what's plummy or not plummy, nor about no bacon rind, what you've got mountains of and grudges a little bit; yes, even so much as a smell of. No, it wasn't about any of these things, as well I would have let you know, but for all my words being so snapped off short in a way as makes my blood boil. No, it was about our friend as I come to see you about . . . our friend as we needn't name the name of. There's been dark doings, that's what's what, and if you was to follow me, instead of talking quite such a lot, it would be thatter and whatter."

He turned to go, still smearing his mouth with the back of his paw. Kay followed him out of the bedroom into the deserted corridor, and then down the stairs to the hall. Kay did not know what time it was. He thought that it could not be very late, because the governess was still at her music in the library. The rat opened the hall cupboard door. "It's in here, master," he said in a low voice.

When they were both inside the cupboard, the rat closed the door upon them. He produced a piece of phosphorescent wood, which gave a faint light. "It's in here, master," he said again. The panel at the back of the cupboard came out. Behind it there was a gap in the wainscoting from which one could step onto the cellar stairs.

"They've got him down here," the rat said. "Chronic, I call it, padlocked up in that old dog kennel."

"Old Blinky?" Kay asked. "Is it old Blinky?"

"Ah," said the rat, "that's what."

He led the way down the cellar steps into the darkness of the cellar, which was only lit by a ray of moonlight from a grating and by a sort of dimness about two other gratings higher up. Kay could see the faint bulges of a line of barrels against the wall and smelled the stale beer in the saucer underneath the spigot of the cask in use. It was a creepy place even in daylight.

"There's dark doings goes on down here," the rat said. "Those cats comes down down here and they makes a night of it, as they calls it. An honest cellarman can't get a wink at night sometimes, though they leaves pickings too. This is where they put your friend."

He led the way past the wine cellar to a corner, where, as Kay knew, an old dog kennel had been stored.

"There's a place to put a fellow," the rat said. "It gives one the thought of mange even to see. They've clapped a padlock on him too. Trying to make him tell what he's got to tell."

Kay heard the moaning of poor old Blinky inside the kennel.

"I say, Blinky," he said, "I'm most awfully sorry. Is there anything I can do?"

"Never you mind about me, Kay," Blinky said. "But you'd better know the truth about the treasure. I got the message and then the Pouncer and Abner and another of them came down upon me. It was Blackmalkin who betrayed us."

"I thought it was," Kay said.

"They're trying to get me to say what I know," Blinky went on, "but they never will. Now, you bring your ear close to this hole in the kennel, and I'll tell you just the story that was brought to me."

Kay did as he was bid and old Blinky began his tale.

"You were quite right about it being buried by an earth-quake," he said. "The red mudbank was toppled right over it and the river changed its course. It was under the ground for years and then somebody found it."

"Was it Sir Piney Trigger who found it?" Kay asked.

"No, it was a farmer called Old Man John who found it. Old Man John found it while he was digging his cellar in the house he built right over where it lay. He didn't call it treasure though. He called it 'sin-and-heathen idols' and left it all propped up against the cellar wall. It stood there for years.

"Then some people, two men and a little boy, all with the same name . . ."

"Abner Brown," Kay said.

"That was the name . . . they came to the district to look for it. They dug for it for years without coming anywhere very near."

"Yes," Kay said, quoting the old lady, "yon Abner was theer, digging for t'brass and finding nowt."

"Then after a good many years there came that man whose name you just mentioned. Please don't mention it again, for it is one of those gunny names which I can't abide. . . . Well, he, that gunny man, he found out where the treasure was, and oh, my goodness . . ."

"I say, how you made me jump," Kay said. "Whatever was the matter?"

"Kay," Blinky asked, "what was that footstep over there?"

"It was Rat, moving away, wasn't it? Is that you, Rat?" There was no answer. "What sort of a footstep was it, Blinky?"

"A sort of a stealthy footstep," Blinky said. "I shouldn't be surprised if that Blackmalkin had crept up in the dark and heard all that I was saying. Oh, if I could only get out and make sure."

At this he beat against the sides and roof of the kennel. Kay, who was peering into the darkness, heard someone hurry up the steps.

"Stop, you beast," he cried. But the thing, whatever it was, had now gone.

"Kay," Blinky said, "we've been overheard. They'll kill me now that they know my story. Can you move the roof of this kennel? It seemed to give when I bumped against it."

Kay thrust at the roof. "Why, it lifts off," he said. "I believe I can shove it sideways. Mind, while I shove." He gave a great heaving shove. The roof slid off and crashed upon the floor.

"Thank you, Kay," old Blinky said. "I can leave the cellar through the gratings which the cats use." As he spoke, he floated down the cellar on his wings and drifted through the grating into the night.

"And he hasn't told me half the story now," Kay said. "He stopped just where it was beginning to be thrilling. Well, he's safe, that's one good thing. I'd better get back to bed."

He groped his way to the stairs, wishing that Nibbins might come to guide him. He stumbled over a cask stave, which surely had not been there when he came in with Rat. Then he bumped into an empty barrel and sent it slowly rolling into the middle of the cellar. "I'm making a fearful row," he thought. "And she hasn't gone to bed. She'll hear me."

However, he reached the stairs, climbed up them, and paused inside the hall cupboard. All was silent in the hall. Someone had left the kitchen door open so that he could hear the cricket chirping to the silent house. "She's gone to bed," he thought. "I do believe she's gone to bed."

He very cautiously peered out. All the lights were out. That was a sure sign that she had gone to bed. The moonlight was streaming into the hall through the windows. None of the midnight people was there. All was still. He crept out of the cupboard and up the stairs to his room.

He noticed that a light was burning in his room, but this did not surprise him, because for these last few nights a marvelous light had always burned there. He looked out carefully for Blackmalkin or a witch. Neither seemed to be about. At last he plucked up his courage, made a dash for his room, and rushed straight into the governess, who was standing there, waiting for him, just within.

"You've been in the cellar, you naughty little boy," she said. "You know as well as I do that that's forbidden. Haven't I told you, I don't know how many times, that I won't have you in the cellar? And look at your pajamas, sir, all cobwebbed and whitewashed. Now you'll have to put on a clean suit. What were you doing in the cellar, sir, to begin with?"

Kay did not quite know what to begin with—he was upset by

being caught thus. Luckily she did not give him any time. She went on:

"What did you do to the owl? Don't you dare to say you let him go."

"I did let him go."

"You *what?*"

"I let him go."

"You . . . let . . . him . . . go?"

"Yes, he was down there in a dirty old dog kennel that Joe's going to burn, and he was frightfully unhappy, so I let him go."

"And how did you know he was there in the first place? You could only have learned that he was there by listening and prying. You've been at the keyholes, sir, don't tell me, instead of going to bed."

"I haven't been at the keyholes."

"Yes, you have been at the keyholes, sir, don't contradict me. You listened and you pried, and then you crept down to thwart us. I suppose you know what owl it was?"

"Yes, it was Lady Crowmarsh's. I was talking to her about it after tea."

"Yes, it was Lady Crowmarsh's. And I suppose you know that Lady Crowmarsh would have given hundreds of pounds for that owl. We took it this evening out of the claws of the cat, and put it in the cellar because I knew that it would prefer the dark, intending to take it over to Lady Crowmarsh after breakfast. Now that you have let it go it will fly away and never come back, now that it has been frightened here. I shall tell Lady Crowmarsh whose fault it is that her pet is lost. Nicely you've repaid all her kindness to you, letting her pet go!"

"It was a wild owl. It wasn't a pet."

"Yes it was a pet. It was her pet owl that she had had for years."

"It was a wild owl," Kay said.

"If you go contradicting me," the governess said, "I shall write a letter to the schoolmaster and ask him to bring his cane. Now here are your clean pajamas. Take off those you're wearing, and get into bed, but don't think for one moment that you've heard the last of this from me, because you haven't. You and I tomorrow will go through our accounts together, and if I find you've caught your death, going down to that cold cellar, woe betide you."

The light had long since dwindled into the light of the governess's candle. She now flounced out of the room with it, leaving Kay to change his pajamas and get into bed in the dark.

"How on earth did she know that I was in the cellar?" he wondered. "If she heard me, why didn't she come down to stop me? Those steps that we heard must have been Blackmalkin on the sneak again. He ran up and sneaked, that was it. But if she's in with Blackmalkin, she's in with the witches, too, that's certain. Listen!"

Down in the hall Blackmalkin was wailing under a spanking. "Hark," Kay said again. "I believe she's spanking the little sneak. That's his voice, anyhow!"

The governess paused for breath in her spanking. "Another time," she said, "when I send you down to listen" (Kay had now opened the door, so as to hear), "when I send you to listen, you'll wait till the end of the story, and not come away with the best of it not told. You shall have no milk for a week."

After Blackmalkin had gone away, whimpering and growling, saying "I'll be even with you before long, you'll see if I'm not," Kay tried to sleep but could not, because he felt sure that somebody was weeping just outside, in the garden. It was not Blackmalkin, it was somebody saying "Oh, woe, woe, woe. I can't make anybody hear."

Then he distinctly heard the voice of Miss Susan Pricker Trigger say, "Drat my wig, my sweet pa, that boy is in his bed there. Sing out to the horrid little toad—I mean the darling cherub—to buck his stumps and come and open the door. Wait, I'll do it for you. Boy, if you don't want to be skinned alive—I mean my pretty little love, if you want to be thought a little angel—will you jolly well—I mean most obligingly—open the door to my sweet and no longer livery pa, and to me the pretty lady who loves little boys?"

Kay looked out of the window. It was very odd, but there were Miss Susan Pricker Trigger and a cloaked man. "I believe it's Sir Piney," Kay thought. "If they go on making this noise the governess will hear them."

"No, she won't then, my smart young sir," Miss Piney said, as though she had read his thoughts. "She will not hear, being at this moment elsewhere engaged. But bang my cannon, boy, don't keep a lady waiting."

"All right," Kay said, "I'll come down and let you in." So he did. He showed them into the drawing room and asked them to be seated. The room was brightly lit, though the clock said a quarter to one.

"My pa and I have taken the liberty," Miss Trigger said, "so that you may know. The very first time my pa and I have promenaded we come to see Mr. Harker. Isn't that so, my pa-kin?"

"It is, ma poppet," Sir Piney answered. "Mr. Harker, tha is beset with Abners and evil. Mr. Harker, ah did my best to restore it, only ah coom too late."

"Did you find the treasure then?" Kay asked.

"Why, as to that," Sir Piney said, in his North Country speech, "why as to that, it wasna so mooch me as t'other fellow. T'first thing ah see when ah coom there, was where t'Old Man John had doog oop t'earth. And t'first thing ah see was t'gunwale of t'yacht, with ma initials coot, wheer ah'd coot them when ah was droonk.

"So ah thinks, no need to look further. Old Man John has doog up t'boat, he'll have t'brass in his cellar.

"Old Man John was a foonny chap. So ah oop to him. 'You've got t'brass,' ah says.

" ' 'Tisn't brass,' he says, 'it's sin-and-heathen idols.'

" ' 'Tisn't yours,' ah says, 'it's Captain Harker's.'

" ' 'Tisn't Captain anyone's,' he says, 'except Captain Belial's or my Colonel Mammon's.'

" 'Old Captain Harker is dying for this,' ah says. 'Let the poor old man have it.'

" 'Many die for the likes of this,' he says, 'so here it will stop, out of all harm's way.'

"Ah, hadna coom all that long way to be talkt to like yon, but, tha see, ah had to be coonning; ah did what foxy does to goosey. 'That's talking,' ah says. 'Tha's got some sense, lad, oonder the cap,' ah says, 'as well as soom religion.'

"But ah had to think quick. Tha see, yon old farmer was daft; he might take up t'brass any day and doomp it in t'sea. Then ah'd have been fair scooppered.

"Then yon papgoose Abner was in the land. He might find oot aboot t'brass any day. He might shoot t'old farmer and take all t'brass to hissen. Then ah'd ha' been fair scooppered.

"Ah was vara weasely. Ah wasna going home without yon stoof for Captain Harker. Vara coonning ah was.

"So when ah was all ready, with ma bonny wee dukey all ready for sea, ah call ma Indians. 'Coom on,' ah says, 'ma lads, 'tis to glory we steer.' So off we all go to t'Old Man John. Ah wasna going to hurt him, tha oonderstand, nobbut joost a bang and a bag.

"So when we coom oop to t'Old Man John, he says, 'Art going to yon revival meeting?' he says. So ah walks roand him, to get t'soon into his eyes. 'That's reet,' ah says. 'The revival meeting.' Then ah oop with bang and ma wee bonny Indians they oop with bag."

"Now, my pa," Miss Trigger said, "the first time we take a sweet evening walk, I am quite sure we ought not to remember unpleasantness. It's very nice to see this little cheraph, but I'm sure he wants to hear where the treasure is now, not what you may have done when provoked. It's the pepper in you again. When you feel inclined to give way to pepper you must fight it down. You must sing one of your nice songs now, about" (here she sang):

"As I was a-walking in the green month of May,
I met with my true love and thus did she say,
'Oh, sweet grows the clover and blythe grows the corn,
And the nightingale sings in the bonny white thorn.'

" 'O true, love,' I answered, 'But what can I care
Since the . . .'

"Now join in with me and sing from there."

"Ah was only telling Mr. Harker in ma own way, ma Piney,"
Sir Piney said. "Ah was nobbut beginning at t'beginning."

"My sweet pa," Miss Piney said, "that kind of beginning is
over for you now forever, it is ended. We are beginning such a
lovely time, don't let us mix it with any bangs or brandy. Put it
out of this little serub's mind with a song, begin at:

" '"O true love," I answered.' "

"Ah daresay tha's reet, ma Piney," Sir Piney said.

Kay saw Sir Piney rise to his feet, draw breath, beat with his
hand, and look at his daughter for the signal to start singing.

Somehow the song did not begin, though Miss Piney was
nodding and her father was beating with his hand. Something
made Sir Piney flit rapidly over to the table. His daughter
opened her mouth very wide.

Then both Triggers faded swiftly, the drawing room faded.
But, no, Sir Piney was shaking a book on the table, saying
"Page 275." He seemed angry about something, the book shook
and shook, until it was as indistinct as the leaves of a tree all
blown together on a windy day. "All right," Kay said, "I'll
remember the page." At this he rolled over, wide awake.

"It must all have been a dream," he muttered, for the
Triggers were gone. He was in his bed in the dark night, not in
the drawing room at all. "He seems to have got the treasure,"
he thought. The church clock struck one.

He was glad that it was not midnight. A cock, probably Mrs.
Gossip's cock, roused in his roost by the booming of the bell,
flapped on his perch and gave a halfhearted crow. A horse
stamped on the path just below the window. Someone reined
up there, blew a horn with a flourish, and cried in a clear voice,

"The harvest moon is rounding. King Arthur holds court this First Night."

At the stamping of the horse, Kay had been afraid, lest it should be the Nightmare, which Ellen's father had seen, trotting on the road, not making a sound, but with a tongue of pale fire lolling over her teeth, and eyes of blue flame. At the sound of the voice all Kay's fear left him. He hopped out of bed and looked down.

There were two gray horses, one of them led. The rider of the other was a hatchet-faced man, clear in the moonlight, with rather long, yellow hair falling over his shoulders. He had a horn slung over his shoulder and a sword at his side.

"Are you for the court, master?" the man cried.

"May I?"

"The horse is sent for you."

Kay ran downstairs, opened the door. The man helped him up into the saddle of the led horse. A sword was hanging from the saddle.

"You may need that," the man said. "If the Black Knight's at the ford, we'll have to fight our way."

"Will it bend, if I chop with it?" Kay asked, thinking of the sixpenny swords which did bend.

"It's Gareth's sword," the man said. "It will cut through steel and the bone beyond it."

"Could I chop off a person's head with it?"

"That's never an easy chop," the man said. "Your man's shield is generally up to his ear."

"Could I if it wasn't?"

"So many mails are double at the throat," the man said.

"Could I if it were single?"

"Your man is generally looking out for a chop," the man said. "And a chop takes such a long time, you can see it coming."

"But suppose he didn't see it coming?"

By this time they were in the broad, open green which ran between the lines of the houses of the village. The moonlight

was very bright, and, lo, a marvelous thing, all the fronts of the
houses were gone, just as though they were doll's houses. Kay
could see the shops and the living rooms laid bare, with all the
people in bed: Mr. Spiceman, the grocer, and old Mr. Specta-
cle, the clockmaker, and Mrs. Sweetlips, who made such sugar
candy. There they all were, and floating about them as they
slept were the loveliest people Kay had ever seen. They were like
people made of light and of rainbows, and with exquisite faces
and hands. They were soothing the sleep of all there, driving
away little black annoyances and bothers, and giving lovely
dreams instead.

"What are those people?" Kay asked.

"Those?" the man said. "An old man called St. Alpig, down
by the river, always sends those. They are quite real. They go
about the world and help people. Now there's the ford, and
. . . yes . . . there's the Black Knight. Take your sword in both
hands, that's the way."

"Halt there," the Black Knight called. "Come up one by one
and render up your weapons." Kay could see him in the blackness of the ford as a big black man on a black horse reined up in
midstream. The steel gleamed on his lowered helmet and moving sword. He stood stock-still. The water gleamed as it flowed
round the horse's fetlocks. It was all still, moonlit night, not a
cockcrow, not an owl's cry, not a fox's bark, no whisper of
wind, nothing but that grim form in front and the water
tinkling away past the fetlocks.

Kay thought that he saw the black form incline forward in
the saddle as though to urge up his horse.

"Charge him, Kay," the messenger cried. "Chop him on that
side, I'll chop him on this."

Kay felt his horse leap forward with a splash into the ford. He
had long since dropped the reins, so as to have both hands on
the sword. He trod down deep into his stirrups and leant
against the back of his saddle . . . then . . . swosh . . . he
lashed out sideways at the Black Knight's head just as he lashed
out to a ball on the leg side at cricket. He had a lovely feeling

that he had made a magnificent hit. As his horse came out of
the river on the other side, Sir Launcelot caught his rein. "Well
hit, Kay, well hit," he said. "There goes his pagan head. Look."

Turning around, Kay was just in time to see the Black
Knight's head, spouting blue fire, rolling splash into the river.
His black horse, carrying his body, galloped away into the night.

"He'll come back to put his head on again, presently," the
messenger said. "Merlin ought to deal with him."

"Merlin is going to deal with him," Launcelot said. "But
meanwhile, Kay, that was a superb chop. You got in every
ounce of your weight just in exactly the right spot, and, then, it
was so perfectly timed. I never saw anything so neat. There was
his head, and then . . . flash . . . there wasn't his head."

"You ought to tell King Arthur about it, Sir Launcelot," the
messenger said. "For a midnight chop there's been nothing like
it since you fought that mad giant Ugg, the one with boar's
tusks, in the thunderstorm. I'm used to midnight works, but I
missed him altogether. I tell you, Sir Launcelot, this Kay will
make a knight, and oh, won't our present Kai be jealous."

By this time they had ridden up the hill into the dark lane,
overshadowed by yew trees, which was still called King Arthur's
ride. The lane was a good place for wild Canterbury bells,
which were now in full bloom. Every Canterbury bell was now
lit with a glowworm so that the lane glittered.

At the gate of the Round Table camp it was as light as day,
but inside the camp it was brighter than any day. All things
seemed so soaked with light that they glowed.

"I see that King Arthur is over there, hearing petitions with
Merlin," Sir Launcelot said as he dismounted. "But in the
meantime, Kay, you come along with me and see the camp."

First they put the horses into the stable which ran down one
rampart. There were seven hundred horses, all white, cream-
colored, gray or piebald (none darker than that). They were
picketed in long lines, eating grass from the Holy Meadow,
which is always green. Each one of the seven hundred was so
gentle that Kay could feed him by hand, or slip between his

legs, without any fear of a kick. Many of the horses knew
Launcelot, for he had the gift of drawing beasts and birds to
him. When he came into the lines, there was a general whinny
of welcome.

"Oh, I wish that horses would whinny to me," Kay said.

"But they do," Launcelot said. "They're saying Wh-wh-wh-
whelcome, Kay."

"Please, what do you do here?" Kay asked.

"This is King Arthur's court, where all people come who
care. Many come, as you can see. It's hard work here all the
time. Ah, there is the queen . . ."

They were standing near a little covered well or trough of
bright running water. A chariot drawn by two white, small,
very fiery stallions, with harness of red enamel, drove rapidly
up. There were two ladies in the chariot, one of them a
sweet-faced, sad woman in a black dress. "That's Brangwen,"
Launcelot whispered. "The queen is driving."

Queen Guinevere was standing to drive and urging her lovely
horses like energy itself. She was a somewhat fierce-looking and
splendid beauty, with the marvelous red-gold hair that gave
light in the darkness. The fierceness of the drive had brought
color to her cheeks and made her eyes glow like violets. Her
mouth was of an exquisite beauty, a little parted now from
excitement.

> Guinevere's beauty has had peers
> But none has matched her mouth and ears.

Her hair was plaited, then heaped on her head and held there
by what looked like a twisted strand of gold leaf. She wore a
dress of rough green linen with a crystal neck clasp.

"So you've brought Kay to us," she cried, half reining in. "I
welcome you, Kay. Arthur and Merlin could see him now,
Launcelot, if you would take him there. And some day will you
drive with me, Kay?"

"Oh, I would love to," Kay said.

She looked at him very earnestly and smiled. "We will drive," she said. "We will drive the Holy Road next Midsummer Night, against Uther's Spirit Horses. He drives there against any who come, eleven miles on the grass. You must not forget that you have promised the queen."

"Indeed I will not forget," he said.

She smiled and drove on towards the end of the horse lines. Launcelot led him away towards the king. "She is the queen of all horsewomen," he said. "She is the daughter of an old king in Shropshire."

Indeed, everybody in the court seemed happy. The people who had brought petitions were going joyfully away, some of them with parties of knights who were going to see their grievances set right. All the troubled people had been comforted, and all the friendless little children were receiving the loveliest toys from the Lady Vivien. There were horses and chariots, but the little tiny horses were real. Then there were tame bullfinches and linnets which perched on the children's fingers and sang to them. But the most beautiful of all were the bird kites made by Merlin. These were like real big birds, which flew. On their backs were little boxes with seats in them in which the children sat as they flew. Some of these birds sang like skylarks when they were high in the air. Then near the gates of the camp, Kay saw parties of knights returning from quests, with prisoners whom they had set free, or with evil kings and tyrants whom they were bringing to judgment. Then in one place there were most lovely people all shining with light and colors, some of them singing and all happy. "Those are the best people of all," Launcelot said. "Remember that if you call them ever, they will come to you."

"Will they, really?" Kay said.

"They have promised that to the king. *All* those lovely people will come to you whenever you call."

They were now drawing near to the central space of the camp, where the king sat with his counselor Merlin. The king was unlike anybody Kay had ever seen. He could not see Merlin so well, because he was bent over a map which a very muddy traveler was showing to him. Something in the shape of the muddy traveler, or his attitude, seemed familiar to Kay. He was pointing out places on a map and asking Merlin about them. Merlin looked up suddenly and said something to the king. Kay saw Merlin clearly as he looked up. He had a strange, troubled, happy face as though he were always having very difficult puzzles set to him and always finding the answers. The king turned, spoke to the traveler, and then told a couple of knights, "Go with him, will you, to see if you can find this treasure? It ought to be restored."

He nodded (and Merlin smiled) to the traveler, who at once rolled up his map and turned away with the knights to his horse, which was being held at a little distance.

"Now, Kay," Launcelot said, "it's your turn. Come along and speak to the king."

He drew Kay forward through the crowd, and the body-guardsmen cleared a path for them. He saw King Arthur look at him with a smile of welcome. . . . Then, suddenly he heard his name called:

"Kay . . . Kay . . ."

Looking to the caller he saw that it was the muddy traveler who had now mounted his horse. The muddy traveler was Edward, his beloved Edward, Eduardo da Vinci, as he was called . . . and his horse was Petter Horse, the best of all horses . . . and they were all waving and calling and whinnying to him.

"Edward," he cried. "Edward . . . how are you?"

"Why, Master Kay," Ellen said, rolling him awake. "Don't you know my name's not Edward yet? Do wake up, there's a good boy. It's almost breakfast time."

"So that was only a dream, too," he said, "just as I made sure that it was Edward. But now it's real. . . .

"And now I shall be simply frightfully punished, because of old Blinky last night." He went down to breakfast, with his heart in his boots.

*P*resently the governess came down, glowered at him to show that she had not forgotten, said an awful grace in Latin, and . . . instead of speaking or eating, she became deeply interested in a letter which had come for her. It was a very queer letter written in green ink on yellow paper with very untidy writing. The governess read it through three times. She never ate much breakfast, today she ate none, though she sipped away three big cups of strong China tea, each with four lumps of sugar and a third of the cream. She said no word about Blinky. She never noticed when Kay ate the third egg. She never gave him his coffee.

Then, just before lessons, a very smart carriage came to the door. She was evidently expecting it, for there she was in the hall, all dressed for going out. "There'll be no lessons today, Kay," she said. "And I shall be out for lunch. Mind I hear no bad reports of you when I come back." Then out she sailed to the carriage, where a footman opened the door, and a lady who dangled and glittered (Kay could not see her face) welcomed her. Away they drove, with two very shiny gray horses, and the footman sticking out his elbows.

Blackmalkin came purring along the hall after Kay.

"Yes," Kay thought, "you're to give reports of me when she

comes back, aren't you? You shall go into the stable, my son, and do an honest day's mousing for once." So he popped Blackmalkin through the stable window into the harness room and left him there with the mice and a saucer of rainwater. "He is the sneak," he thought. "All the sneaking has been done by him."

"And now," he thought, "I'll look at the book in the drawing room which Sir Piney shook so hard."

The book was on the table just as it had been when Sir Piney had shaken it. It was a fat, drawing room sort of a book in a worn binding of imitation green leather. It was called *Aunt Susan's Compendium of Pleasant Knowledge, 1841-2.* He looked at page 275. It seemed very dull, being directions how to make a pretty and useful penwiper out of scarlet flannel and a merry-thought bone. "It was only a dream," he said. He left the book on the hearthrug.

"What I really want to know," he thought, "is what she has to do with the witches. I'll bet she is in with them. Of course she is in with them, she used Blackmalkin as a spy. And of course she invites them here to supper."

"Hoity, toity, child," said Grandmama Harker's portrait on the wall above him. "If you think that, you should deal with her. Search her room, bless us and save us. You must be the master in your own house. Don't let a witch take the charge of Seekings. This is a house where upright people have lived. Let's have no Endorings nor Jezebelings in Seekings. Bell her, Kay. Book her, boy. Candle her, Grandson, and lose no time, for time lost's done with, but must be paid for."

He looked up at her portrait, which was that of a very shrewd old lady in a black silk dress. She was nodding her head at him so that her ringlets and earrings shook. "Search the wicked creature's room," she said, "and if she *is*, send word to the bishop at once. It's more than a rector's work to deal with an Endor."

"All right," Kay said, "I'll go. I *will* search."

To the west of Kay's room, up a small flight of stairs, there was a corridor, into which he never ventured, it was so dark and awful.

On both walls were dark old portraits and the doors of the rooms where their originals had lived and died. When these doors were shut, the corridor was as dark as the cellar. He knew that the doors to the right and left, at the farther end of the corridor, were the doors of her rooms—her bedroom to the left, her study opposite. His heart thumped and his mouth became very dry as he went up the flight of stairs, past the large-scale old yellow chart of the port and bay of Santa Barbara, towards what might be a kind of dragon's den.

To his great joy the corridor was light. Her study door was swinging open, with a bunch of keys dangling from the key-hole. And this was strange (and even awful), because he knew that Ellen had never seen the inside of the study since the governess had taken charge—it was always locked. Why was it open now? Could she have crept back unknown, unheard? Was she inside the room, like a spider in her web, waiting for him to appear? Would Greymalkin, that mysterious cat, who was so seldom seen, be on guard there, ready to fly at him? Would there be worse guards—fiery dogs or a python? Or would there be secret guards, who would watch him through portraits, say nothing to him, but report all his doings on her return?

Very timidly he tapped upon the door, half expecting that she would answer. No answer came, all was still within, save for the blind flapping near the open window, a cruising wasp, and a butterfly trying to get out. He took his fate in his hands and walked boldly in.

There was not any sign of Greymalkin; the room had no visible spies. There were no portraits on the walls for spies to look through. There were a good many books in the shelves, and some portfolios of drawings propped against the wall, for she was always sketching (rather well). On her writing table was a round case full of colored disks, which looked very odd and gave Kay a queer feeling; he was glad to turn away from them. Even then, he didn't like the look of them. He covered them with a cloth. On the desk was . . . what . . .?

On the desk was the handbag which Mrs. Pouncer had carried when she had come into his bedroom with Blackmalkin. He would have known that bag anywhere, because it was black, with steel moon and stars worked on it. Beside the bag lay the Roper Bilges's copy of *The Sea Gunner's Practice*, but it had been tampered with. All the written pages at the end had been neatly removed—they were no longer there.

"I say," he said to himself, "how on earth did she get this from Mrs. Pouncer?"

How indeed? It was not so easy to say.

He stood in the middle of the room, staring round him. It looked innocent enough, but was it? There were some strange little woodcuts on the bookshelves. When he looked at these more closely they frightened him, much as the disks had. Then there were some most strange playing cards with Latin underneath their figures; he did not like the look of these. Then the books were not quite all that they might be. He only opened one—it had hieroglyphics instead of print. He put it back in its place and opened one of the portfolios of drawings. He did not like that at all: the drawings were of strange black figures upon red paper. He began to be very much afraid.

Then he thought that it was not very nice of him to come spying on her, when her back was turned, so he went out of the room.

Then he thought that Grandmama Harker was right, that he ought to make sure that his home was not being used for witchcraft, so he went back again. He had not yet looked into the cupboard.

The cupboard (as he knew from Ellen) was really a room, being what was called a powdering chamber.

"And supposing," he said to himself, "supposing Mrs. Pouncer is really her sister . . . and supposing she is in the powdering room, living there . . . that would account for the way the things go from the larder." He looked through the cupboard keyhole. It was dark within—he could make out nothing. He flung the door wide open, crying "Aroint thee, witch," in case Mrs. P. should be there.

Mrs. P. was not there. No one was living there. The little room was in use as a clothes cupboard, but what were the clothes which hung from the pegs? Ah, what indeed?

There was a row of seven crooked pegs.

From each peg there hung a witch's complete outfit, thus:

1 long scarlet cloak
1 black stick with a crooky handle
1 tall, black pointed shiny hat

And attached to each hat there was something . . . he had to turn up the nearest hat to see what it was. It was marked inside Sylvia Daisy. The outside was a marvelous wax face of Mrs. Pouncer.

"Now I know all about it," he said. "*She* is Mrs. Pouncer. This is her mask . . . and look at all her magic and witch things on the shelf. She is a queen witch. She'll take a whole archbishop to settle . . ."

He looked at the magic things on the shelf. There was a magic lantern which lit the cupboard like daylight when he touched a button; there were magic baskets labeled Wish; there were magic ladders and ropes, which pulled out, and out, and out, to any length you pleased; there were fox-eye and cat's-eye spectacles for seeing in the dark (he pocketed a pair of these); there was a gallon tin of invisible mixture; there were seven pairs of one-league shoes, seven pairs of seven-league shoes, and seven pairs of forty-nine-league boots (these last were screwed down to keep them still). Then there were green and scarlet and yellow bottles, labeled Snake Bite, Dragon's Blood, and Pouncer's Best Bewitching Mixture. Then there was an ivory box labeled "Ointment for turning little boys into tomtits" (Kay did not touch this). Then there were bowls of gums and herbs for incantations. Then there were books, oh, such books with such titles:

Broomsticks, or the Midnight Practice
Spells and How to Bind Them
The Beginner's Merlin
Merlin's 100 Best Bewitchals
Werewolves, *by one of Them*
Shape-changing for All, *by M. Le Fay*

And at the end of the shelf was a small red book: *Why I Am a Witch*, by Sylvia Daisy Pouncer.

"I say," he thought, "that is confession. She glories in it. I'll write to the bishop. I don't care if it is sneaking. She has no business to be doing this kind of thing.

"All the same," he thought, as he looked at the row of scarlet cloaks, "it would be rather sport to try on Mrs. P.'s things."

He hesitated for an instant, then he lifted the cloak from the peg. The outfit came down in one piece. He put it on before the mirror. The cloak was rather long, but when he said "I wish it were shorter," it shrank to the right size. When he looked at himself in the glass, lo, he *was* Mrs. Pouncer, hooky nose, crooky chin, and wicked, black, piercing eyes which could see further into things than his own eyes, as he very soon found. They were eyes like gimlets.

"I say," he said, "I look exactly like her. Now I will just watch myself conjure." And at this he put his left hand on his heart and struck the crooky stick downwards on the floor.

Instantly he felt himself lifted into the air, off his feet, and through the open window. He had not time to catch hold of the rose trellis, he was carried so quickly past. He went floating along the drive, over the gate, over the Crowmarsh estate, past Blinky's tree, over the manège where they were lunging the chestnut colt, then faster and faster, past the house where the poor mad lady lived, past the milestone on Racecourse Road, past the white rails of the course . . . on, on, on . . .

"Oh, dear," Kay cried, "it's taking me straight to where all the witches are . . . and they'll turn me into a tomtit. Stop, stop. I charge you to stop."

It didn't stop, he didn't stop. He went faster and faster.

Soon the second milepost was passed, then the third. The stick began to point downwards towards a wooded hollow where the house called Russell's Dene stood. The stick was pointing towards the house; nothing that Kay could do seemed to have the slightest effect. "I can't turn it or stop it," he said. "It's going straight to those windows." The house was a big brick building of the time of Queen Anne. It had a gloomy, heavy look as though it were drunk and wore a wig.

"I'm going straight to where all the witches are," Kay thought. "They will bewitch me into a mouse and set the cat at me. Oh, dear. Oh, dear."

The stick carried him swoop through one of the upper windows into a big, gloomy room, paneled to the ceiling. There were two open doors in this room, one on each side of Kay. People were talking just beyond one of these doors. Kay heard his governess's voice saying "What was that, that came through the window in the next room?"

"It was my cat, Jouncer," the milky voice of Abner Brown replied. "He always comes in that way."

"Really?" the governess said. "By the pricking in my toes I thought that it must be one of us."

"No, dear Pouncer," Sister Aconite said, "my toes pricked, too, but I distinctly heard the cat's feet go patter-patter."

"Jouncer *is* one of us," Abner Brown said. "He knows our moonlight games and loves them. But . . . more coffee, dear Brother Venom?"

"No, I thank you, Master Abner."

"How time has slipped away, my dear seven," Abner Brown said, "in listening to Sister Pouncer's thrilling story revealed by this owl. What a pity that her faithful spy Blackmalkin did not wait for the end. It might have spared us so much trouble. We might have learned the whole truth. And this Harker child released the owl, you say?"

"Yes, imagine it. I'd a very good mind to tomtit him there and then."

Here the other witches joined in with "It's a pity you didn't." "The idea of such impertinence." "Just as we might have learned the whole truth, too," etc., etc.

"Wait," Abner Brown said. "Does this Harker child know more of the owl's tale than we do?"

"He may. He may know the whole truth."

"So I think," Abner said. "I am sure, or almost sure, that old Trigger got the treasure. What he did with it is the question. *I* think he gave it back to old Harker, who put it under that big hearthstone which you say is in his room. We'll look there this afternoon. But in the meantime I have been preparing a peep show into the past. The spells for that must be almost working now. We *may* be able to see exactly what did happen. I *saw* it as a child, remember, but was too young to know, and neither my pop nor my lamented grandpop ever explained it to me."

At this instant a gong began to beat in a room somewhere on the other side of the house.

"Hark," said Abner Brown. The gongbeats changed to a voice which cried, "The spells are working. The past is laid bare. I charge you to come see it."

"There is the call," Abner said. "Now, if nothing blurs the picture, we may see what happened. Let us come along, then. Will you not wear your wrap, dear Pouncer?"

"No, thank you."

"This way, then. Through the door . . ."

"Oh, oh," Kay thought, "they are coming here. They will catch me."

He had no time to think what to do. Since the stick would not take him back through the window, his only possible way of escape was through the door beside him. He slipped through it into a corridor just as the witches entered the room where he had been.

The corridor was long and white, with doors on each side. Quite close to Kay was a small steel door standing ajar. It was very heavy. He slipped past it into a narrow passage and closed it behind him. He just had time to draw the heavy bolts before the witches were pushing at it from the other side. Kay went along the passage into a small room, brilliantly lit, although it had no window. There was a second steel door. When Kay had shut and bolted this, he could hear no sound of the outer world, not even the witches hammering on the steel outside.

"I am a prisoner now," he thought.

*T*he room had steel walls, some of which were hung with red velvet, all marked with magic. There were eight chairs in a row facing these red curtains. Kay sat down wondering what he was to do next. Suddenly fiery letters appeared one by one across the curtains, spelling out the words

OPEN US.

"All right," Kay said. "I will." So he walked across and opened the curtains. Behind them was a recess in which stood a tall red pedestal the height of a man. On the top of the pedestal was a man's head, made in gold or other bright metal. This head was fitted with spectacles and earpieces of a magic kind, so that it might see and hear the past.

"I have seen and heard," the head said. "Remove these trappings from me."

Kay removed the spectacles and earpieces. As they pricked his fingers, he dropped them to the floor, against which they burst. After this there was a silence, till the head said, "One minute is past, question me."

"What have you seen and heard?" Kay asked.

"You shall see and hear," the head answered.

The room became suddenly dark, except for a glimmering about the head.

"You are looking into the past and hearing it," the head said.

Instantly Kay saw a tiny shining picture, of waves beating on a beach. But, no, it was not a picture, it was real. The waves broke and the trees beyond the sand were shaking. It grew larger, till it was like the scene itself. The surf was bursting, the sun glaring, and the hard leaves of the trees clacking on each other.

A man came out of the jungle onto the sand. He was dressed in gray cotton clothes, and wore a tall straw sun hat. He was staring along the beach. Suddenly he turned his head and looked straight at Kay, so that Kay saw his face. The words of Miss Pricker Trigger came into his mind at once: "a white, sweet, sanctified horsedealer . . . a cherry-lipped poisoner." The man in front of him was so like those descriptions. He had long white hair and beard, a rosy face, and a smile. His eyes had a way of turning up, as though looking at heaven were his chief delight. His hands were plump and white. He smoothed down his beard with them. Yet when his eyes turned up, Kay felt that the man was watching out of the corners of them. His outside seemed all woolly white lamb, and the inside all bitey rough wolf. "That is old Abner Brown," Kay said. "It could not be anybody else."

Abner Brown poked into the sand for turtle eggs, found some, and then sat down to suck them.

"Yes, my Benito Suarez," he said, in his milky voice, when he had sucked the eggs. "I thought I recognized you when you came by three days ago. I was sure that you were my Benito and so you are. And you are looking for what we looked for all those years ago . . . just as I am. Now, as no one seems to be about, I'll look at these papers of yours, which I made so bold as to pinch from your room at the inn this morning, while you were fishing."

Here he settled himself comfortably, pulled out some letters and read.

"Oho," he said, "so your real name is Trigger, is it? Sir Piney Trigger, of Trigger Court, England. . . . You must be a rich man, yet you come looking for my property.

"Well, if I don't find my property soon, I'll see if I can't squeeze a little of your wealth out of you. I guess you'll be quite glad to pay little Abner not to tell what he knows about you. So.

"Though I guess we are on the brink of finding my property, now that we are digging that red clay . . ."

At this point he stood up, muttering "I may be Millionaire Brown even now." Shading his eyes, he stared at a big, strong wooden ketch, with tanned sails, which had just swung into sight on her way to the sea.

"That's the wherry that was at Watford's Farm Landing," Abner said. "I wonder what she's doing. She was to have taken Watford's cotton, but not till next week. I may be wanting her myself if all things go as I hope. But she is laden and seems to be making for the sea."

After this Abner picked some berries from the shrubs, as a dessert to the turtle eggs. "Well, well," he said at last, "I have had my little walk. I'll be getting back to the great work. Today may repay me for all my troubles."

At this moment there came a loud cry of "Popper, Popper, are you there, Popper? Hey, Pop, where are you?"

"I'm here, Ab," Abner called. "Don't make such a noise, boy, even if you have found it. What are you yelling murder for? Have you found it?"

A man of about thirty years of age appeared through the scrub. He was dragging by the hand a boy of about five. Both were like old Abner in the face, being plainly son and grandson. Both were scarlet from running, and gasping for breath.

"Speak, can't you?" the old man said. "Have you found it?" Young Abner panted and waved towards the wherry.

"He's got it . . . in the wherry."

"Who's got it? Got what? What wherry?"

"The man Ben, all the treasure. He tied Old Farmer up

in a bag and took the lot. He's taking it to sea in his barge there."

At this old Abner boxed his son's ears. "Don't bring me a crazy tale like that," he said.

The son took out a pocket telescope, focused it, and handed it to his father. "Take a see for yourself, Pop," he said. "That's Ben steering. . . . And now, little Ab, don't you stand there grinning as though this were something good to eat." At this he boxed *his* son's ears, which set him howling.

Old Abner took one hasty glance at the steersman. "It's he," he said. "It's Benito. Trigger. There's only one chance, and that's a poor one. He's going about now, there are his headsails shaking. He will make one short tack almost to that little point. If we run there like smoke we'll get there as soon as he will. As he goes about, you hail him, Abner; he may not know you."

"What am I to say?" Abner said.

"Yell out Danger, or Murder, or ask a passage, or say a snake's bit you. Yell Help."

"He won't pay no heed," the son said.

"Anyway, he'll look at you. And while he looks I'll give him all the lead I've got in my shooter. Run, now, run. Let the brat stay here. Stay here, Ab, and eat berries. Pop and Grandpop are going in swimming."

They left little Ab on the sand while they ran as fast as they could towards the channel. Kay saw the barge leaning over, with all her sails wrinkling full, and a white streak spreading at her bows. She was making good speed, for the current in midchannel helped her. Son Abner ran for the point, the old man ran more to the left. Kay saw his white hair blowing and saw him draw his revolver.

In a minute Abner was crouched behind a shrub. Abner, the son, was hopping from rock to rock to the water's edge. He flapped the rocks with a bough to scare the snakes which were sunning there. His father, a much more poisonous snake, was now making a rest for his shooting arm.

The barge came rapidly nearer. Her bows gleamed in the sun, her long, green windvane streamed away to the leeward. Kay saw an Indian crouched in her bows. The sails still hid the steersman, but Kay kept saying to himself, "The steersman is Piney Trigger, or Twiney Pricker. I shall see him, for this is he alive, this is what happened." Young Abner was now knee-deep in the creek, with his arms lifted as though pleading for help.

Something seemed to trouble the ketch. The white streak at her bow suddenly dimmed to gray. At the same instant the full, wrinkling, swelling bag of the foresail crumpled up, shook, and banged. The wind went out of the mainsail an instant later, then her wet side swerved itself round and Kay saw the helmsman stoop as he pitched some gear across and let the boom jibe. The foresail flapped and filled on the other tack. Young Abner (just an instant too late) shouted, "Hi, brother, for any's sake. Hi, hi, hi, give me a passage." The steersman, whose eyes were on the sail, cast a glance at him. Young Abner cried again, "Hi, brother, take me down with you." Then bang, bang, bang went the shots from the old man's revolver. A white streak suddenly appeared on the barge's side, where a splinter had been knocked off by a bullet.

A fourth shot followed (it flew wide somewhere), then the revolver jammed. By this time the barge was moving fast away on the other tack. Piney Trigger shook his left hand at them as he swept far out of shot. The breeze was freshening, out there in the estuary. Little bright splashes flew up on the barge's side as she hurried away. In less than a minute she was fairly out to the sea, heading away from the land.

The two Abners met together and watched her. They said nothing till she was out of sight. The old man fidgeted with his revolver, and as he could not open the catch, flung it far out into the creek.

"There, he's gone," he said at last. "I'd have shot him full of holes if the running hadn't made my arm shake. Then just as I'd got the bead well on him the wheel jammed. Where's he making for?"

"England, I reckon."

"Go on with our England. He's off for one of the islands."

"Well, couldn't we tell the coast guard at Crab Point, and have him headed off?"

"He'll be twenty miles at sea before you get there, and what good would it do to us if they did head him?"

"Well, at least they would stop him having the stuff."

Abner answered this with a snarl. After a pause he said, "Now that we're cooler, answer. How do you know he has the stuff?"

"I was digging in the new place," his son replied, "when I heard some wagons coming along. They were going along the pike to French-fellow's Pier. I didn't look up till they'd passed. Then I thought they looked like Old John's wagons, and I thought that one of the men in the second wagon was this Ben fellow. I just thought, 'He's getting a lift to the pier to do a bit of fishing.' I went on with my digging and dug quite a piece. I found one of these Indian arrowheads."

"Sit on it," his father said. "Get on."

"I suppose an hour later, Old Farmer John came running up, pretty near out of his mind. 'Did my wagons go past here?' he asked.

" 'Sure,' I said.

" 'Was that man called Ben or Trigger in them?'

" 'I guess so. What's the matter, John?'

" 'Matter?' he said. 'That fellow and his Indians. You call him Ben, but his real name's Trigger. He and they knocked me flat, tied me up, and took all the stuff I had outen of my cellar. It was that gold and silver which I guess you've been looking for. I had it and they've took it . . . loaded it up on to my own wagons and said they was going to the pier. But I'll pier them yet,' he said. 'I've sent to the marshal. I've called Joe. I've got my gun. You call your pop, quick now, and we'll get him at the pier before he can be off in that yawl of his.' He was pretty near dead with rage and running, but off he went for the pier and I came looking for you."

Old Abner sat on the rock swaying from side to side. "When first we came here," he moaned, "I thought of trying out by John's farm there, but them Indians put me wrong. And it was there all the time. And that fox, Old John, had it in his cellar and watched us digging for it twenty years. I've gone harvesting there and drunk a horn or two with him a dozen times and he grinned and said nothing. He had us fooled all the time, the worst kind of fools. What was he planning to do with it?"

"Keep it from doing harm, he said."

"He's been fooled himself now, pretty good," old Abner said. "But he'll answer to me for the fool he made of me. . . .

"But how did the Trigger find where the stuff was?" he asked after a pause.

"John told me that," his son said. "He found bits of the boat in John's yard. Found it first go off. He never had to dig nor nothing. He had us fooled all the time. Now he's got it."

"He won't have it for long," the old man said.

"I don't know for that," his son said. "Old John won't stop him. Old John, I reckon, will just let it go without a word, as soon as his dander goes down."

"Well, I won't," his father said. "I'll get this Benito Trigger, sir, wherever he comes ashore. I'll have the stuff yet, or my fair half of it, or he shall squeal for it. I'll start this day. He ain't done with me yet, he's only begun."

At this point, little Abner broke in upon them with "I guess I wanna go home."

"Well, get home. Walk," his father said.

"I guess I don't wanna walk."

"Well, I guess you'll just have to."

"I guess I ain't gonna walk."

"I guess you are. How else are you going to get."

"I guess I wanna be carried."

"Who's gonna carry you?"

"I guess you are."

"I guess I'm not."

"Then I guess Gran'pop's gonna carry me."

"I guess he ain't," Gran'pop said.

"Then I guess I'll stay here an' yell." Saying this, he started to yell. His father boxed his ears, to give him, as he said, something to yell for. Old man Abner said, "I'm off, for Trigger's home. When he gets there he'll find me waiting for him." At this the picture suddenly dimmed, the figures of the three Browns blurred into the background. Kay saw the surf and the waves of the sea, and then, lo, the shining head said, "That is all," and the picture vanished. Kay rose from his chair. At the same instant the scarlet cloak which he was wearing turned into a scarlet canoe. It floated him up from the floor, bored a big hole in the wall, floated him through, and then sped him home like a bird. In a minute the outfit was on its peg and Kay was in the drawing room, looking at *Aunt Susan's Compendium*.

*T*he book was on the hearthrug, open, but somebody must have handled it since he had left it there. It was open in the middle to show him that there were two volumes of *Pleasant Knowledge* bound together (for 1841 and 1842), and that therefore the book contained two pages numbered 275, one of which he had not seen. He turned to page 275 for the 1842 volume. It bore a chapter heading: Secret Writings. It went on thus:

Though in the enlightenment of modern times the need of secret methods of correspondence has become less frequent than in the past, it may still fall to the lot of our readers to want the knowledge of such methods. It may not be generally known that an effective secret writing can be made very simply, by using, instead of the letter needed, a letter some distance before or after it in the alphabet. Thus, instead of writing CAT, write BZS or DBU. With a little practice people can become ready writers in these changed alphabets. . . .

"That's queer," Kay thought. "Perhaps Benjamin used a secret writing when he wrote those notes about the treasure." He

had not time to prove it at the moment, because Ellen carried
him off to dinner, but after dinner he took an exercise book
and a pencil to his lair below his dressing table. Then with
great care he made several alphabets in columns. After a little

juggling with these, he found that the letters $\dfrac{\text{SSS}}{\text{JGZ.RPC}}$

might possibly represent not those letters, but two letters later
in the alphabet, thus:

$$\dfrac{\text{U.U.U.}}{\text{LIB} \quad \text{TRE}}$$

It was very perplexing work, almost as troublesome as *acer*,
and the result was odd. Still LIB TRE did seem to spell something, whereas JGZ seemed like initials, and what English name
began with Z?

He was about to try another combination of alphabets, when
he heard a carriage in the drive. "She's coming back," he
thought. An instant later he heard her in the hall, with others.
"She's brought the witches here, or is it only Mrs. Gossip?" he
asked, as he listened. Abner's voice told the footman to wait.

"It is the witches," he thought. "What has she brought them
here for?" He heard her bring them along the hall, up the stairs
to the corridor outside his room. They did not seem to be more
than five.

"Wait here a moment," she said, "I must just see if anyone
has been in my room." You may imagine how Kay felt when he
heard her say this.

While she was gone the others muttered together. "We must
get to the bottom of it." "She had one of our cloaks, for I saw
the red skirt flick past the door." "Well, we shall find who it
was, and then . . . snip . . ."

The governess came back from her room. "Come on in
here," she said, leading the way into Kay's room. "It is safe in

here, we can't be overheard in here. This is the child's room, where Captain Harker slept. Some of you must set on the bed, there won't be room for you all on the sofa." She made sure that both doors were shut.

When they were all seated, she said, "It is true that I left my window open, but I have looked at the robes, they are all cool; it cannot have been anyone from here."

"Then who was it?" Abner asked. "Someone, in one of our robes, was listening to us while we lunched, and got before us to the image, and all our spells were wasted. Worse than wasted, for the knowledge must have gone to an enemy. I ask, who was it?"

"Not one from here," the governess said. "We will make an incantation tonight to find out who it was . . . and then. . . . short shrift."

"Yes," Abner said. "If it won't then be too late for short shrift. However, this is the room, you say. Let us have a look at this hearthstone."

At this he pulled back the carpet so as to show the stone.

"No doubt about it's being big enough," he said. "And it certainly hasn't been disturbed in recent years. We're in plenty of time if it's buried here. Off coat, Uncle Venom, and then we'll get the cold chisels at it."

Kay heard the two men take off their coats and settle down to work.

"The stone's leaded in," Abner explained. "We will chip out the lead and prize the stone up with our crowbars."

Kay heard them chip at the lead, while the three ladies said, "How fast you're doing it." "It won't take long at this rate." "What can we bring you for refreshment?" etc., etc.

"This is only Quaker leading," Abner said, after they had chipped for some minutes. "We'll have this up in no time. It is a thin melting of lead to cover the boltheads. I can prize the bolts out now with the jimmy, if you'll hand it to me, Sister."

"Here's the jimmy, dear master."

"Thank you. Yes. It is as I said. Here come the bolts, they

pull right up. It's a good deal easier than I'd expected. Now, Uncle Venom, if you'll take this crowbar, I'll take this one. It seems to me that one good heave will make her swing on her axis."

Kay heard them heaving and panting. It wasn't quite so easy as they had expected. At last Kay heard them say "It's giving. There it is. Now then." Kay heard the stone swing back. All five people were intent upon what was beneath. Kay could just see their bent bodies craning forward into the hollow.

"It's not just under the stone," Abner said. "The space seems to me to be right underneath the fireplace. There's a room of sorts."

"Is there anything in it?" Sister Aconite asked.

"I'll soon see," Abner said. "It'll be something of a squeeze to get down."

Kay could see him squirming down, legs first, into the opening. Presently his head disappeared.

"Is there anything there?" the two women asked.

"Nothing," he said from below. "It's an empty room. The stuff hasn't been here, at any rate not for many years. It's dry, empty and dusty. Not a thing in it, except this."

Kay could not see what "this" was, but it was evidently a small thing. He heard it being passed about.

"It's only the handle of a sword," Sister Aconite said.

"It's not even that," Abner answered. "It's the handle of a cutlass worth about ten shillings when new. Well, there's a disappointment. Or rather, one more false trail removed. We know that it isn't here at least. But what on earth was the room made for? That beats me. Is there any other place in this house where old Harker could have put it?"

"None, that I know of," the governess said.

"Nothing in the cellar?"

"Nothing. I've searched."

"Well, where did Trigger put it, if he didn't give it to Harker?"

"Where indeed?"

"Well, we must go on with our incantations till we get another clue," Abner said.

"We're spending a small treasure in gums and herbs," Uncle Venom said. "It's my belief that Miss Susan Pricker Trigger has it, all the time."

"Maybe she has," Abner said. "But I don't think she has. Anyway, that will be easy to prove, as things turn out. It must be somewhere, and we must get it, and we will get it."

Kay could see him sweeping the particles of lead and brick displaced by the work down into the opening. Presently the stone was rolled back, and the carpet replaced.

"Our young friend will notice that these two bolts have been unleaded," Abner said.

"He won't," the governess said. "He's the most unobservant boy I've ever met."

"The maids will notice, though," Sister Aconite said.

"A very good imitation can be made," Abner answered, "with candle grease and soot from the chimney."

In a few minutes he had covered the two bolts with melted grease and soot.

"They won't notice that," he said. "And now we'll be moving."

He gathered up the crowbars.

"I suppose that there's no clue on the sword," Sister Aconite said.

"It's all rusted deep," Abner answered. "If anything ever has been scratched on it, it's rusted out now."

"What shall we do with it?" Sister Aconite asked.

"Well, the young shaver might like it."

"No, indeed," the governess said, "that might be giving him all sorts of ideas."

"I'll take it with me, then," Abner said. He put it in his pocket. They all left the room.

"Well," Kay thought, as they went downstairs, "they are just about cool enough."

*   *   *

After tea Kay was sent to hold skeins of wool for Ellen, because the Women's Winter Knitting Club would soon be meeting and boys ought to make themselves useful. Ellen talked of old times as she balled off the wool.

"Things were very different in my father's time," she said. "They call them the good old times, but I don't know, I'm sure, what my father found good in them. Oh, the dreadful things he used to tell. For it wasn't then like it is now, Master Kay, with so many things done for poor people. No. Why, the farmers used to beat the boys black and blue, and pinch their ears till the blood ran.

"And then there was the wartime, fighting against that Boney. Oh, the money there used to be then. Never anyone sober in the parish on market nights; everybody had the French brandy, by what they called the Night Hawks. They used to bring the brandy by night right up the river, and then bring it about to people's houses, and so cheap. But the Night Hawks were bold ones; they killed poor Mr. Parminter. There was a lot of them hanged for that. They hung them up on the top of Cop in those days. My father used to show me the sort of like a hollow where the gallows was, but the boys have all altered it now, scrabbling about for poor people's bones and that, which they say keep you from drowning, but I don't know I'm sure.

"Then they put Boney on his island in the end, and then there wasn't any more French brandy, nor nothing else. Oh, dreadful it was, and bread so dear, my father said. Many's the time he was glad of a bite of oats out of the horsebin. And then like men came down from the cities, my father said, to tell the young men not to stand it, because the French didn't. So then they got what they called the Liberty Tree out in the wood . . ."

"Liberty Tree," Kay said. "What was that?"

"It was that big beech tree, Master Kay, in the middle of Corselaydead Wood, where the four big rides meet. We went past there with Rose and Will, if you remember, the day we walked to the flower show. They called it the Liberty Tree, my father said, because there's Liberty cut on it, and that's what they did in France. They put a red cap on it, and that made it Liberty, and then they took their oaths. The Liberty men were bold ones, too; they burned a lot of ricks and that, till they were sent to Botany. My father had the red cap that was on it, till mother wanted it for crawlers. There's not many knows about these things now, for the old ones are gone, and the young all go into the towns and never care."

*W*hen Kay went to bed that night he knew that Benjamin's writing meant a hundred yards south of the Liberty Tree, but he could not understand what the S.S.S. meant, even if the S.S.S. stood for U.U.U. Then, just as he was falling asleep, it came over him in a flash. "Of course," he cried, "I see what it means. What an ass I was, not to see it before. It means a hundred yards south of the Liberty Tree under three big yews. That is it, of course. I wonder if there *are* three big yews. I cannot remember. But of course there will be." His mind at once made pictures of enormous yews with interlocking boughs growing over "the sort of like a hollow" where Benjamin's treasure lay. Soon they began to cover Kay with shadow, so that he fell asleep.

He had not slept for long before a shrill crying sounded in his ears. When he woke, the room had something in it that was fluttering and battering against the ceiling and the walls. When his eyes grew accustomed to the light he saw that there was a bat in the room. He had always loved bats, because of their bright eyes, cocked ears, and nice leathery umbrellary wings and the little hooks to them. He had always longed to be a bat, so that he could fly in the twilight and hook himself up head downwards somewhere high up in a steeple when he was tired. Now here was a bat actually crawling along his bed to him.

"Good evening, Kay," the bat said. "I've come from my friend Tom Otter. We thought what fun it would be if we could persuade you to spend an evening with us. We live in an interesting old place which you might like to see, and I've brought you a suit of wings, in case you care to come."

"I'd love to come," Kay said. "It is most frightfully kind of you to think of me."

"Hurray, he's coming," the bat said. "We hoped you would. Now I'll help you to put on the wings."

"Just try flying from the bed to the window ledge," he said, "and then fly back once or twice. You'll soon get the hang of it. It's really very easy."

Kay found that it was quite easy after the first attempt. "Come on, then," the bat said. "You keep by me. It isn't far, really, to our place. I generally go this way."

Kay put on his pair of fox-eye spectacles and followed him. It was amusing to see his friends the grocer and the carpenter walking in their gardens, and to fly just over their heads. It was eerie to hear them say "The bats are very bold this year. That one nearly knocked my glasses off." Then Mrs. Grocer said:

"When bats grow bold
We shall have cold."

Mrs. Carpenter said:

"When bats fly low
It's going to blow."

Both the husbands said the same thing: "Well, I wouldn't be surprised if we did have it a bit cold, if we did have it a bit blowy."

Presently they came in sight of the river, at a point which

Kay longed to spend days at, exploring, but was never allowed, as it was dangerous.

Some twenty years before, there had been a mill there, with two wheels. The mill was now vanished to its foundations, but the millrace head was still there in a quiet pool forty yards long, in which water lilies were spreading. The shoots of the wheels still dribbled water even in the hottest summer. Beyond the mill shoots was a causeway or bridge, under which the main river ran over a lasher. At the further end of the lasher was the lock by which the barges had passed on their way up or down stream. The railway had now put an end to all this traffic.

Above the mill and bridge the river was a shallow basin, a hundred yards broad, broken up by islands and withy plats, where there were swans, kingfishers, many moorhens, sometimes a heron, and now and then wild duck, or duck that had escaped (these were the ones that Kay loved to think of) and gone wild. Below the mill there was a deep, turbulent, foaming pool from which the current sped away upon its course. There was a big idle back eddy at one side of it, where bubbles, like glass teacups upside down, sauntered back towards the lasher, and then either ran at once into the current or were driven back to saunter round again.

The causeway was pleasant in calm weather. You could put in ships above the lasher and watch them go down the falls and through the rapids, or round and round the wheel of the pool. But in times of flood it was wonderful, and terrible, when all the hatches were wide, and the roar of the weir could be heard for a quarter of a mile. Then you could imagine yourself beside the Maelstrom or Niagara, and the fountains of the great deep being broken up. It was there that he had seen Dr. Gubbins's pig swept past, a cutthroat corpse, in the great February flood of two years before. Jane had said, "All pigs cut their throats in the water," yet Kay could not understand how they could, as they never had any razors. Jane did not know how they could, either, but affirmed the melancholy fact.

The bat swerved down towards those foundations of the mill

which overlooked the eddy. "Come in after me, through that hole where the big stone has fallen," he said.

The bat led the way along the hole into what once might have been a part of the cellar of the mill. It was a rather damp, dark place, lit by a greenish glitter, which Kay did not understand. A hairy thing, which smelt very strongly of fish, rose up out of the gloom.

"Come in, Master Kay," Tom Otter said, "and welcome to our poor abode. Damp but pleasant, as we say. That greenish light that you see is the water. It comes right up here and the moon shines through it, which gives that effect. Would you like to taste a bit of fish? We've got very pretty trout. Or what you might prefer is to put on otter pads and a skin and come on down for a swim."

"I'd love that," Kay said.

The otter produced an otter skin with pads attached. Kay put it on.

"There's really nothing like the water, is there?" the otter said. "I'll show you some queer things down there beneath the water. You'll find that you'll be able to see when you get down."

"I'll just take a cruise above the falls," the bat said. "The gnats are at their best in this weather."

After he had gone the otter led Kay into the water. In a moment he found himself in the eddy, from which he could see the current of the stream running away in glittering streaks.

"Dive now," the otter said. "There's nothing so lovely as the water at the foot of the fall, where it comes down all white and goes up as bubbles. And stuck there in the crevices of the hatches you'll find all sorts of odd things."

Sure enough, Kay did see all sorts of odd things. The bones of Dr. Gubbins's pig, the skeleton of a pike with his teeth still fixed through the webfoot of the skeleton of a duck, two addled swan's eggs, bits of old branches as white as bone and the bow half of a tin gunboat, which had once been the joy of his heart, now sunk beneath the waves fast by her native shore.

"Of course, things are quiet now," the otter said. "We don't get the fishing nor anything else that we used to have. The river used to be much wilder, but still in a flood it's wild enough for anyone. A thing that you'll like is to dive down here and come up in these little twists and eddies and then dive down again. Of course, we can't do that when the spates are on."

When they were weary of this happy pastime, the otter said, "Now I'll show you another thing. Those beastly otter hounds have been after me more than once. They never can make out where I go to. I go to a place here, which they have never suspected. The entrance is a spring in the riverbed. Come on down with me."

He dived down into the heart of the current into an upward eddy of water far colder than the water of the river. Kay could see a fissure in the rock of the riverbed, from which this cold water gushed. Some little fish, which were tickling their bellies with the chill of the eddies, darted away as they drew near. Kay shuddered at the cold of the spring and had to strike out hard against its force. It was pitch dark down there in spite of his glasses; Otter seemed to be taking him down a deep well. Suddenly he shot upwards into a glimmery cave and clambered up onto rock strewn with river drift.

"Here is a place," the otter said, "which no hound yet has ever come near. There's light, if one feels the need of that, from the chink in the rock there. There's nearly always a fish or two where the spring comes up, at the place where we dived. I could live here all the year round, only that one misses the noise of the falls. Take a look about you, Master Kay. It's a snug little place. I've dodged the hounds here twenty times, if I've dodged them once."

Kay saw that he was in a little cave or hollow among rocks. The floor of it sloped a good deal. A sort of glimmer showed from a fissure in the rock, but one could not see through the fissure from either side. At one end of the cave the wall seemed to have been cut or wrought by men; there was a sort of shelf in it. Over the shelf, fixed to the rock, was a very old broken bone cross. "I know what this has been," Kay thought. "A hermitage. It's the cell where old St. Alpig lived. That is his bed or his altar, and then, I suppose, the steps or passage he used fell in. There seems to have been a fall of rock there." Then he said aloud, "I say, Mr. Otter, did you ever come across any bones of men here?"

"No," the Otter said, "All men have been gone from here for years."

At this moment they heard a strange scraping and scratching noise in one corner of the cave. It seemed to come from beyond the fall of rock. "Someone digging," Kay whispered. "Is it a rabbit?"

"No, that's not a rabbit," the otter said, showing his teeth. "No rabbit ever dug like that."

"Can it be men?"

"No," Otter growled. "Men clink when they dig, and stop to talk, and then pass round a bottle and begin again. No . . . I don't know who this could be. It's big, whoever it is. It might be Stoat. I don't exactly want Stoat coming round here. He may be all very well, but he hasn't the name for it. Down here we often get blamed for things we'd never dream of taking. But Stoat never dug like that."

"Could it be Badger?"

"Badger?" Otter said. "Well, I hope not. But that isn't Badger's digging. Badger growls and grunts as he digs, and sings his beastly digging song."

"What is that?" Kay asked.

"Mind, I say nothing against Badger. To see him go for a wasps' nest is to see real courage. Then his teeth are simply superb—there's no other word for them. But he is rather a joke. He growls down into the ground before he begins—'I'm as good a man as you are, and so I'll show you.' Then he scuffles out the earth and sings to it.

> "First I'll dig a this way,
>   Then I'll dig a that way,

> Then I'll dig a criss way,
> Then I'll dig.
> Then I'll dig a one way,
> Then I'll dig a two way,
> Then I'll dig a run way,
> Then I'll dig."

The scratching noise continued.

"Don't tell me that that's Badger," the otter said. "Badger never dug like that. I don't at all like that snuffling noise, that sort of woofing noise."

"Why, what do you think it is?" Kay asked.

"I hardly like to say," the otter whispered, "but it's that beastly kind of woofing noise that the hounds make when they go blowing along at the holes on the riverbank. If they find a way in from that side, which they never have before, this place won't be safe. He's coming nearer, too."

Presently the unseen digger stopped from his scratching and scrabbling. He cleared the earth from his muzzle and began to sing in a most unmusical voice:

> "When the afternoon's quiet brought peace to the soul
>   I spied a white duck on a pond,
>   I asked the sweet creature to come for a stroll,
>   And, though she did peck a bit,
>   I wrung her white neck a bit,
>   Ho says Rollickem Bitem.
>
> Then, strolling along in the field by the mill,
>   I spied a gray gosling at grass,
>   Who found me all hungry and left me all still,
>   For a goose in digestion
>   Solves every harsh question.
>   Ho says Rollickem Bitem."

"It's Bitem," Kay said. "Is that you, Bitem?"

"Yes," said Bitem on the other side of the stone.

"Is that you, Kay?" Nibbins's voice asked. "What are you doing?"

"I'm in here with Otter," Kay said.

"Well, look here, Kay," Nibbins said. "Do please shove this stone aside, if you can get at it from your side. We've been having adventures, Bitem and I, and we're dead beat. Can we get out your way?"

"You'll have to swim for it," Kay said.

"Well, shove the stone aside, Kay, and let's have a look. Even a swim is better than what we've been having."

With a good deal of trouble Kay managed to get the stone to one side. Bitem and Nibbins came pushing through into the cave. Both were out of breath and covered with earth. They lay down panting.

"They've turned poor old Bitem out of his quarry earth," Nibbins said. "Roper Bilges sent the news of it to the hound master, who had it all stopped up for the season, just as poor old Bitem had got it all into order with all the bolt-holes bored. So I told him that I knew of a place near the old lime kiln here, a place that I've sometimes come mousing in. I did a bit of batting there, too, when I was young, but we don't mention that to Bat. Well, we came along to look at it and prowled around in it. Then, while we were grubbing for a bolt-hole, suddenly, bang, the floor gave way beneath us and down we came. I never saw such a place. We fell fifty yards, I should think, by the feel. We couldn't get back through the hole that we fell from—we couldn't reach it, or near it. Then we both thought that our only chance would be to dig down to the river this way and then swim for it, but the stone was so hard that we'd almost—at least, I'd almost—given up hope. Of course, it takes a lot to make old Bitem give up hope."

"You'd both be the better for a bit of fish," the otter said. "Would you like it fresh or some that's been hung a bit?"

"I like it well hung," Bitem said. "But Nibbins here would like it fresh, I'm sure."

"Well, I'll bring you a bit of both," the otter said.

While Otter was fetching the fish, which took a minute or two, Nibbins said, "I'm not at all sure, Kay, that you oughtn't to have a look at what is beyond there. There's a very queer smell."

"Do you think it's treasure?" Kay said.

"Well, it's a very rich smell," Nibbins said, "a cellary smell. You ought to smell it, anyway."

"What sort of thing is it that smells?" Kay asked.

"There's round things and there's square things," Bitem said. "Neither is good to eat."

"You've got things like that," Nibbins said, "in the cellar, Kay. Take a look."

It was not so easy to take a look. Kay pushed through with Bitem and Nibbins into the cave, which was pitch dark, but very much more spacious than the one in which he had been sitting. He could see little there. There was hardly a ray of light. He groped with his hands and felt walls of rock. Groping downwards, he felt something like bales of sacking tied with strips of leather. Further on were some small casks lying on their sides. A fragrance that was sweetish, heavy, and rather sickly came upon him from these barrels. It was a little like the smell in the decanter cupboard of the sideboard when the stoppers had been left out.

"That's the kind of thing that we came down on," Bitem said. "However, Nibbins always falls on his feet, and I've been used to falling anyhow since those beasts in red first came after me."

"But where did you fall from?" Kay asked. "Do you mean to say that you fell through the roof?"

"I should think we did," Bitem said.

Kay put up his hand, but could feel no roof above him.

"It's getting lighter now," Nibbins said. "You'll be able to see in a minute. There. Perhaps you can see now. Yes, there's the hole we fell through."

Far above their heads was a hole in the rock of the cave. Part of a broken and rotten ladder was still fixed to it: men must at one time have used the place as a cellar.

"It's a wonder you weren't both killed," Kay said.

"I'd never suspected a place like this," Nibbins said. "It's just a little ordinary sort of place up above, that you have to squeeze through."

By this time, Kay was able to see the cave. It was like a very dark old church, with stalactites dripping from the roof. In the lower end of the cave were tiers of barrels and cases.

"I know what this is," Kay said. "It's the cellar where the moonlight people put their brandy and tobacco, and those are some which they never removed. Now, Piney Trigger worked the moonlight business—supposing he brought the treasure here. . . . Supposing it isn't brandy but the treasure . . . ?"

"I say," Otter said, "it's almost sunrise. You'd better be off, Kay, with Bat here. Slip off your otter skin and put on your bat's wings."

Bat helped him to put on his wings. "Come quickly," he said. "It's a great deal later than I thought." As he led the way up through the hole by which Nibbins had fallen, Kay called to him, "How will Nibs and Bitem get out? They'll be drowned if they try to swim, and they can't climb."

"Otter will manage something," Bat said. "Come on quickly, I've only got a few minutes left. Creep along this passage here. Now, here we are in the ruined limekiln."

They crept out over some fallen stones of the kiln (which still smelt of the warm, rank taint of Bitem's passing) into the overcast summer morning not yet light. The leaves of the trees hung heavily, occasionally dripping. There was a good deal of mist about. Not far up the road, as they flew, Kay caught sight of the backs of four laborers, with pickaxes over their shoulders, shambling drowsily to their work. They were going very slowly. Two of them carried lanterns, one of them had a coil of rope slung about his neck, all four were plastered with the rather pale clay of near the river.

"They're going early to work," Kay said.

"They're going from work," Bat said. "They've been working by the river all night. Look how tired they all are."

Indeed, as he spoke, the four exhausted men sat down on a heap of stones by the road. One of them seemed to fall asleep at once. The other three were dazed stupid with tiredness and nodded forward as they sat. Kay knew them as he flew over them. Two were the knights whom Arthur had sent with Edward "to see if they could find the treasure," only the night before; the third was Edward; the fourth, the sleeper, was poor little Brown Bear. Could they have been looking for the treasure in the river? They were sopping wet. They looked so utterly miserable and discouraged that it was plain that they had found nothing. "That's where the treasure will be," Kay thought, "sunk in the river, deep in the mud, where no one will ever find it. I never thought to ask Otter about it."

"O Edward," he cried, "cheer up. And do come home. . . ."

Edward lifted his weary head and stared stupidly at him.

"I'm Kay, I'm not a bat," Kay cried.

"Come on," Bat said, tugging him with his hooked wing. "We haven't got a weenit to weese."

"But I must speak to Edward."

"Queek, queek," the Bat said, in his shrill way. But lo, it wasn't the bat that said queek, queek. Kay was sitting up in his bed in full daylight. The curtain rings were saying queek, queek as they clinked in the wind.

"A very good morning," somebody was saying, "for a dance round the Liberty Tree." There was nobody there. The bat, the heap of stones and the four dog-tired companions were all gone, yet somebody had said those words, "dance round the Liberty Tree."

"I don't know about dance," Kay said. "But I'll go to the Liberty Tree. I'll take a measuring tape, I'll see if there are three big yews, and I'll have a trowel to dig with, in case."

*I*t did not take him long to reach the Liberty Tree in Corselaydead Wood. As Ellen had said, "There was Liberty cut on it," though the bark had almost overgrown the cuts. Sure enough, a hundred yards south from the Liberty Tree brought him to the center of a space between three big yew trees. Ten minutes of troweling there brought him to . . . There in the earth among the yew roots was a roll of something much decayed and worm-eaten, containing something heavy. It was a mildewed, rotted leather, wrapped round mildewed, rotted tarpaulin, wrapped round something that had once been wood. Inside the wood was more leather, which might once have been a moneybag. Inside this was a tin box about the size of the saddle soap box in the harness room of the stable. Inside this was something done up in an old silk handkerchief. Inside this was something of a sort that he had seen in the clockmaker's shop, an old gold watch fatter than the governess's table clock. It was very big; it had a dial for the seconds as well as for the hours; there was an engraved inscription on the back:

Presented to Sir Hassle Gassle, Bart., by the members of the Condicote Hunt, as a small tribute to his manly Probity and truly British Sportsmanship, in which the

Virtues of the Citizen and the Cheerfulness of the Companion have been signally united. April 17th, 1810. God Save the King.

"I know what it is, then," Kay said. "Of course, this is Benjamin's treasure. This is the repeater watch which he took from Sir Hassle Gassle, 'that Sir Hassle mourned to his dying day,' as Ellen said. I'll take it at once to the present Sir Hassle."

The church clock was chiming for nine o'clock when he passed beneath the baronet's arms upon the gateway. The arms were three hassles gassle's, muzzly, and the supporters two gassles showing their teeth. Kay's heart sank when he heard the chimes—he would be at least an hour late for breakfast.

He crossed the flagged courtyard to the door, where a long bell handle of twisted iron, when vigorously pulled, made a faint ting to sound in the east wing of the house far away. Presently, after he had rung half a dozen times, a footman opened the door and told him that there was no need to have rung so often, since people weren't deaf, and what did he want, ringing like that? Kay recognized the footman as Roper Bilges's brother, who had been at the ducking of Blackmalkin.

"Please," Kay said, "I was afraid the bell wasn't working properly. I want to see Sir Hassle Gassle on very important business."

"Sir Hassle is at breakfast. What is your business?"

"It's private."

"You'd best write to Sir Hassle, then," the man said, "and make an appointment when to see him. That's the rule with private business. You ought to know that." He was about to close the door when young Lady Gassle, dressed for riding, crossed the hall on her way to breakfast. She was a very beautiful young woman, with eyes so bright and teeth so white that she always seemed more alive than anybody in the room with her.

"Why, it's little Kay Harker," she said. "Don't shut the door, Bilges. What is it, Kay? Do you come to see me?"

"No, please, Lady Gassle. I wanted to speak to Sir Hassle."

"Well, come in," she said. "We're breakfasting. Have you breakfasted?"

"No, not yet, Lady Gassle."

"Come in, then, and breakfast. What a pickle you're in, though. Have you been taking a toss? Let me just mop you up a little and get some of the earth off."

When she had tidied him a little, she took him into the big, bright breakfast room, which had a red and blue Axminster carpet on the floor, shining red mahogany furniture, six big paintings of Thoroughbred hunters, a gleaming globe of the world, and Sir Hassle at breakfast, with *The Times* propped against the coffee pot.

"You owe me that gold watch and chain, my Polly," he said. "Kem is in for the Grasslands."

"What majority?"

"Sixty-seven, a very near thing. Hullo. Who's this? Kay Harker? Coming to breakfast? Right. Are you a pork-pie man or just an egg man?"

"Please, a pork-pie man, and, if you please, I've found your grandfather's gold watch, that Benjamin the highwayman took."

"Well, I'm blest," Sir Hassle said.

"That will just do for the gold watch and chain I owe you over the election," his wife said.

"Of all the things I ever knew happen," Sir Hassle said, when he had examined the watch, "this is just about the neatest. It's the thing my grandfather worried over till he died, and it worried my father, too, and it's a great pleasure to me to get it back. And all the hunt will be delighted too. It has been very well preserved too; it will be possible to get it to go again. I shall owe you a big debt, Kay. What can I do for you? You must think, and let me know."

"Please," Kay said, "when you go hunting, will you please not hunt a fox, who is a good fox, really, and very nice, who may live somewhere down not far from where the old mill once stood."

"Well, if he's a good fox and very nice and a friend of yours," Sir Hassle said, "and you tell him not to go goosing and henning among the farms down there, I dare say we shall be able to do without him."

It was now half-past ten, an hour after lesson time. He could not imagine what she would do to him. Lady Gassle guessed that he might be wanted for lessons. She asked her husband to take Kay in front of him on his hack, which he did. Kay rode all the way, and learned a lot about horses, how this one was called Old Joe, and how they remembered everything, and how clever they are and how nervy.

"But if you're so fond of horses," Sir Hassle said, "you ought to come up on Wednesdays and Saturdays, at eleven, and ride with my little boy, Bill. Would you like that?"

"Oh, I should think I should."

"Well, come along then on Saturday."

"Please, I don't think I should be allowed."

"That's all my eye and Betty Martin, you won't be allowed. I'll get my wife to write about it."

When they reached Seekings House, Ellen was in a fine taking. "Whatever have you been doing, Master Kay, going out like this without your breakfast and never a word?"

"He's been breakfasting with me," Sir Hassle said. This was excuse enough for the moment, but when the Hassle Gassles had ridden away she turned on him again.

"It's lucky for you that your governess had to go off to Russell's Dene again," she said. "They sent the carriage for her just before breakfast, so she doesn't know about you. Otherwise I don't know what she'd have said. And whatever have you done to your pajama coat to get it all over fish scales?"

This came from wearing otter skin, Kay thought, but before he could answer, Ellen went on: "I couldn't let you wear it again in that state, I'd have to wash it. And then, another thing, poor little Nibbins is missing. He wasn't in last night and he hasn't been in all morning. Jane and I think that Bilges the

Keeper has shot him, for he always shoots cats, though he's got no business to. And I don't know what we'll do without little Nibbins."

"Yes," Kay thought, "Abner has sent for her because he has found some clue. And the fish scales on the pajamas show that last night wasn't a dream, but real. And the treasure is down in the cave by the mill, and poor little Nibs and old Bitem are down in the cave and can't get out, unless they try swimming and get drowned. And if Abner *has* got a clue by incantation, and goes to the cave for the treasure, he'll find them both there and shoot them. What am I to do?"

"Ah, that's what," said a voice behind him. Rat, the cellarman, was standing there, smearing his mouth with his paw. He looked much more seedy than formerly, having newly come from the dustbin.

"Well," he said sourly, "and what are you looking at *me* for? *I* ain't done nothing. I never didn't, not never. It wasn't never Rat done it. You thinks acos I don't wear no pajamas all over fish scales as I larders and I sculleries. But I don't. I only dustbins. Except sometimes I rubbish-heaps. And what's dustbins? Glass bottles, mostly, what's empty. What's rubbish-heaps? Old tins what's been under the tap. And what's life? That's what."

"I've saved a bit of bacon rind for you," Kay said. "It's here, in my soap dish."

Rat took the bacon rind without joy and without thanks. He ate it in a greasy sideways sort of way, with a good deal of bolting. However, when it was down he was a different being.

"As neat a bit of rind," he said, "as ever I stummikked. He put me in mind of a bit of rind as maybe you, what lives on such, may have forgotten, but what a pore cellarman, what don't get, no not the smell of rind, not twist in a year, does well on down in the dark, ah, many a long day. He wasn't thrown out on no dustbin, but took to the hens, and the sun cooked him beautiful, ah, he *was* a rind, he was. But what I says is a cellar's a cellar, ain't it, and a friend's a friend, ain't he?"

"Yes," Kay said. "Certainly."

"Ah, you admits it now," Rat said, "and nicely you shows it. You ain't stirred neither paw nor tooth for your friends, though you've been back hours. Here's Bat come digging at me, saying 'You go and see if he's gone to help them, acos they're down there and can't get out, unless they gets drownded trying.' So I says, 'But he knows they're here, he'll help them.' 'No,' Bat says. 'He mayn't. He may be took by such. And I can't go,' Bat says, 'acos I can't see in this here flaming daylight that is my distraction. But Nibbins and Bitem,' he said, 'is down there in agonies, and what'll help 'em if Kay don't?' That's what."

"But how can I help them?" Kay asked

Rat didn't answer this, but walked to the door and beckoned to him to follow. Just outside the door he shoved back the tread of a stair and motioned to him to enter the opening. Kay found it fairly light inside. In the darker corners some bats hung, fast asleep.

"Them's them as bacon rind is flung away on," Rat said. "They thinks scorn of rind. Gnats is their joy, and they're partial to a midge. But here's what . . ."

He had opened a panel in the wainscoting of a little room which Kay recognized at once.

It was Mrs. Pouncer's cupboard. There were the magical books, the gums and unguents. The cloaks, masks, and hats had been removed. "They will be doing magic in them," Kay thought.

"That's what," Rat whispered.

"Of course it is," Kay said.

He saw at once what to do. He took down from the shelf a pair of one-league shoes, the magic lantern, a ladder, a rope, and an extra pair of spectacles.

"And him," Rat said, pointing to one of the baskets.

"You mean, to carry the things in?" Kay asked.

"No, I don't mean," Rat said.

"What then?"

"Acos," Rat said, "I seen her one time say to one of them 'Goose,' and in come a cold goose with sassingers. Then she said, 'Rabbit pie,' and in come a rabbit pie. And if you was to say 'Raw goose' and 'raw rabbit' when down there with your two friends, it might be the saving of their pore lives."

"I'll certainly do that," Kay said.

"Ah," Rat said. "Yet I notice you never stop to think what you might say so as to rejoice a poor cellarman what toils in dustbins for a living he don't get."

"What can I say for you?" Kay asked.

"There was a thing come here once in the summer," Rat said. "He come done up so he wouldn't burst, but he did burst, and he was to have come quick, but he didn't come quick, and so the sun got at him. And he was very baggy and people called him a Naggy. And he made folk go very white at dinner time, so you flung him away, but I didn't fling him away. No, I put him away and wished he was more. Now you just come into this little passage and hold that basket. Then if you will say Naggy, perhaps he'll come for you."

"I know what you mean," Kay said. "The haggis. . . ." He went into the passage, held the basket, and said, "Haggis."

Instantly there came a puddingy flump in the basket. A cold, bulging, blobby thing had fallen into it. "Here you are, Rat," he said. "Take it, will you?"

"Ah, that's what," Rat said, taking it. "Now you put on your shoes in here. You can get out at that jackdaw's place at the end." As Kay sat down to put on the shoes, he heard Rat passing along the passage to the cellars singing a song:

> "Of all the foods as good as tart,
>   There's none like pretty Naggy;
> He warms the cockles of my heart,
>   Though he is cold and baggy.

"What though the wise eat mutton pies,
  Or pasties made of staggy,
  To all the wise I make replies,
  Give me my pretty Naggy.

"O let my jaw lay down and gnaw
  Until my teeth are jaggy,
  Both cooked and raw the Scots whae ha
  My ain braw sonsie Naggy."

Kay was not sure of the last lines, because when Rat was singing them he was whisking through the jackdaw's place under the eaves, holding his laden basket. He had slipped on the one-league shoes, which were like scarlet galoshes of soft leather, then he had stamped one foot down, to make his shoe fit into it, and lo, away he had whisked, through the hole, over the garden, over the hill, over the wood, across Mile Meadow, which was said to be the best grass for milk in the seven counties, then along Yell Brooks, across Foxpits, then down, quite out of breath, at the third milestone. He had just time to say "That makes one league" when he was off again. This time it was fun, because he was up among a company of rooks, who were changing their pasture. He had always longed to be among rooks.

"Hurraw," they said, "Hyaw's Kaw," meaning, "Hurray, here's Kay." But in an instant Kay was past them and coming down by Seven Springs to Condicote Old Mill, to the ruined limekiln where the entrance was. Luckily no one was about.

He slipped off the red galoshes lest they should take him further, then he put on his fox-eye spectacles, then he tied the basket round his neck, then he took out the lantern and examined the entrance. It seemed to him that no one had been there since he had left with Bat. He crept into the old cellar or stable from which Nibbins and Bitem had fallen. He peered down through the gap in the floor, and called, "Nibs, Nibs, Nibs,"

"Is that you, Kay?"

"Yes, are you all right?"

"Well, we're feeling rather lost, as we couldn't face the look of the river when Otter showed it to us, and didn't quite know that you'd be able to help. But don't speak quite so loud, if you don't mind. We'll explain why presently."

"I'll come down," Kay said.

He was pulling out the ropeladder to a proper length when he began to puzzle how to secure the end. "I wish," he said, "I wish I had somebody here to tie the ends to the rocks so that they won't slip." Instantly an invisible someone took the ladder from his hands, secured it to the rocks near him, went down it, secured the lower ends below, came back up it, said, "Ladder ends tied securely" (in a tinny, clicky voice, like a biscuit-tin lid being put onto the tin), and disappeared. That was one of the results of having a wish basket.

Kay went down the ladder. Bitem and Nibbins were overjoyed to see him. Neither Bitem nor Nibbins was hungry, as Otter had given them a trout. He heard a noise as though a pickax were being plied against the wall of the cave from somewhere on the other side. He heard the click of the pick and the falling of stones after each blow.

"That is why I said don't speak quite so loud," Nibbins said. "They've been at it ever since daylight. They're digging into the wall from some other cave. If you come over here you will hear them."

Kay went quietly to the wall of the cave. There the noise was so clear that it was possible to hear the voices of the workers when they stopped working. Whoever they were, they were not Edward and the guards. Kay could make out that there were always two pickaxes working at the same time, for five minutes at a spell. Then there came a pause, during which the broken stone was shoveled away. Then the picking began again.

"They're a lot of people there," Nibbins said, "and they're making as little noise as possible—you'll notice that they don't sing—and they're getting within the last yard. Those picks will soon be through."

"They will," Otter said. "They will be through in no time, and that will mean another way into my place where I've been so snug. It may seem very selfish of me, but do you think, Kay, that you could block up the hole you made into my den, so that it won't be noticed?"

"I'll try," Kay said. "You go back into your den, and I will wish."

He had no sooner wished than invisible someones came silently, blocked up the approach to Otter's lair, tinnily reported "Entrance blocked securely," and disappeared.

"That's your third wish," Nibbins said. "You'll get nothing more out of that basket this time until you've gone a league and crossed running water. That's how those things work."

"Nibs," Kay whispered, "do you think that the diggers there are the Pouncer seven?"

"They may be."

"If they are, why don't they use the wish basket?"

"You can only use a wish basket for good things," Nibbins said, "so you may be sure that they don't use it much."

"Where's Bitem gone?" Kay asked, looking round.

"He never says when he's going; he goes," Nibbins said.

The picks at this moment struck some rotten piece of rock. One of the workers cried, "Look out, she's coming." On the instant there came a crashing fall as though all the roof had given way. There was a half-minute's pause, then the voice of Abner Brown sounded very distinctly through the rocks as he tapped with a hammer.

"That was a good clearance," he said. "Hark at the taps. Two or three more like the last will fetch us through. You can hear how hollow it is on the other side."

The man called dear Brother Venom began to sing:

> "Now Midnights all, my fellow six,
> Just one more little spell of picks.
> My right toes prickle on the mold,
> Which shows that they are near to gold.

My left toes twiddle in their shoe,
Which shows that there is silver, too."

"Now, no singing," Abner said. "When we've copped the
dibs we'll carol. Come on, picks all."

The voices and the pickaxes seemed so near that it was like
having them in the next room.

"They'll get the treasure now," Kay thought, "if it's here. But
is it here?"

He held up the lantern over the casks and cases stowed at the
lower end of the cave. He counted twenty-nine small wooden
tubs, thirteen small puncheons of green glass, and eleven flat
wooden boxes, some of which had rotted through, showing
mildewed silk, rotted lace, and fungus where tobacco had been.
"This is not the treasure," he said. "These are things left by the
moonlighters."

"Well, come along," Nibbins whispered. "Quick, before
they break through upon us. Don't let us be caught by the
seven."

"Wait a minute," Kay said. "I must just look round."

"Oh, don't. Come along."

"No. I want to see."

"Well, I'm going," Nibbins said.

Kay let him go while he looked round the cave. There was
no other treasure than the spirits. "It isn't here," he said. "It will
be a fine squish for the seven when they break through."

He noticed that at some time, long before, there had been a
heavy fall of rock at the landward side of the cave. Thinking
that the fall might have buried the treasure, he walked to that
side to look at it. Something was there, lying on the ground.

It was not treasure but the skeleton of a man, lying on his
side in the rags of his clothes. He clutched a rusty knife in one
hand and the tin door of his broken lantern (which lay at a little
distance from him) in the other. He had been scratching
something on the tin at the time of his death. Kay picked up
the piece of tin to read the writing, but at that instant—oh,

horror—there came another crash of rock followed by a cheer of "Hurray, the pick's gone through."

Kay did not wait another second. He pocketed the inscribed tin and hopped up the ladder after Nibbins. When they were at the point of coming out into the open air, Nibbins suddenly stopped him. "*She* is there," he whispered. "Just outside."

Almost on the instant the voices of the pickax men, Abner and Venom, were heard outside calling "Mrs. Pouncer . . . Mrs. Pouncer . . . come on down. We've put a pickhead right through the rock into a cave as big as a wine vault. We'll all be through into it in an hour or two, like into Tom Tiddler's ground, picking up gold and silver."

"How wonderful," Mrs. Pouncer said. "But what are those things you are carrying?"

"Yes, what *are* they?" Abner said. "We found them in the outer cave. People had been digging there only this morning. Perhaps you can tell us whose they are."

Mrs. Pouncer seemed to be examining the things.

"A handkerchief marked *Edward*," she said, "a collar marked *Brown Bear*, an old hat marked *Robin Pointnose*, a knight's cloak buckle with the device of the Plow stars, and a colored waist-coat marked *Bruna Bree*. No . . . I really cannot say whose they are. But they must be the things of enemies, for, do you know, just as you began to bring them here I began to feel that pricking in my toes which tells me that enemies are near, about to thwart us."

"Let us get back to the digging, then," Brother Venom said.

"Yes, come. It's just upstream from here, and I pity whoever tries to thwart us now."

As soon as they had gone, Kay slipped on the scarlet shoes, took up Nibbins, stepped out with his foot, and in another minute was in his bedroom. Nibbins ran away at once to purr to Ellen for the milk and sardine which she always gave to cats which had been missing. Kay looked at the piece of tin which he had taken from the dead man's hand. The oblong door of the lantern had been scratched with a knifepoint thus, on the inner silvered side:

Abner Brown followed me here, thinking this was the treasure. He shot me because I wouldn't share. I am dying. The treasure is in the little South Cave. Give it back to the priests. My dear love to Susan.

T.P. called Pine Trigger.

"There it is," Kay said. "Abner followed him into the cave and shot him. That is poor Piney Trigger himself that is lying there."

"That's what," Rat suddenly answered at his elbow.

"How do you know?" Kay asked.

"Acos I knowed the party and seen the deed," Rat answered. "You think acos I got yellow teeth and a tail as I wot not what's what, but I wot's that which, howsomedever.

"I was marine cellarman in them days. I come up the river in a barge wot had strong smells in it, but not good to eat, only to sniff when faint. There was floods and bangings, and the water come into the barge, so I says, 'I'd better get out of this,' so I climbed ashore along a rope.

"Ah, and I need to hold on, too, doing it.

"There was a strong smell when I come ashore, so I followed it.

"I got down into a cave by the smell, and was just settling in, when in come a stout but pale party, with a lantern. He goes all about, looking at the casks and things and making notes and muttering. 'So you're a cellarman, too,' I says.

"Suddenly in come a white-haired party with another lantern. 'Now, Ben Trigger,' he says, 'I've tracked you down,' he says. 'Are you going to share? I want half.'

" 'You can want,' the other says. 'You'll get nothing out of me except another tooth out."

"Then BANG goes the white-haired man's pistol, and the

other party falls. I was so scared of the bang, it did so clang, that I run out into the night.

"Bye and bye the white-haired man comes out, all shaky and twittery. 'I've killed him dead, and after all it isn't there . . . the treasure isn't there . . . and now I'm a doomed man. . . . Oh, what shall I do? Oh, why did I shoot? I didn't mean nothing, except just to scare him. . . .'

"And at that he goes too close to the bank, which was all rotten with the rain, and the bank had a bush on it, and bank, bush, and he went swoosh into the river, which was all one foaming roar. It spun him right out into the white, and he go on screaming just like a pig, but not for long in a roar like that.

"I went back to the cave. The pale man had broken his lantern, so I ate his candle and come away. I don't like being cellarman where there are bangs, but if you ask what was what about what you know, I say that that's what."

"Yes," Kay said, "that was what, I see it all. And by this time, I expect the seven will have found the little south cave, and taken all the treasure.

"Oh, I wish that Edward and the others could have found it.

"I wonder who would stop the seven from having it, because it isn't theirs. Who could stop them?"

The day passed as he puzzled over the question, who could stop them. The governess was not there for dinner, nor for tea, but just as Kay was going to bed two carriages drove up, with herself and seven others. They were all very dirty, hot, and cross. "They haven't found it after all," Kay thought.

They all came into the house. Jane was ordered to build up the fire, as everybody was to have a hot bath. After the baths they were to have a high tea for eight, with sixteen poached eggs, and Ellen was to go to Farmer Chesses and bring two pounds of fresh butter and a quart of cream, because they had had such an exhausting day exploring the ancient history. "And mind the tea is strong," Abner said, "for we shall all be up all night at this."

"Yes, please see that the tea is very strong, Jane," the

governess said. "And, Ellen, you might call at Mr. Clove's for a pound of his special tea, and Mr. Brown would like some of the invalid's brandy that is in the cellar to mix with his tea, so please bring up a bottle, or rather, two bottles, for the others might like a little too. And as we are rather short of cakes, please go to the bakers and ask for any fresh crumpets, for there is nothing more delicious than hot crumpets thickly buttered and spread with sugar."

As they were now beginning to come upstairs, Kay hopped into bed, where he very soon fell fast asleep.

*H*e had slept for some little time when he felt himself rudely shaken by the arm. He woke up to find the room full of light, as before. Nibbins was on his bed, shaking him.

"Wake up, Kay," he said, "wake up. We haven't got a moment to lose. I've only just been able to dodge her and get here."

"What is it?" Kay said.

"No more witchcraft for me," Nibbins said, "after what I've gone through this evening. They caught me fast asleep in my chair after they'd had tea, and they took me up to their black room, as they call it. I knew when I saw the black room and all the seven, as well as Abner, that they were going to do something awful . . . and I can tell you they did."

"But what did they do?" Kay said.

"Do?" Nibbins said. "What didn't they do? First they tried all the simple witchcraft. A fellow wouldn't object to that. There's nothing in that, it's rather fun. But when that didn't do any good, they said that they'd have to use stronger measures."

"But I still don't understand," Kay said, trying hard to wake up. "What were they trying to do?"

"Why, to find the treasure, because they said that others were working against them, and they meant to find it first. They

tried things that make my blood run cold, awful things, but
they could get no clue. Then Mrs. Pouncer said, 'Well, we'll
find out who it is that's thwarting us,' so they tried that. They
asked it three times, and each time they got the answer 'Kay
and his friends.' Then Abner said, 'Oh, indeed. Really. Right.
We'll give Kay and his friends such a change as they little
expect.' They'll be here in a minute—any minute. Come along,
Kay, quick."

"Where to?" Kay said.

"Out of here, first. Quick. There are their steps in the
corridor."

Sure enough, there were their steps. Kay and Nibbins had
barely time to slip through the little door in the wainscot, and
bolt it behind them, before the seven were in the bedroom.

Kay and Nibbins ran down the corridor into the garden. As
they came out into the night, they ran into someone. They
thought for an instant that it was Abner, but it was Bitem
eating a rabbit. He knew at once that the hunt was up.

"Right," he cried. "Jump on my back, Kay. Hold me round
the neck. I can manage. . . ."

In a minute they were over the wall, the church clock then
striking one.

"Down into the town, Bitem," Nibbins said. "They'll never
think we went there." They saw the lanterns of the seven in
the garden, all moving away from them. "I was only just in
time," Nibbins whispered. "We'd only a minute to spare."

In a few minutes they paused for breath in the street of the
little town, which stretched to right and left in the silence of
the moonlight. All the townspeople were abed, even Pimply
Whatto. All the houses were shuttered, no lights shone in the
windows, not even a cat moved along the broad green shaded
with trees, where the stocks still stood beside the whipping
post.

"We're not pursued," Nibbins said. "It's all right."

"I don't know that it's all right," Bitem said. "This isn't
exactly the kind of place that's all right for me. They've got

scores against me that you little wot of, Nibbins, all of them. I'd a guinea fowl out of that one. I'd three hens and a cock out of that one. At least you can't count the cock—he was the toughest I ever. Then, that one with the gate, he was turkeys, very innocent young things, very mealy. Then that one was ducks, just the three, if I remember. Then that other one was a goose, and that one was a clutch of chickens. Then there was tame rabbits there, very juicy they was, only furry to the gullet, if you understand. There was only a guinea pig there, nothing on him, but worth it just to try. Then in that one she thought that she'd shut me out, but she'd really shut me in. Nineteen they counted the next morning, but she didn't see me, because I got out while she swounded."

"What we ought to do," Nibbins said, "is to cross running water. That upsets magic."

"Well, we have crossed running water," Bitem said. "There's an underground brook runs under here. Many's the time I've gone along it."

"Are you sure of that, Bitem?" Nibbins said.

"Well, of course, I'm sure."

Nibbins stopped still and began to shake.

"It's all very well," he said, "to be free from them for the moment, but we've got to go back. It's tomorrow morning that I'm thinking of."

"Never you think about tomorrow morning," Bitem said. "You just be thankful that you're not caught today. If you'd been hunted like what I've been hunted, the hounds coming on you in the middle of your sweet sleep and you not expecting them nor hearing them, no, but just dreaming of your last juicy bit of gosling, all yellow fat . . . Ah, if you'd gone through that and heard the horn and the horse, and seen their sharp teeth, and run all day in front of thirty of them . . . Ah, if you'd done that and got away at the end, you wouldn't think about any tomorrow. No. 'Let tomorrow fend for itself,' you'd say, 'but this is bliss.' "

"What in the wide world is this?" Kay asked, interrupting.

Coming up the center of the road that led from the river was a procession of small carts drawn by sturdy horses under escort. Kay looked at the carts and recognized them. There in front were the two which he had owned. They were very good ones which tipped up and had tailboards that came out. Then there was little Bill Gassle's cart and little Dick's cart from the rectory and Charles's and Brian's carts from the squire's. Then there were all the brand-new shining blue, yellow, and scarlet carts from the village toy shop, and a lot more carts, which he didn't recognize at all. But marching in front of the long procession of loaded carts was a figure whom he thought never to see again. It was Edward in his fullest uniform, in his coat with the piping down the edges, his gun slung in a bandolier and his rapier at his side.

"Edward," he cried.

"Ha, Kay," Edward said in his usual extravagant manner. "I've got the treasure. We've jolly well got the treasure for you, Kay. We've been a long time about it, but when I give my mind to a thing, I carry it through."

"You mean you got it from the little south cave?" Kay asked.

"Yes, out of the little south cave, and it's going under the hearthstone in your room before tonight's much older. And don't you have any fear, Kay. We're the guards, we are. We hear that the house has gone all to sixes and sevens since we left it, but that's going to be remedied now."

Nibbins burst into tears of joy.

"Edward and the guards come back," she cackled. "Now there won't be any more witchcraft."

"And are you going to the house now?" Kay asked.

"Going straight there. Come on."

"Look out, then," Nibbins said, "for they're all there, looking for us."

"There's nothing I like better," Edward said, "than to have my enemy looking for me. Then I don't have to look for him. Come on, boys."

When they reached the garden, Nibbins said, "Be careful,

now. Halt the carts. They'll have sentries posted at the doors, you may be certain. Yes. Look. There, those little green lights near the holly. That's Blackmalkin—those are his eyes. Greymalkin will be on the other side of the house, guarding the other doors."

"Right," Edward said. "Bitem, let you and Tom creep round through the grass till you see Greymalkin. He'll probably be under the yew. Take a sack and scrobble him up in it. Don't let him squeal. We'll settle what to do with him later."

"He shan't squeal," Bitem said. "Nor yet won't he not gurgle."

"We'll give you a full minute's start," Edward said, "to give you time to get round. Then Dogg here, and Peter Dogg, and you, Nibs, shall creep in with another sack on Blackmalkin there, scrobble *him* up and not let *him* squeal. We'll settle what to do with *him* later. Off you go, Bitem and Tom. We'll get in as soon as the guards are sacked."

Kay saw Bitem and the rather melancholy-looking lad known as Tom steal away through the long grass. "He's first rate for a night attack, Tom," Edward said. "He's so unexpected."

After what seemed a long long time, the two Dogg cousins crept away with Nibbins. Presently Kay saw Blackmalkin's eyes glow up green. He had been pacing to and fro, and now had turned to stare in their direction. Edward nudged Kay's arm. "Now watch," he said.

Kay saw the green eyes become a little brighter as Blackmalkin took a few steps towards them. Then suddenly the two little lights went out. There was no squeal, nor any sound of a scuffle, only a little sigh as though somebody very thirsty had just had a cool pleasant drink. Edward nudged Kay again. "They've bagged him," he said. In a few minutes the two sets of scouts returned, bearing the two sentries, both neatly tied up in sacks. The water rat appeared at the secret door. "You can go in," he said. "I've just been up part of the way. They are in a great tear and taking, all setting off for the river or somewhere."

Kay and Edward crept up the secret stair into Kay's room. There they heard the voice of Abner Brown calling "Haven't you got them, Mrs. Pouncer?" and Pouncer's voice replying "It's too provoking. I must have put the lantern and rope somewhere, when I was tidying, and then, my one-league shoes are gone."

"Well, come on," Abner said. "We must do without them. After all, we've got some lights and a rope and the carriages are here."

"I must just look a moment longer," she said.

"Really you mustn't stay a minute longer," Abner answered. "We've got to get to the river and into the cave. It will be daylight before we lift anything at this rate."

This seemed to convince Mrs. Pouncer, because she went downstairs muttering "It's too provoking," and Kay heard her pass along the hall and out at the front door. Soon the noise of carriage wheels was heard on the gravel.

"That's it," Edward said. "They've learned where the treasure was by their magic, but they've learned it a little too late. Now come along, boys, let's get busy. All the stuff in these carts has to go underneath this hearthstone before daylight."

There then followed a great bustle among the guards. One by one the carts were brought up and unloaded. The treasure was then carried up by hand and laid under the stone. All worked with a will. After two hours of hard work it was all stored safely away.

Kay stood with a light in the secret room looking at it as it was carried down. First they brought in the gold and silver people which had so pleased the mermaids. Three of these were knights with swords, and one a queen-knight, leaning forward, with her hair blown back from her helmet. Then four were Bringers of Blessings, like King Cole of England, King Alfred of Wessex, Saint Nicholas of Bari, and Saint Augustine. Four other were lovely, calm women, Forgiveness, Mercy, Peace, and Pity. "According to the list," Edward said, "there should be one more of these people, but he is not there."

"He is under the sea," Kay said.

After the images came the great gold and silver candlesticks that the goggle-eyes of so many fish had gawped at. Then came the censers and the church vessels. Then, when these had all been stored away, there came the marvelous caskets, each made like a church of gold or silver, with spires and pinnacles specked with jewels. The roofs of these churches opened like doors. Inside were colored glitterings from jewels, for each church was a box of precious stones, pearls, blue sapphires, yellow sapphires, opals like jewels with fire inside them, rubies like the heart of fire, emeralds like the depth of the green sea, diamonds like raindrops in the sun. Here and there on the treasures were relics of their travels, such as bits of the grass mattings from Santa Barbara; chalk marks and numbers put on them by Captain Harker or his mate Hollings, when they were brought on board the *Plunderer;* springs of coral, dried seaweed, and a few spiky, pearly shells from their under-the-sea time; and much of the dried red mud of Old Man John's farm. On the last of the caskets was an old envelope with the following inscription in ink:

> Brought up the river, and safely landed by me at midnight, January 25th, 1850.—P. Trigger

"I don't know who helped him," Edward said. "Probably his Indians, whom he paid and sent home afterwards. He was a rough customer, Sir Piney, but he did do his best to make amends for it."

It seemed to Kay and Edward that they heard a North Country voice say, "Tha's reet, ma son." Then, a moment later, they heard the same voice and a familiar female voice (now sweeter and fuller than it had been) singing in the garden:

> "After long years alone,
> Ironed to flesh and bone,
> It is most sweet to pass
> Like wind above the grass,
> Free ever, and to find
> The waiting mind.

"Then to set forth together,
To know the new strange weather,
And where the new road leads;
To put old burdens by,
And have the wind and sky,
Light as the wild duck's feather
Or dandelion seeds."

When the song had died away in the distance, Kay asked if
he might speak to the guards. They all came in, in their dusty,
rough, muddy working clothes. They were very much sunburnt
and wind-tanned. It was lovely to see them all looking so well,
and to have them there again. Kay spoke to each one and
thanked them all.

"You must have had a dreadfully hard time," he said.

"We had a lot of disappointments," Edward said. "We followed so many false clues. And I must say that yesterday, after
all night in the mud with those two men whom Arthur lent, I
must say that we came near to despair. It was little Maria who
kept us at it. She made us all lovely beef tea, and whipped up
eggs in milk (and in cream for poor Brown Bear), and it was she
and Susan who thought that there might be that cave to the
south. I can tell you . . . when Otter gave us a hint, and it
proved to be the fact, when we peered in and saw the treasure,
it atoned for any troubles we may have had. I must say, that
was a moment.

"But, however, we have found it. It is safely stored, and this
stone is sealed. What I have to say now is . . .

"Up, guards, and at them.

"It's time to set this house to rights.

"You, Lenda, take Jemima, Susan, and Maria into this
Pouncer's room, seal her cupboard, then lock everything up, so
that she won't get in again.

"You, Peterkin, Snowball, and James, and you, W. Brown,
break open that magic room, fling everything that you find
there out of the window and burn it in the bonfire.

"And the watchword, till further orders, is Keep Awake."

While they were hurrying to obey, there was a scuttering in the passage. Otter came tumbling into the room.

"I say," he said, "there are such doings down by the river. The eight of them came, with that man Roper Bilges and his brother, and the pimply man, and Brassy, who sets the traps. They have all been digging in the mud for hours. They're all filthy, blistered, and as cross as two sticks. Then they got into the south cave and found the treasure gone. Then they got into the middle cave and found a body. Now they're all fighting, quarreling, and blaming each other."

"Serve them right," Edward said. "But tell me, Otter, as you came here, did you see any coast guard men?"

"I should think I did," Otter said. "Dozens of them, some on the roads, others in boats, all creeping in on them."

"Right," Edward said. "My plans are working just as I could wish. John, just run down to the study, will you, and bring up yesterday's paper?"

Edward opened the paper and read: "His Excellency the Dictator of Santa Barbara, accompanied by the archbishop of Santa Barbara and a numerous and distinguished suite, will arrive in London early tomorrow on a short visit to the metropolis. They will be stopping at the Hotel Glorious."

"There," Edward cried. "On the very day the treasure is found, the people arrive to take charge of it. I noticed that announcement yesterday, tired as I was. That shows you the kind of brain I have."

"I showed it to him," Maria whispered.

"I'll send them a letter," Kay said. "Come along to the drawing room, where the embossed notepaper is kept."

In the drawing room, Kay wrote his letter:

DEAR LORD EXCELLENCY AND ARCHBISHOP:

I hop you are quite well.

All the church treasure which was trusted to Capt.

Harker, my great-grandfather, is now safely here. Please come with safe men to take it.

I am quite well.

KAY HARKER

"I'm afraid he'll never come for that," Kay said. "He'll think it's a rag."

"Well, let's send it by someone who will make him come," Edward said. "Not Ernest, he's such an ass. Bruno Bree is the man. Bruno, mount Peter Horse, gallop to London to the Hotel Glorious, and give this letter to the dictator's hand. Tell him it's deadly serious and he must come at once."

"I must put in a P.S.," Kay said. "The statue of St. George is under the sea."

After Bruno had galloped off with the letter, Edward said, "I must say that your guardian has been an ass, Kay. However, someone else will be here this morning. Then, perhaps, something can be arranged.

"Now I'll just post some guards, and you'd better get to bed for an hour or two."

*I*t was very late when Ellen called Kay that morning.

"Oh, there have been doings," she said. "Your governess and a whole lot more of them have been taken trespassing down in a cave where they were smuggling. And what's worse is that there's a dead body where they've murdered someone. And, oh, the brandy they've found. Joe says it's enough to make the army blind and the navy mellow. And Sir Hassle has had to telegraph to your guardian."

There were no lessons that morning, but a great deal of coming and going.

But long before lunch, at about eleven o'clock, there came a much greater surprise. While Kay was in the schoolroom wrestling with a portion of Mrs. Markham, Ellen came to say that he was wanted in the drawing room. This was usually a message foreboding punishment. Today Ellen brought it all smiling. "Who is there, Ellen?" he asked. "You are a tease not to tell a fellow."

"You go down and you'll see," she said.

He went down in a drag-leg sort of way, and opened the door. There, to his amazement, was the beautiful lady who had taken him to the weathercocks and to Miss Twiney Pricker. She came up to him and kissed him. "You don't know who I am," she said. "But I know who you are. I am Caroline Louisa, who loved your mother. I could not come before, but now I am going to live here and look after you. Will you like that?"

"Will I like that? I should rather think so. But what will she say?"

"She won't be here."

"Oh."

At half past two that afternoon they were playing cricket in the garden, when His Excellency the Dictator, with the archbishop of Santa Barbara and two other very important-looking men, drove up to the door in the fly from the Cock and Pye. They were all as nice as they could be. Kay had the great pleasure of taking them to his room, rolling back the carpet, and showing them the stone. The two men procured crowbars from the ironmonger's shop in the village. They hove the stone aside. There was the treasure neatly arranged as the guards had left it. Kay told them all the story of it.

They guarded it that night and then carried it away.

As for Abner Brown, Mrs. Pouncer, and the others, they were all examined by the magistrates for being found unlawfully assembled, with arms in their possession, with intent to defraud the Queen's Majesty by removing certain articles of contraband, to wit brandy, lace, and tobacco, from where they were to some other place, the said articles not having paid any duty. The magistrates were much puzzled by the case, because the people were not smugglers, and had not smuggled the goods, yet were plainly there with ropes, hooks, and carriages to remove the same. The seven were at last dismissed with a good scolding for taking part in a foolish frolic, but they were fined a large sum for trespassing in pursuit of game.

Abner Brown paid all the fines. Mrs. Pouncer left the district that afternoon.

Roper Bilges was discharged from his place for poaching. In revenge, he and his brother, Sir Hassle's footman, poisoned all the otter hounds. For this they were sent to Dr. Gubbins's Remedial Home for Scoundrels, where parts of them have been cut out, cleaned, and then put back. They are already much improved. Dr. Gubbins has great hopes of them.

Pimply Whatto and Brassy are now keeping a little pig farm.

Sir Hassle wears his grandfather's repeater, which goes as well as ever it did. He takes Kay for a ride three times a week, out of the hunting season. He is going to give Kay a lovely little pony mare, called Christine, for his birthday, but of course this is a secret. Sir Hassle never draws for a fox down by the river.

The squire will not buy any more otter hounds. Otter hunting has therefore come to an end there. Water Rat and Otter have the river to themselves. They are very happy there, as the salmon have begun to come back.

Joe has taken the pledge, and is keeping it.

Bitem is very well. He has a fine summer lair in the hollow of Spring Hill. So far he has had one of my hens and three of my ducks this season. In the winter he goes down to the cave near the river where no hounds ever come. I hear him singing from time to time.

Blackmalkin and Greymalkin have turned over new leaves, but of course they will never be so nice as Nibbins, who is the nicest cat there is.

Old Blinky is still there. So is Bat.

Ellen and Jane say that they are never going to marry, but stop where they are to look after Kay until *he* marries.

Kay and Caroline Louisa are as happy as the day is long. Last year they went to spend the winter as the guests of the dictator of Santa Barbara, where they had a most happy time. While they were there, the archbishop showed them the treasure, or some of it, in use, as it had been of old, the candlesticks on the altar, the images against the screens in the quire, and the vessels in the side chapels. Many of the precious stones from the caskets had been sold to build and endow a great college for the study and cure of disease.

While at sea, both going and returning, Kay was quite sure that he saw the mermaids.

The guards are very happy too. You may be sure that there is no more witchcraft in the house, nothing but peace and mirth all day and at night peace, the owls crying, the crickets chirping and all sort of fun going on among

THE MIDNIGHT FOLK.

Afterword

Madeleine L'Engle

John Masefield's *The Midnight Folk* was in my bookcase when I was a solitary only child growing up in New York. From this and other books I was made familiar with the world of the English orphan in the charge of a guardian and brought up by a governess. Governesses were either beautiful young women who had fallen on hard times—and who usually ended up marrying the guardian (if the guardian was nice) or the hero who took over the guardianship when the horrid guardian's vile deeds were uncovered—or tall, handsome women who were very wicked, and it didn't take me long to guess that young Kay Harker's governess was a witch.

This witch and her wicked companions were after the treasure with which Kay's great-grandfather Harker had been entrusted and which, through a series of misfortunes, he had lost.

As a child I gave a willing suspension of disbelief to Kay's travels through time and space, first with the good cat, Nibbins (there are two bad cats, involved in witchcraft, which Nibbins has put behind him), then into Great-grandfather Harker's portrait.

Great-grandfather Harker tells Kay that he needs his honor restored. He had been entrusted with the great jewels of the churches of Santa Barbara, and he will not rest until they are returned, though they were lost through no fault of his own but through mutiny, shipwreck, capture. When Captain Harker returns to England, many people assume that he has not, in fact, lost the treasure but has been living off ill-gotten gains, and that most of the treasure is hidden somewhere on his estate—quite possibly under the great hearthstone in what is now Kay's bedroom. Of course this is what the wicked governess thinks, and she is determined, by hook or by crook, to get the treasure for herself and her evil companions.

Masefield makes no bones about calling evil people evil. The nastiest one of all, Abner Brown, is described as being "like a white, sweet, sanctified horsedealer, or a hymn-singing cutthroat, or any cherry-lipped poisoner who will drop a tear at your pain and put ratsbane in your beer at the same breath." John Masefield, the poet, makes it possible for the reader to accept the convoluted and perhaps overly complicated plot—though when I was a child such complex interweaving of strands delighted me more than they confused me, and I doubt that they will daunt the young reader today.

Masefield, writing at a time when the British Empire was triumphant and people could believe in the "white man's burden," had some ironic comments to make. Miss Twiney Pricker, whose father is part of the plot, though not quite as dastardly a villain as Abner Brown, says of her pa that he got "Negro servants from savage parts to places where they could go to school and wear proper trousers instead of the fans and things . . . which they were accustomed to where they lived in their heathendom. He . . . brought many heathen savages into the advances of civilization. Sometimes they died, of course."

I missed the radicalism of this when I was a child, and I wonder if one has to be an adult who was alive during the time of the vast Empire to understand now how very advanced Masefield was in his thinking.

Moonlighting, too, means something very different today. Back a century ago in England, it was bootlegging, which was done by moonlight. Miss Twiney Pricker explains it to Kay as "what

comes by moonlight, French brandy and tea and this burgundy."
She explains to Kay that her pa had seven barges with false
bottoms which he took "right through a lock that the queen
herself was opening."

The young American reader may find the world of Kay's
England (now vanished forever) difficult to recognize. Boys
were usually educated at home until they were sent away to
school, sometimes when they were as young as nine or ten.
Even when children came from loving families, they saw far less
of their parents than their counterparts in the States. But it
will not be difficult for the reader to understand Kay's affection
for his stuffed animals, which of course the wicked governess
has confiscated, but who, with the other good midnight folk,
come to help him as he tries to find the treasure, and to restore
his great-grandfather's honor, and the honor of the Harker
name. If the desire to honor the name is less familiar today
than it was before two world wars ripped western civilization
apart, it is not a bad desire to bring back. We need to regain a
sense of honor, and I am grateful to Masefield for pointing out
its importance.

And of course Kay's own sense of honor helps right to
prevail. The treasure is found and Kay, with the help of his
midnight folk, is able to rescue it, keep it from the witches,
and give it back to the archbishop of Santa Barbara. The
witches are routed, the bad cats reform. The evil midnight folk
vanish with the dark, and the good midnight folk, the stuffed
animals, the real old owl, the water rat, are all there to help
Kay do his growing up.

This poetic book makes demands on the readers, but it is
well worth the trouble, and the child with imagination will find
many delights.